Happy
Birthday
Sam and
all the best

DANIEL JONES
DOOM

MARK KING

First published in Great Britain 2014 by Rethink Press
(www.rethinkpress.com)

© Copyright Mark King

All rights reserved. No part of this publication may be reproduced, stored in or introduced into a retrieval system, or transmitted, in any form, or by any means (electronic, mechanical, photocopying, recording or otherwise) without the prior written permission of the publisher.

The right of Mark King to be identified as the author of this work has been asserted by him in accordance with the Copyright, Designs and Patents Act 1988.

This book is sold subject to the condition that it shall not, by way of trade or otherwise, be lent, resold, hired out, or otherwise circulated without the publisher's prior consent in any form of binding or cover other than that in which it is published and without a similar condition including this condition being imposed on the subsequent purchaser.

This is a work of fiction. All characters in this book are fictitious. Any resemblance to real persons, either living or dead, is entirely coincidental.

Cover image © SOURCE

Dedication

This book is dedicated to Dennis King, my father; to William Cassidy, my step-father; to David Cragg, my father-in-law; and to Andrew Bagshaw, my friend. Four men who have had a positive influence on my life that I shall never forget and for which I will always be grateful.

1

JACK

A slap to the face brought no respite from the shouting.

'What about my son?'

A hard punch to the nose brought silence as the man slumped to the ground. His hands were un-ceremoniously tied together with rough twine and then to a rope attached to the horse's saddle from which he would be dragged to captivity.

A couple of kicks to his backside brought him back to consciousness and, as he struggled to his feet, a rag was stuffed into his mouth. He mumbled futile words of protest, but his gagged pleas fell on deaf ears as the Hunter lifted himself onto his horse's saddle.

'I should have executed you for disobeying Procedure Six, but I think we shall take you to the Achievement Centre. Our masters can make up their own minds about what to do with you.'

The other gang members laughed mockingly as they trotted off down the road dragging their crying captive behind.

Under the protective cover of a ruined building his young son watched in silent terror.

2

THE HUMAN HORSE

Beads of sweat swept free from the flesh and splattered the dry earth, leaving behind a visible trail of human endeavour. Two lines in the dirt marked the passing of cart wheels. Gasps of exhaustion escaped dry lips, and the sharp intake of breath with panting regularity signalled the human horse was near to collapse.

The corner was turned and the Tribute hut at the Three-ways came into view, with its low arched roof like an over-turned bowl. It showed the halfway point to home had been reached.

As the creaking wooden cart was dragged ever closer John finally slumped to the ground, then crawled the final painful feet before he could rest his aching body against the supportive stone structure. He wiped the sweat from his brow with the long sleeve of his shirt, but realised it could no longer absorb the moisture that flooded from his flesh.

He closed his eyes and visualised Duster, his old companion and friend, and wondered how his horse was coping with its new master. He could see the powerful muscles covered in a brown coat spotted with white dots, with his long shaggy mane, and again around all four hoofs. How John wished Duster was with him now so he didn't have to pull the wood-laden cart any further.

The sun was setting and John knew he would have to make a

move before it got dark. He had no choice but to lumber his large frame from the comfort of the ground, and once again pull with all his might until the cart rocked itself into motion.

Slowly, through gritted teeth, his body weight began to gain speed on the slow descent from the cutting grounds. Overhanging branches gave brief respites of shade from the sun, but was no substitute for the images of cool water that now sloshed around John's dehydrated brain.

The first whiff of wood smoke made him look up from the ground, and through straining eyes his home came into view.

Before he could reach the barn his mind gave up the fight for the final push as his body cried out for refreshment. Leaving the cart where it stood he staggered to the water trough before collapsing head first into the inviting clear liquid that glistened enticingly.

Gulping like a mad man he drank until his belly could take no more, before crumpling on the ground, his hair dripping wet, eyes closed, breathing heavily as he tried to regain his stamina.

'Daddy, Daddy what's wrong?' asked a concerned Sarah as she walked out of the barn carrying an empty slop bucket. 'Speak to me, Daddy!'

John didn't want to speak to anyone. He didn't want his young daughter to see him in such a vulnerable state, but a reply seeped from his cracked lips.

'Nothing is wrong, my little darling. Nothing at all.' With a shaky hand that clasped the side of the wooden trough he heaved himself up, then pressed both his palms against his aching back. 'Be a good girl and tell Mother I'm back.'

Sarah turned and ran towards the door of the larger round hut, then disappeared inside shouting. 'Mummy! Mummy, Daddy is back.'

John returned to the laden cart and for the final time today he pulled with the last of his will power, until at last it reached the two large open doors of the barn. The wood that nestled on top, and which John had been labouring on all day, would need to be stacked against the mud walls were it would be protected by the overhanging thatch roof. But that would have to wait for later, for now it was time to eat.

Straightening his back John tried to walk confidently through the door. Mother was already spooning vegetables from the clay pot that simmered over the open fire into wooden bowls, and once John had washed the day's grime off his body he sat down at the table with Mother and Sarah.

He ate in silence, too hungry to join in Mother's small talk. He left the table once finished and walked out, calling behind, 'I need to get the wood unloaded. Sarah, once you're finished round up the animals, and get them inside.'

Cornelius the albino cockerel was perched on the log pile reviewing his harem of hens that pecked the ground beneath him, and wasn't pleased with having his brilliant white feathers ruffled as John waved him off his advantage point. Soon Sarah had joined her father, flapping her arms in the air, shouting at the chickens, ducks and geese as she chased them into the barn. The sun had now set, leaving behind a soft red glow on the horizon as John made the final inspection of all the animals, and once he was satisfied they were all safely inside he heaved shut the stout doors.

The fire was raging and was a welcome sight as a chill filled the air. Swipe the cat was stretched out in front of it, and raised his head slightly to note John's arrival as he sat down in his favourite chair with its soft cloth cushion filled with feathers. John's head, with its shock of dark hair interwoven with ever increasing streaks of silver, was soon slumped to the side as he fell into an exhausted sleep.

'Wake up John.'

He snorted out of his slumber. 'Where's Sarah?' he asked, only half awake.

'She's already asleep. It's time we were too.'

He rocked his frame into a standing position and clasped his lower back in pain. 'Thirty nine seasons I have lived, and in just a short while I will have no more worries.'

Mother held out her hand and took hold of John's before leading him into the smaller hut. The bedroom was darker and the warmth of the dying fire that glowed placidly in the distance was fighting to keep the cold away.

Sarah was asleep, breathing gently, snuggled under a sheepskin rug behind the wicker divide that separated the smaller hut in two. Soon John was lying on the straw strewn across the floor with his arms wrapped around Mother as once again he fell into an exhausted sleep.

3

THE MASTER OF PROCEDURES

John awoke to the sound of the cockerels. He brushed the loose straw from his thick stock of messy hair as he pulled his sheep skin rug off, and slowly lifted his aching body off the dirt floor of the bedroom.

Walking out of the hut he crossed the track to the barn opposite and disappeared around the back. Letting his trousers fall to the ground he relieved himself against the mud wall before opening the barn doors to check all the animals kept inside overnight were safe and sound. He made a careful inspection and all looked well until his gaze came across the empty stall that was once the home of Duster. In a sudden rage his thoughts went back to the day when he was violently robbed of his horse at the Three-ways. Taking in a deep breath of the crisp early morning air, he turned and walked out.

Mother was up by the time he walked through the door, leaving it open to refresh the room. John called out for Sarah but he got no response. Calling out a second time was returned with a small murmur before a third, and more angry call, finally had Sarah walking through rubbing her sleepy eyes, while moaning under her breath.

Dried wood was added to the fire and soon the remains of last night's meal bubbled itself into a broth that would be gulped down for breakfast, dipped with stale bread. Only the sound of slurping filled the air and when the final spoon had been finished Mother arose from her wooden bench.

'OK. If we're all finished then we better start on the chores before the Procedures.'

John went back to the barn while Sarah helped Mother. The sun was rising into the sky. Soon the call to Procedures would be heard from the well situated in the middle of the village.

Mother placed a small bowl of leftovers from the pot onto the floor. Swipe the cat had his head buried inside within a flash, with purring delight as he chomped on his breakfast.

Bang, bang, bang.

Bang, bang, bang.

The sound of wood beating against wood resonated around the assortment of huts, barns and yards that was the village, and which for its inhabitants constituted life as they knew it.

Bang, bang, bang.

Bang, bang, bang.

'Hurry up, come on everyone. Hurry up. I haven't got all day.'

Bang, bang, bang.

Bang, bang, bang.

The village folk walked hurriedly over to the well in the daily manner with which they had followed all their lives.

'Gather around, you lot, and hurry up.'

The children sat on the ground while the adults stood around in a natural order with the shortest at the front and mostly men at the back.

John let go of the plank and it came to rest against the mud brick wall of the well. Next to it was a bale of straw. He clambered onto it so he stood above the crowd, and called out in a loud voice, 'Silence. Silence please.' He was waving his hands in a downward motion. 'Everyone: silence, please.'

The ensemble slowly quietened down until all that could be

heard was the occasional cheep of a bird and the rustle of the wind that flowed through the trees, blossoming in their late summer foliage.

'The Seven Procedures: this is the reason we are here. We gather every day to recite the Procedures as instructed by our saviours.'

Somebody sneezed and the crowd began to murmur. 'Silence please.' John was still waving his hands in a downward motion. 'Let's have silence.' His pleas were heard and he carried on. 'Every day we gather to recite, so I will lead and everyone must repeat after me.'

'Procedure One,' he called out. 'The Over-seers saved humanity from its own destruction and this must never be denied. Failure to comply will lead to summary execution.'

Everyone gathered repeated the sentence.

'Procedure Two: the Over-seers must be obeyed without question at all times. Failure to comply will lead to summary execution.'

Once again the crowd repeated the sentence.

'Procedure Three: no harm will be caused to any Over-seer or their property at any time. Failure to comply will lead to summary execution.'

'Procedure Four: on your anniversary of the fortieth cycle of the seasons you must report to the Achievement Centre, where you will receive your just rewards. Failure to comply will lead to summary execution.'

A loud cheer went up from the crowd when the words 'Achievement Centre' were mentioned.

'Procedure Five: work sets you free. On the seventh day, one tenth of the produce of your labour will be given in Tribute to the Over-seers and left at the Tribute huts. Failure to comply will lead to summary execution.'

John lowed the tone of his voice as if to emphasize the importance of the next sentence.

'Procedure Six: to enter or dwell in the desolate lands is forbidden for ever. Failure to comply will lead to summary execution.'

Everyone now repeated in one loud voice the final Procedure.

'Procedure Seven: the Procedures will be spoken every day and obeyed without question. Failure to comply will lead to summary execution.'

John clapped his hands. 'Well done, everyone,' and the rest of the villagers clapped in unison. 'Is there any more village business before we end today's meeting?'

There was silence. No one moved and with a final clap of his hands the Daily Procedures had finished. John silently walked back to the barn, and along the way was joined by his best friend Badger. 'Wait up, John.'

John stopped and turned around to greet him. Badger's smile was a welcoming sight although it could just about be seen through his bushy beard.

'John, I know it must be hard having Duster taken from you.'

Before Badger could finish John snapped back in an annoyed tone. 'Taken... he wasn't taken with my consent. He was stolen by those damn Hunters.' John eased off and his cheeks, flushed red with rage, now glowed with embarrassment. 'I'm sorry, my friend, for snapping at you, but it's hard at the moment, not only with what happened with Duster, but also Daniel being away doesn't help.'

Badger's semi-toothless grin reappeared. 'Don't worry about it. I understand. That's why I want to speak to you. I'm the only person now with a horse in this village, so why don't you borrow it?'

John thought for a second, but before he had a chance to reply Badger asked, 'So how is Daniel doing?'

This was one question John didn't want to answer quickly, so he tried to change the subject. 'OK. Anyway... your offer... thank you, but I must decline. You still need it for ploughing the fields.'

A disappointed look showed in Badger's eyes. 'Look John, who was there for me and my family when we had that terribly bad winter a few years back? Who gave us wood to heat our home? You did! Who shared their precious supply of food during the snow, which stopped me and my family starving? You and Mother did, that's who! Who lent me the great pile of wood so I could use it to barter for my horse in the first place? You did! I'm not having another word from you on this matter. It's yours to use and that's final.'

Badger held out his hand, worn rough from many years labour with the plough, working for others while sharing part of their crop as payment. It was hard work, but he had successfully brought up a large family, and was glad he was now able to repay his friend's kindness.

John shook Badger's hand. 'Agreed, and thanks.' He turned and walked back to the barn while Badger went in the opposite direction to fetch his horse.

Sarah was being chased by hens eager to feed from the corn she held in her hand as John approached. A trader had arrived from the village at River-mouth and was waiting, eager to barter the dried fish skewed to poles that he had slung over a mule's back.

'Hello John, my friend,' he called out, and soon the pair shook hands in greeting before settling down to the game of brinkmanship that each used in trying to get the best value for their wares.

'I need a cart loaded to the top with dried wood for the fire to cure my fish, with spare to stockpile for winter. I will give you twenty of these finest smoked trout in return.' He smiled gently as John stood in silence, rubbing the whiskers on his chin in contemplation.

'A cart load of the best seasoned wood is worth double that amount. I will swap you half a cart load,' and John smiled back.

The bartering began in earnest and a deal was near to completion when Badger came strolling over holding a leather bridle with his work horse in tow. 'Greetings, Tom. I see the fish catch has been kind to you this month. How is life in River-mouth?' Before he received a response Badger fired another question that shot a stab of fear through John's heart. 'And how is young Daniel Jones doing with his apprenticeship at River-mouth?'

Tom looked puzzled at this last question.

'Daniel? I didn't know he's at River-mouth. In fact I've not seen him there for some weeks.'

John knew he needed to jump into the conversation before it would lead to even more dangerous questions, and his mind spurted in and out of thoughts before a stuttering answer came from his sun-chapped lips.

'Oh, Daniel's not finishing it in River-mouth. I sent him out of the vale so he could broaden his horizons a bit.'

He could feel his cheeks blushing with guilt at the blatant lie he had just told, and was fishing for another reply which would change the subject quickly when Badger enquired again.

'So where did you send Daniel too?' John was hopelessly lost in panic knowing his secret would be discovered. 'So John, will he be back for your great send off on your up and coming Achievement Day?'

John was stumped for words, frantically looking for a way out, when Swipe, living up to his name, grabbed everyone's attention by lurching at the mule. In full flight with his claws out he swiped at one of the fish, and managed to dislodge a whole pole which dropped onto the ground. In a second the feline was ripping at the dried flesh, gulping down his opportunistic meal before he was finally chased away by John.

'I'm sorry about that, Tom. Put that fish on my order. Now I have use of Badger's horse I will have a cart load of wood brought over this afternoon. Please excuse me. I'd better get loading.' With that he walked off towards the barn entrance before stopping. 'Thanks, Badger, for the loan of your horse. Can you fasten it to the cart?' With that final remark he disappeared inside the barn giving silent thanks for the timely intervention of Swipe.

Once the cart was loaded John visited all the hamlets dotted around the landscape, swapping his wood that he had chopped down by hand from the cutting grounds for other goods that the family didn't produce: bread from the baker, some patching cloth from Eudora the weaver, and grain from Badger's store.

Returning to the barn he reloaded the cart for a second time before making the longer journey to the village at River-mouth, where he paid off his dues for the dried fish he had purchased from Tom earlier in the day. Then he made a hasty retreat from there before anyone asked any awkward questions about Daniel's whereabouts.

The sun was setting as the cart rattled its way home with John on top. His body gently rocked from side to side with the motion of the wooden rims of the wheels that slowly moved over the rutted track. John's mind kept being summoned by his breaking heart to the image of Daniel's face, and the mystery of his son's sudden, and unexplained, disappearance.

So far he and Mother had been able to fool everyone by lying. This was bad enough in itself, but since the Over-seers had shown their wrath with their unwanted and destructive visit to their village with their demands for someone's blood they had no choice. He couldn't be sure Daniel was involved, but with losing his axe, his horse, and his son in the space of two days John was not going to take any risks with his chance of entering the Achievement Centre, and in receiving a lifetime of the rewards that were promised.

When finally home came into view his thoughts changed to the image of his awaiting supper of steaming vegetables and cured fish. Once he had returned Badger's horse, checked on the livestock and shut the two great barn doors, his hungry and tired frame strode through the door.

4

MAD-DOG

The flames licked their way up the wooden support, and were soon eating into the thatch of the roof. Thick black smoke that had engulfed everything inside with choking death started to billow from behind the wooden door that had been kicked in, and which now just hung on one of its hinges.

'No, no, no.'

The screams of despair faded into an uncontrollable sob. Floods of tears dripped onto the dried earth bleached grey by the sun, turning brown with human misery.

A terrible sound of fear pierced the air over the crackling sound of burning wood which called out to the gates of hell to open and release the poor suffering soul who was tied to a chair inside the hut as flames ripped through his home, raging into an inferno.

'Where is Dangerous Butch?' A hard kick to the gut brought only muted cries of pain in response. 'Where is Dangerous Butch?' Another kick to the belly only brought more tears.

'Look, you silly woman, if you tell me where he is, not only will you live, but there is still time to save your husband before he is burnt to death in your pitiful hovel.'

A pleading, tear-stained face looked up to her tormenter as he towered above her outside her burning home. 'He passed this way about six sunsets ago. He went that way.' Her head nodded to the right indicating his last known direction. 'Now please get my husband out of there, please, please,' came the begging, distraught, response.

'Tie her up to the horse she can come with us.' And the assembled men began to laugh.

'What about my husband? Please get him out of there.'

Laughter followed. The shouted cries for help that emanated from within the burning hut now turned into one long scream of agonising pain as the flames consumed the poor man's flesh as it burned like oil in a lamp.

'You dog!' screamed the woman. 'You're nothing but a demented dog.'

'You're nearly right: not demented, just mad. That's my name: Mad-dog.'

5

LIES

The fish made a nice change for supper. Its smoky flavour left behind a salty savoury taste that lingered after each mouthful, even when followed by a gulp of water freshly fetched from the village well that had kept it nice and cool, deep in the bosom of mother earth.

Chunky potatoes boiled in the pot with an assortment of herbs with their various shades of colour, picked straight from the vegetable garden, helped to give substance to the meal, along with the bread baked fresh that morning, smothered with a thick layer of creamy butter that the family milking cow had helped to provide.

Fruit picked from the surrounding trees that grew wild in nature's wood provided a sweet dessert which helped to finish off the meal to everyone's satisfaction.

Once John had said his thanks to Mother and Sarah for all their hard work he left the table, lowered his aching back into his favourite chair in front of the fire. Soon his head was bobbing to the side until eventually he slumped into an exhausted sleep.

His rest didn't last long. Once the chores had been finished Sarah sat on the floor as Mother joined John in the chair next to him, and then started to wake him gently with a soft nudge to the arm. John snorted out of his slumber and rubbed his tired eyes.

'Right, sleepy head. It's time we had a talk with Sarah.'

John straightened his back and gave Sarah a soft smile as she sat, legs crossed, with her back to the fire that glowed with a placid light.

'Yes, Mother. You're right.' He leaned forward and gently rubbed Sarah's hair. 'You know we love you, and you will always be my pride and joy?' Sarah nodded sweetly in appreciation.

'We need to discuss your future. As you know I'm near to the anniversary of my fortieth season, and I'm looking forward to going to the Achievement Centre to receive my just rewards.' John turned towards Mother holding out his hand which she held with a tight squeeze.

'As you also know Mother still has a season to go before her big day of reward, but we have always wanted to celebrate together, and it was always our intention for both of us to go at the same time.'

Mother blew John a kiss as he continued.

'Now we have always brought you, and Daniel, up not to tell lies. While Mother going early to the Achievement Centre is a bit of a white lie when it comes to the Over-seers, this had always been what we have planned. I hope you can understand why we are doing it?'

Sarah silently gestured she understood.

'We expected Daniel to become head of the family and would have looked after you.' John paused and returned his gaze back to Sarah. 'But as you are aware Daniel has disappeared, and we don't think he's going to return soon.' John's face softened as he sighed.

'Now, I need you to keep a secret just like you have with your grandparents treasures.' Sarah again stayed silent, engrossed in what was being asked of her. 'We believe Daniel has been in some trouble with the Over-seers, and has had to run away. He may be hiding in some desolate lands far off somewhere.'

Sarah suddenly chirped up and asked, 'But I thought Daniel has been away finishing his apprenticeship?'

John sat back into his chair. 'Your mother and I have had to tell a few more white lies lately.' He now felt awkward and hoped it didn't show. 'This is what we have told everyone, and luckily so far no one has questioned it.' John paused. 'Until today that is. Badger got a bit too close for comfort. This is why we need you not to say anything especially when we both go to the Achievement Centre, and you go live with Badger's family.'

Sarah changed the subject with a question of her own. 'What's life like in the Achievement Centre?'

John and Mother looked at each other with raised eyebrows. Silence fell over the room. Mother looked at Sarah, then back to John who sat still, unsure what to say, before she looked back at Sarah with a confused look on her face as she tried to answer her question.

'I'm not sure. Are you father?' John shrugged his shoulders. 'All we know is that for everyone who keeps to the Procedures they will be showered with rewards by the Over-seers. No more toiling with back-breaking work, no more worrying if there will be enough food to get through winter. Maybe there's no more disease either.'

Mother looked back to John, but Sarah soon had another question for her. 'So where does everyone go, and where do they live?'

Mother was even more baffled with this question than she was with the first one Sarah had asked. 'Ur...' She hesitated. 'Ur...' before she glanced towards John looking for his help.

'Why don't we have a final look at granny and grandpa's secret treasures?' suggested John as he lumbered his frame out of the chair and stood up straight with his palms pressed against his lower back. 'I feel as stiff as an old board,' and with that distracting remark he went to retrieve a knife.

Soon he was kneeling in front of the fire using the knife to lift up the side of the blackened hearth stone sunken into the ground. Once he had gained a hold he tossed the knife onto the dirt floor, and then used his free hand to feel under the stone until he found what he was looking for.

'Here it is.' He clambered his body into an upright position while holding a leather pouch, then lowered his backside onto the soft feathered cushion that rested on his chair.

'Sarah, can you just add another log to the fire before I start?' She did as asked and as she returned her gaze a gasp of joy escaped from her lips. John had spread over his open palm a gold linked chain. At its centre was a glass-covered round disk and under this twelve clear stones that sparkled with light from the fire, each with a different number next to it. 'Mother, we know this is for you.' He passed it over and she eagerly placed it around her wrist.

'We never did get to find out what this spelt,' as John pointed to the word 'Rolex' imprinted on the timepiece. The next object out was a key attached to a small piece of red leather with a yellow metal insert on which was printed the picture of a black stallion prancing on its hind legs above the word 'Ferrari'.

'I never did find out either what this key unlocked!' exclaimed John while his hand was fumbling in the pouch for the final object.

'Here it is.' He pulled out a picture of a young couple standing proudly outside their stately home in front of two large white doors. 'Never did find out where my parents came from either.' John stated brushing the picture gently with his finger as if he could once again feel his parents in the flesh.

His concentration was broken when Sarah enthusiastically asked, 'do you think granny and grandpa will be waiting for you in the Achievement Centre?'

Unsure at first what to say he looked thoughtful before replying. 'I hope so, but I was young when they went, about the same age as Daniel. It was many seasons ago, and nature may have taken its own course by now.'

Sarah turned, gazing into the fire as she gentle stroked Swipe. The room fell silent except for the crackling noises that spat free from the burning wood, radiating in glows of gold and furious reds. When she returned her attention back a flood of curiosity came forth from her young mind.

'Why did granny and grandpa never come from the Achievement

Centre to see me? Why would they leave such a lovely home to move here, and why do you have to go to the Achievement Centre? What about if you don't want to go, what if you don't want to stay?'

John knew his, and Mother's, continuous shrugs would not be enough to answer her curiosity so Mother once again jumped into the conversation. 'My little one. Time for bed.'

'But Mum, I don't want to go yet.'

John heaved himself free from the chair as he collected back his parents' treasures while Sarah continued to protest with a raised voice.

'Look, young lady, there are certain things you just have to accept, like the Procedures, and it's very dangerous to ask questions when the answers have already been provided for us.' Towering over Sarah he glared at her. 'Do you understand?'

'Yes, Father,' Sarah replied half-heartedly. She got up and, after a goodnight kiss, wandered into the darkness of the bedroom. John returned the treasure to its hiding place, then rejoined Mother as she sat looking at Swipe while he licked his black fur, still lying on his side with his back warming to the fire.

Once slow heavy breathing could be heard from the bedroom, indicating that Sarah had fallen asleep, the conversation resumed.

'Sarah does ask some funny questions.' John agreed with Mother's suggestion.

'You're right, Mother, and a wiser man than me might ask the same questions too, but I've worked too hard, and kept to the rules too long, to take the risk of finding out if all the answers to life aren't what they seem. All I know is that we have lived by the Procedures, and we will die by the Procedures, hopefully once we have both enjoyed many years of rewards as promised by our saviours.'

Mother took hold of John's hand, squeezing it as she looked into his eyes. 'I hope you are right, Father, but by the tone of your voice I sense doubt in your mind.'

6

NIGHTMARES

Doors to the left and doors to the right, all identical, all closed. Each one illuminated as if daylight was on the other side helping to light up the passage way that extended into the far distance. Another handle turned and again the door failed to open. Another step forward to another set of doors.

A door to the left and a door to the right, once again identical to the others, once again illuminated like the others, once again offering the tantalising prospect of finding an escape route from the never-ending passage. The round handle on each door was turned, and once again failure was the reward. Another step forward to another set of doors.

A door to the left and a door to the right, nothing had changed, the same glowing white doors, the same round handles, the same opportunity. The handle of the right door was clasped tightly and slowly turned. A small click was heard. The handle kept turning and with a slight push the door swung open. A blinding light filled the passageway. A voice called out to enter. It was a welcoming voice and one that was recognised.

Another step forward, but this time the doors were left behind. In front was a large brightly-lit cavernous room. With every step forward the blinding light eased as a lone metal table came into view.

Another step forward revealed a naked man lying motionless on top, held fast by two prongs that clasped around his upper chest and lower torso. Next to it stood a silent Over-seer. 'Come to me, my son. I want to see you one last time. Speak to me, son. I want to hear your voice one more time.'

But responding was futile. A wailing siren echoed off the walls, drowning out any replies. The air turned stale and the whiteness of the room was flushed by a scarlet light. The flesh of the hands turned pink as the veins underneath throbbed a violent blue.

The poor soul on the table pleaded for breath in the toxic air, but the son was unable to help, riveted to the spot as if being held by an invisible force.

The beast gazed at the son who stood transfixed, and started to wail a cruel laugh as the nails on each of its hands began to grow in length like a cat's claws before the kill.

The son stood helpless. The father lay pleading. The Over-seer started feeding. It slashed at the flesh of the stomach, and ripped it away like cream off a cake. Lifting its head it lowered the living skin into its gasping mouth then the jaws started to chew as stinking saliva dripped onto the floor.

Once finished the Over-seer set its gaze at the son, laughing at his helplessness, before once again tearing at the live feast that wriggled in agonising terror on the table. Meat with sinews trailing was ripped from the bone and consumed. Screeches of pain so dreadful that the angels themselves guarding the gates of heaven would have closed them in terror echoed their excruciating pleas around the chamber.

The Over-seer lowered its head over the doomed soul and started to sup on the warm blood that spurted into the air from broken veins, and when it lifted its head it gurgled with delight on the lifeblood of humanity. The final delicacy: eyeballs freshly pulled from quivering sockets that dangled on the end of extended nails like sausages on tooth picks were chewed with purring delight.

The son stood paralysed as his father was eaten alive by the Over-seer.

Daniel awoke with a jolt. His heart was beating fast. Small droplets of sweat clung to his forehead. For a fraction of a second he was unsure of his surroundings until he wiped his brow and looked up. The last dregs of a fire glowed at his feet while sitting opposite him with her back resting against the wall was Mary.

'Still having nightmares, young Mr Jones?'

He nodded at her question, and then replied. 'We need to get out of here. I need to return to my home village as soon as possible. I need to save my father's life.'

Mary sat in silence at first, as if contemplating the situation, before she gave her considered opinion. 'If you do that then you will put him in danger. You know if the Over-seers capture you, not only will your father be in serious trouble, but so will your whole family.'

Daniel was determined. 'You don't understand. My father is in great danger now. It will soon be the anniversary of his fortieth season.' He pushed himself up from his sleeping position and joined Mary in resting against the wall.

'Very soon my father is blissfully going to the Achievement Centre to receive what he thinks are his just rewards.' Mary's mouth opened slightly in surprise as Daniel continued. 'He is totally ignorant of the truth. He doesn't know there are no rewards. He doesn't know that he will end up on the dining table of the Over-seers so they can devour him alive. I can't stop these images invading my sleep, the never ending corridor with all the locked doors, trying desperately to find a way out that I can never find. Why can I never find a way out?'

Mary shook her head from side to side as she tutted.

'You're right, Daniel. We must return as soon as the coast is clear. We must warn your father.'

Their conversation was broken by the sound of approaching footsteps. Daniel instinctively reached over, picking up the axe that had not only saved his life, but had also brought prosperity to two generations of his family until he had taken it. A shadow darted off the walls following the light of a flaming torch as a voice echoed.

'It's all right. It's only me.' Gwendolyn appeared out of the shadows. A bow and a quiver were strapped across her back, and strung across her waist were two dead rats.

'I've had a successful hunt. Not much to go on, but once these rats have been skinned they will add a bit of meat to the pot.'

Daniel's stomach began to tighten up. He had never got use to this cuisine, but in the present circumstances he had no choice other than to starve. The three of them had been underground hiding for over a month, and without Gwendolyn catching what she could by using her skill at archery there would have been nothing to eat. The last decent meal had been a tin of porridge found the night before they were last above ground. How Daniel wished he could now be back in the fresh air, but since he had used the Golden Shield to defeat his nemesis they had no other option because the ground above them swarmed with deadly enemies whose only purpose was to find and execute them.

'When do you think it will be safe to leave the caves?' Daniel asked hopefully of Mary, who was already adding the last remaining herbs from her stock to the pot that nestled within the red hot glowing embers of the fire.

She looked up. 'Tomorrow I think. I haven't felt any vibrations for twenty-four hours so hopefully all the Triclops have gone. But there is another reason we need to go. The poor horses are close to starvation. They need to get above ground and feed on fresh grass. Another week down here and they will be too weak to walk. Then you won't have to moan about eating rat anymore because you will have plenty of horse flesh to consume.'

Gwendolyn's heart began to pang at the thought of losing Orlov, and she also knew Daniel would be devastated at losing Champion, especially as he was still trying to get over the fact that Duster had drowned when crossing the estuary. Now guilt started to fill her soul at her hand in Duster's demise. Although Daniel thought it was an accident she still wanted to tell him the truth, but was too afraid of spoiling their friendship, especially as it hadn't started on the best of terms in the first place.

Mary spoke again, bringing Gwendolyn out from her thoughts. 'There may still be Hunters above ground so we will have to be very careful, especially as the horses will need good grazing before they have their full strength back. I'm afraid we will have to go on foot to start with.'

Daniel looked at the white chalk walls of the cave. 'I'm glad about that. I can't stand it in here any longer, all we have had are rats to eat, dribbles of water to drink, and when the fire goes out never-ending darkness.'

He got up from the ground, and started to pace up and down the tunnel. He hadn't enjoyed his time underground. It kept reminding him of the first time he crawled into the cave at the cutting grounds near to his home with his friends. He wished now he had turned back when they did. He wished deep down that he could still be as ignorant as his father, that he had never discovered the terrible fate of everyone who entered the Achievement Centre.

He needed to stay in control of his thoughts, not only for his own sanity, but also for the moral of the other two. His life had been turned upside down since he had learnt the truth about the Overseers and had gone on the run, but the last few weeks hiding in the chalk and flint mines dug by the hands of generations past had been an ordeal as taxing as any he had faced recently.

Mary tried to lighten the mood.

'Why did the banana go to the doctor?' Daniel and Gwendolyn looked at each other confused. 'Because it wasn't peeling very well.' She started to chuckle. 'Oh, you two. Don't you get the joke?'

They both looked at Mary and said in unison. 'What's a banana?'

'How silly of me.' Mary flushed. She looked at her wrist and continued. 'It will be getting dark outside soon. Give me the rats and I will skin them for the pot. While I'm doing that why don't you both scavenge for some firewood? But be careful. Take no risks. Get enough broken branches or wood to last the night because in the morning we will start the return journey to Daniel's village.'

7

THE MASTERS COMMAND

'What do you think of this?'

Wolf looked up from the wooden wash bowl as water dripped off his face. He had noticed Mad-dog's entry, but was in no rush to acknowledge his presence.

'I said, what do you think of this?'

Wolf looked into the small piece of cracked glass that hung from the wall in front of him that served as a mirror, then examined the recently shaved contours of his face.

'Are you listening to me, Wolf?' Mad-dog barked.

He knew his failure to show eagerness would wind up his rival Hunter, and gloried secretly in Mad-dog's frustration. Wolf straightened his back, turning slowly as he wiped his face dry with a cloth.

'Think of what?' he replied.

Mad-dog held out his hand, and between his forefinger and thumb he held a piece of paper covered in handwritten words.

'This!'

Wolf shrugged his shoulders.

'What am I supposed to think? It's a piece of paper with words on it, and as neither you or me can read or write, nor anybody else in camp, what is the point of your question?'

Wolf turned his back on Mad-dog and looked for his response from the mirror's reflection. He could see Mad-dog was getting frustrated.

'Yes, I know that, so the only person we know who could have written this is Dangerous Butch! And as I found this piece of paper only a couple days horse ride away it can only mean he has passed nearby recently.'

This last sentence had caught Wolf's attention so once again he turned to face his rival.

'I thought you and your gang were combing the desolate lands in the east for them two youngsters, and their old lady of a companion?'

'I was but after a month of fruitless searching I decided to give my men a break back at camp. It was while we were on our way back we came across a hut. We stopped to see what refreshment we could find, and I must have taken the couple inside by surprise, because I caught them red-handed, reciting the words from this piece of paper.'

Wolf held out his hand and grabbed the evidence from Mad-dog's clasp.

'So this couple – did they tell you where Dangerous Butch is?'

Mad-dog smiled.

'We had to force it out of them. It took a bit more pressure than normal, but it's amazing how much information a woman will give when she sees her loved one, and home, go up in flames together.' And then he started to laugh.

Wolf enviously handed back the paper. Mad-dog now held the upper hand. Since his own gang had been taken by surprise by the young man with his axe, and that girl with her deadly arrows, who nearly ended his own life, he was in no position to carry out their masters commands. He had lost half his gang, all their weapons and most of the horses. If it wasn't for the kindness shown by that old lady who had patched up his wounds on that fateful day, and had ultimately saved not only his life, but also the life of his best friend and lieutenant, Fat-man, he wouldn't now be having this conversation with Mad-dog.

'So what are you going to do now then?' enquired Wolf.

'I'm going to have some fun first with that woman we brought back with us, and then while my gang take their turns feasting on her pleasures I'm going to go to the Achievement Centre at the Three-ways to inform our masters on my progress. Then after that I will take a few days rest before we resume the hunt.'

It was at this point that Wolf realised that Mad-dog had only visited him so he could gloat not only over his own predicament, but also glory about having news on one of the most wanted outlaws in the land.

As Mad-dog left the hut his laughter started again, but with increased pleasure as Wolf was left behind to reflect in his own failures.

* * *

Fat-man was woken up by a woman's muffled screams that emanated from behind the locked doors of Mad-dog's hut.

He was ready to bury his head back under the animal skins when suddenly the door in front of him slammed open, and in rushed Wolf. The long laces of Wolf's knee-length leather boots hung down, untied. Droplets of water glistened in his short cropped hair, and by the tone of his hurried voice it was obvious he had important news that couldn't wait while he finished getting ready this morning.

'Good. You're awake. Mad-dog's gang are back in camp and he's got some news.'

Fat-man lifted his large frame off his bed, and brushed off the loose straw from his clothes. 'What's all that noise coming from Mad-dog's place?'

'That's what I'm here about. He found a couple trying to learn how to read from a handwritten piece of paper. After a bit of forceful persuasion he found out that Dangerous Butch passed within a couple of days ride from here.'

Fat-man walked over to a small table. He lifted a jug and drank the water contained inside. 'What's that got to do with all the screaming?' he enquired. 'And what's it got to do with us?'

'Don't you get it, Maxwell?' Fat-man shook his head. 'Since we had the disastrous encounter with that trio that overwhelmed us in the Great Forest, we are treading on very dangerous ground. Mad-dog's gang will be out again soon looking for them, and if he also manages to catch Dangerous Butch along the way he will get all the glory.'

Fat-man shrugged his shoulders. 'So?'

Wolf sighed. 'It's lucky one of us has the brains around here. If Mad-dog gets all the success, and the glory that goes with it, the Over-seers will execute us just to remind all the other Hunter gangs what the payment is for failure.'

Fat-man grasped his throat, and gently squeezed it. 'You're right. For some reason I've just gone off the idea of having a shave this morning.'

Wolf nodded. 'Even if they only find the trio we will be in grave danger. If Mad-dog tortures them in his normal way they will spill the beans on how they took us by surprise, and how they managed to take our horses, and weapons.'

Fat-man gulped as Wolf started pacing around the small enclosed space that was Fat-man's home as if in deep thought. 'There's nothing we can do at the moment. We will just have to hope that Mad-dog fails in finding any of them.' And with that remark Wolf walked out the door.

* * *

'The first one to saddle my horse and brings it to me can have seconds with this woman,' barked Mad-dog across the yard as he stood at the door of his hut, tying up the buttons of his trousers. 'I need to go the Achievement Centre.'

Gang members suddenly darted across the yard to the barn, and soon a scuffle of bodies were all pushing at each other to get through the doors, and to Mad-dog's horse. A fight broke out as bodies fell to the dirt floor, rolling about sending dry dust into a whirl of smoke above the scrummage.

A weasel of a figure stood back waiting for his chance, then sneaked past the mass of pitiful human behaviour to gain his prize. The leader's horse was soon saddled; as it was lead out into the open a combined groan of disappointment arose from the pathetic souls that rollicked amongst the settling dust.

'I knew it would be you, Leyland,' laughed Mad-dog. 'There is a reason you are my lieutenant, and it's not just because you can be relied upon to be as deadly as a knife across the throat, but also because you can be as devious as a snake in the grass.' He carried on laughing as he mounted his steed.

'Go on, go enjoy your reward.' With no further encouragement Leyland shot through the door of Mad-dog's hut, and locked it behind him.

It took half the day to reach the Tribute hut at the Three-ways, and after tying his horse to a tree near to the boulder that marked the path to the Achievement Centre he walked up the track under the shade of the overhanging trees, preparing mentally the message he would convey to his masters.

The birds were singing their last tweets of the day when they were suddenly drowned out by the sound of rumbling that emanated from within the grey-coloured doors that were cut into the cliff face at the end of the track, and which indicated Mad-dog's arrival had been noted.

Slowly a gap began to appear and two great doors disappeared into the walls as the dark cavernous interior appeared along with the sight of a silver-suited Over-seer standing at the entrance, silently pointing into the darkness.

Mad-dog followed the instruction, walking in as the rumbling began once again until darkness engulfed him. Only silence loomed along with an acrid smell that always greeted human arrivals. Light suddenly flooded from the ceiling followed by the voice of the black-clad Dominator that echoed off the walls of the inner chamber.

'Report to the Dominator.'

Mad-dog held a steady nerve, then replied, 'The law-breakers you seek have not been found yet, but…' He didn't have time to finish before he was interrupted.

'Unacceptable,' boomed the Dominator.

'But during our tour we did find new information on Dangerous Butch.' Silence followed before the Dominator responded.

'Report.'

Mad-dog once again composed himself. 'I have discovered he passed within two days ride of here, and is heading east.'

All went quiet once again, but this time Mad-dog wasn't going to lose the opportunity to impress his master. 'I have a new plan of action. The trio you seek that have broken Procedure Three headed from the west to the east which is the same direction Dangerous Butch is heading. Two of the trio are before their age of Achievement so must have family. I presume they will try to come back to visit them so I will take my gang half way, and lie in wait for them. Hopefully I will be able to satisfy two of my master's commands.'

He paused, but there was no reply. The silence became deafening until it was broken by the concluding directive of the Dominator. 'Success by Hunters will bring great rewards.'

'And failure?' Mad-dog enquired.

'Summary execution for all involved.'

A sly smile spread over his face as the Dominator started to communicate in clicks. The lights went out, and the rumbling noise began from behind him. Mad-dog knew his meeting was finished.

He hurried down the track as the sun was in its descent, eager to start the ride back to camp before darkness set in. Soon he was mounted on his horse and whipped its behind furiously. As the steed darted off through the woods its path was blocked by a lone man with a cart loaded full of chopped wood. He was sweating profusely as he pulled the great weight with back bent over, oblivious to the approaching horseman.

'Get out my way,' shouted Mad-dog as he nudged his horse past the cart, before lashing out an almighty kick which sent the woodsman crumpling to the ground. He soon reeled himself from the dirt with fists clenched and teeth gritted, but it was too late for Mad-dog was gone, leaving behind the echoes of his mocking laughter.

* * *

The meat was succulent, charred black on the outside, but red and tender on the inside, dripping with bloody juice, and just as Wolf liked it. The picture of her face kept filling his mind, her silver hair; the wrinkles around her eyes which softened her features in a motherly way. Her brown iris which shone with such warmth and her voice, which on one hand contained so much knowledge, but on the other seemed so full of youthful confidence.

He couldn't clear the old woman out of his mind, and the kindness she had shown not only to him, but also to Fat-man. He thought about his own mother who had died giving birth to him, and wondered what she would have looked like. His concentration was broken by Leyland who had wandered over.

'I will swap the woman for poor old Ginger's horse. He's not going to need it anymore, and then you can do what you will with her.'

Wolf could feel the rage swell up from within, but knew it best not to let it show in case it was taken as a sign of weakness. 'Get lost, you little turd.'

Leyland walked off sniggering as he shouted out, 'The first person to bring me a drink can have their turn.'

Wolf's thoughts returned to Mad-dog. They had been fierce

rivals since childhood, and he knew Mad-dog would gladly end his life if given half the chance. Then again he would do the same to Mad-dog.

'We need another horse.' Fat-man looked up from his meal in response to Wolf's remark. 'Now Ginger is dead I will have his horse and once Mad-dog's gang leave camp we will go looking for a horse for you.'

'That's easier said than done,' replied Fat-man. 'There's no one around here with a horse because we have taken them all, and the only way to get our hands on one is to barter for one from a trader. And what have we got to use in exchange?'

Wolf smiled. 'Easy. When Mad-dog and his rabble are gone we will take the woman he brought in, and swap her at the market!'

A grin appeared across Fat-man's face, revealing his diseased teeth

'I like it. I like it at lot.' And with that he turned his gaze back to his meal.

8

MEMORIES

Mary leaned over her duffle bag and rummaged inside until her hands touched the smooth edge of a book, and as she nestled her back against the wall she pulled it out. She was alone. The last few weeks had been unbearable, living in the refuge of the old chalk and flint mines that had lain hidden for hundreds of years under what was once her home city before its destruction.

Reading the dairy that now rested on her lap was one of the few distractions Mary could enjoy. She opened the green plastic cover and ran her finger along the smooth printed first page advertising the wares and services of companies long lost in the dust of history.

'Icarus Hines, not just a butcher, a Bar-B-Q Specialist.' Her mouth was watering as she spoke the words while her eyes darted from picture to picture showing the large selections of meats, sausages and burgers proudly on display.

'How I wish I could just walk into a shop and buy everything on display. You just don't appreciate what you have until you can't have it any more,' she thought, while her stomach rumbled, followed by the slow hunger pain that grew the more she dreamt of sizzling sausages with eggs, beans, fried mushrooms and toast, all washed down with steaming mugs of sweet tea. It was no good. No matter how much she wanted to be able to relive the memories of life before the Over-seers she had to live in the present, so turned the page.

Her attention was next drawn to an advert for artificial grass with accompanying pictures of gardens resplendent in all their fakery. 'How wastefully humanity disregarded what nature provided for free,' she thought. Another few flicks of the pages brought what she was looking for: the handwritten words of a man she had never met, but felt an attachment to. Someone who had lived in a world that only she could remember, a way of life lost in destruction by earthquakes, floods, and fires before being remoulded by the Over-seers. The effects of their arrival in the Orb had caused humanities downfall, and now they lived off its labour as the ultimate new masters while brainwashing their feeding fodder with the Daily Procedures.

A sigh seeped from Mary's lips as a small tear rolled down her cheek. Rubbing it away with the sleeve of her dress she started to read the diary.

'January 1st. The weather has been all over the place recently. One day the wind blows from the equator bringing scorching heat, and then three days later it blows from the pole bringing snow.' These few words, just a sentence long, always sent a shiver through her body as if they had been chiselled from ice. Mary thumbed through to the usual pages

'February 5th. Wedding anniversary. Must book surprise meal at Rushcutters, arrange babysitter for Joe and Lucy.' The name Rushcutters felt familiar, but she wasn't sure if she had ever visited the place when she was just a young child. She liked the name. It felt welcoming, and images of feeding swans by the riverbank shot across her mind. She thumbed some more pages.

'March 24th. I'm concerned about continuing weather problems, not good for business, major problems with transport of goods to and from warehouse.

April 1st. I wonder if it's all one big April Fool's Day joke, all these rumours in the media of approaching objects from deepest space?

April 3rd. What a shock. All the staff are glued to the TV news channels as the UN announces large Orb heading to earth. Aliens maybe!'

Mary didn't know why, but she always seemed to reread the same pages, as if hoping that somehow by magic the wording would change. More than anything she wished they would be just mundane words, everyday appointments, and memories. A world that no longer existed, a world Mary desperately wanted to return to.

'May 17th. Terrible day. Giant tsunami two hundred feet tall wipes Sidney from the face of the earth.

May 18th. Another giant tsunami hits east coast of America. New York, Boston, and Miami all gone.

May 19th. When will it end? Tsunami has hit west coast of Africa and Europe, from Lagos to Lisbon, from Amsterdam to London, up from Hamburg to Oslo, all gone, buried in a wall of water and wiped from the face of the earth.'

These three deadly days were buried deep in Mary's memory from her childhood and now they felt as if it had only happened last week. Mary was brought out of her daze by a sudden loud crackle from the fire. Without realising it these last entries had left her hypnotised, and she knew the next pages were filled with just as much horror. Talking in a whispered voice as if showing respect for this record of history she continued.

'May 20th. Millions around the world have died. It can't get any worse? Can it?

May 21st. First earthquakes felt, not much damage locally but from Manchester to Munich across to Mumbai all left devastated.

May 22nd. Heard on the news that tsunamis and earthquakes are being caused by the gravitational pull of the approaching Orb.'

Mary tutted then took in a deep breath. She stopped for a second but was drawn back to the page.

'May 23rd. The area has suffered increasing earthquakes so I have moved all my family to the works unit as it's made of steel and reinforced concrete so able to withstand the tremors.'

The next entry was the one that hit home what a terrible catastrophe all of humanity had suffered, a disaster so terrible mankind could have followed the fate of the dinosaurs. A fate it could still follow under the rule of the Over-seers.

'May 24th. According to what remains of the media the death toll is no longer being counted in the millions, but in the billions and is rising by the hour.

May 25th. Terrible damage caused by yesterday's earthquake. I have invited all my workers to seek shelter and safety in the warehouse with their families.'

Mary paused, looked up from the page and was suddenly mesmerised with the shadows that flickered off the walls. She wiped another tear that had escaped from the safety of her eye as it rolled down her aged cheek.

'Why didn't we see this coming? Why did we humans think we were so clever we could overcome anything that got in our way? Why were we so surprised when Mother Nature turned on us like an abused wife when a new lover came courting on the horizon?'

Mary riffled under her long skirt and retrieved a handkerchief. After wiping her moist eyes, she blew her noise so loudly it echoed down the tunnel. Once settled she returned to the next entry.

'May 26th. All order has collapsed. Martial Law has been declared. The army is on the street, shooting anyone who breaks the curfew.

May 27th. Most of my workers and their families have taken up my offer. The unit has a generator so we have been able to replace the electricity which was cut off six days ago. We have limited running water, but at least we are well stocked up on tinned food.

May 28th. We now have to seek secure shelter in Storage Area One during the frequent earthquakes. Its thick metal sides and ceiling gives protection. We can just about fit everyone in. There is limited contact with the outside. There is only one government-run radio station left on the air which gives out daily briefings.'

'What a terrible May it had been,' thought Mary. 'Normally it's such a lovely month; spring is in full stride with all the blooms flirting their wares wildly to any passing bishe-barnibees, excited as they hunt for aphids.' Wetting the tip of her finger before returning to the diary she quickly thumbed more pages until she came to the final weeks in June.

'June 22nd. There have been no tremors or flooding for some weeks. The radio says it's like this all around the world and the planet seems to have stopped its convulsions.

June 23rd. I left the unit with a couple of others to scout around and saw the Orb for the first time. It's larger than the moon and is visible during the day, but is even more dramatic at night. It just hangs in the sky. The radio says there has been no contact from whoever is inside.

June 24th. We left the unit again today to seek fresh water. There is nothing now. Not even the army is on the streets any more. We have armed ourselves with tools and makeshift weapons, and keep the women and children in at all times.

June 25th. There was great excitement tinged with foreboding today. Large space ships have been seen leaving the Orb and landing on earth. The radio says they have come to save humanity and that everyone should do as instructed by them.'

Mary's attention was distracted for a second time as the flickering flames flicked lighted sparks into the dark void above, only for them to return as burnt cinders. The pot on top simmered with just two meagre skinless rats inside.

'July 7th. I have seen today what I never expected to see in my life and that was alien beings. They were encased in silver suits and stood taller than any man. I saw them from a distance and thought it best to keep out of their way.

July 8th. There is nothing now. We have run out of fuel for the generator so there is no electricity, no working gas supply, no running water or working sewers, no working communications, and no authorities to keep control. The government radio station no longer plays any music, just a daily bulletin which is repeated all day. There is no other media'

Mary's eyes were now tiring in the dim light. 'It's no good,' she thought, 'I need to put my glasses on.'

With Daniel and Gwendolyn out the way she felt more comfortable wearing them. Delving through the duffle bag until her fingers clasped what she was looking for Mary pulled out a small black cloth bag which contained her golden rimmed glasses. They rested snugly on her nose as she continued.

'August 22nd. The radio has given a name to the aliens from the Orb. It has advised everyone over the age of forty to seek out an Over-seer and one of their transport ships where they can be transferred to the Orb. Two of my staff members who have no family and are over forty are leaving the unit today.

August 26th. The same message has been played now on the radio for the last four days. All persons over forty to seek out the Over-seers for transportation to the Orb. It has started to sound very sinister.'

Mary thumbed more pages and her eyes automatically fell onto the same written lines that she had read time after time in the last month while trapped in the mine like a pickle in a jar. Sometimes she had an image of the writer's face. Although she had never met him she could sense his long-gone presence through the book.

'September 12th. We stopped listening to the radio until today when a new instruction was given. All persons are to leave areas of habitation by October 1st and seek resettlement in camps being set up. Over and over the message plays. It has caused a rift among us. Half our group wants to leave and half want to stay. I'm going to stay here with my family. We have shelter and enough food to last the rest of the year.

September 13th. After much debate it had been agreed that anyone who wants to leave for one of these resettlement camps will go tomorrow, and can take some of the food with them.

September 21st. There has been no more information from the radio, just hissing. All contact with the outside world has stopped. We spend most of our time in Storage Area One, safe from whatever monsters may be lurking in the outside world.

October 1st. Heard terrible explosions outside today. Fred and I went to investigate and were horrified by the sight of giant metal monsters standing on three legs, taller than most buildings. They looked like one-eyed beasts from mythical stories that strode the landscape breathing fire and destruction with laser beams that shot out from their bellies.

October 3rd. I found one last battery that isn't flat and used it on the radio. We didn't expect to hear anything so the surprise was even more enjoyable as we heard the voice of Elvis Presley singing Love Me Tender waft softly out of the speaker. The joy was compounded when we heard a woman's voice who said she spoke on behalf of the resistance movement.'

The mention of this song had Mary thinking of her own parents. It was a favourite of theirs and she could remember it being played around her home as a child. Her father would hum it without realising, and when he cuddled her too. These reflections were no good. They were breaking Mary's heart because she had no mementoes to remember them by.

'October 21st. The destruction has been going on twenty-four hours a day, every day, for the last three weeks. Whatever was not destroyed by the tsunamis and earthquakes is being destroyed by the Over-seers. I now know how it must have felt for them poor people stuck in the trenches of the First World War. The only solace we have is from the resistance radio station, but this is only for half an hour a day as we have to make the remaining batteries last. The only other thing I can do is to write in my diary.'

There were only two months left to go through and they always seemed to cause Mary the most pain. She didn't know why she kept putting herself through it, but it had become addictive in the boredom of hiding for so long underground in constant fear of being found, and with no way of escape.

'November 1st. My wonderful warehouse was directly hit today. I just managed to close the door to Storage Area One as the roof came crashing down. I had left to see if I could find another battery for the radio as it stopped working this morning. The resistance had named the walking beasts Triclops, and one was nearby as I scuttled through the broken glass. It was just destroying everything in its path and I could see through the twisted shutters it was heading our way. I ran for safety and closed the door just as a high-pitched sound followed by a red light burst into the warehouse, and the walls tumbled down.

November 2nd. Today will be my last entry unless we are rescued. We cannot open the door as it is blocked by something on the other side. We are trapped, and worse, I believe the ventilation unit on the other side has been damaged because ammonia is seeping into the room and we are slowly choking to death. The candlelight has nearly died, and once it fades away we will be in the darkness of death. My family is by my side and we are all too exhausted to move. So are the others who stayed. We tried everything to open the door, but I have now accepted our fate. My dying wish is that if my diary is ever found, it is found by a human being, and not by one of those aliens.'

Mary stopped whispering and held a respectful if reflective moment of silence.

What followed this final entry was blank. 'I wonder what would have been written on these pages if this poor fellow had lived?' thought Mary. 'I wonder what mundane everyday entries would have replaced these chilling words if the Over-seers had never shown up?' Her deliberations could have carried on racing off into different scenarios, but the distant sound of approaching chatter sent Mary scuttling to replace the diary back in the bag, closely followed by her glasses.

Pushing hard she rocked herself to her knees, then after another attempt managed to get to her feet before grabbing her umbrella that rested against the wall, and which was her only means of defence.

'It's only us,' called out Gwendolyn as two shadows appeared from the blackness of the passageway.

Mary felt herself relax, knowing her two young friends had safely returned from their trip to the outside world. What also increased her excitement were the two plump pigeons hanging from Gwendolyn's belt alongside a ginger tom cat. Daniel's arms were stacked with thick logs.

'Well done, you two.' said Mary. 'Daniel, you stoke the fire, and Gwendolyn you skin the cat. I will pluck and gut the birds. We will feast tonight and so will the horses.'

Mary began pulling at the grey feathers from the flesh of the birds and hummed a joyful tune as the darkness was beaten back by the rising power of the fire that roared ever louder with every piece of wood added to it. Smoke floated above their heads like a shroud hung from the ceiling, before slowly seeping its way through the network of tunnels that spread out in all directions.

Gwendolyn had soon completed her task as she explained what the situation was like above ground.

'It's very quiet up top. I couldn't see a single Triclops, and Daniel scouted the whole area and didn't see any Hunters. Did you, Daniel?'

He agreed while prodding the fire. 'I think we are in the clear, and whoever was after us has given up, or just moved on thinking we must have done the same.'

The pot of water was bubbling away as the cat, rats, and birds boiling flesh filled the air with its aroma, and with dried herbs added to the mix their rumblings of hunger would be satisfied once again as they tucked into their meal.

'That was lovely!' exclaimed Mary as she slurped the last dregs from her bowl before wiping the dribble from her chin. 'If it's as safe on top as you claim, Gwendolyn, then you can take the horses outside to graze.'

Gwendolyn noisily finished her meal. 'Honestly Mary, we didn't hear or see a soul. That's why I was able to shoot so much game. I laid the bait expecting only to get a rat or two, and when these pigeons turned up looking for some scraps I couldn't believe my luck. Once they were dispatched I left them were they lay, and behold, not soon after that big ginger tom turned up thinking it had another easy lunch. But what it didn't know was it would end up being the lunch.'

Daniel couldn't join in the joke as both Mary and Gwendolyn chuckled to themselves. He had no choice at the moment other than to eat whatever could be caught. It was only a couple of months ago that he could look forward to roasted chicken with vegetables, and fresh baked bread finished off with sweet fruits from the berry bushes and trees that grew around his home. His thoughts, as they always did, turned to his family. He hoped they were safe and no harm had come to them since he had killed the Over-seer. He knew Mother would be worried for him and that Sarah was probably too young to understand, but it was his father he was most concerned about. Life would be hard for him now that not only had he lost his axe when Daniel took it while fleeing, but also the demise of Duster the beloved family horse. His feelings turned a dark grey as the memory of Duster's drowning while they crossed the estuary came flooding back. Although he now had Champion to take Duster's place it still couldn't take away the pain. It was no good. Daniel had to take his mind away from the past before it fell into a deep well of depression with no hopeful means of escape.

'Like I was saying Daniel… Are you listening to me Daniel?' He was brought out of his trance-like state by Mary's question. 'Like I was saying, we will scout before first light while the horses stay here and regain their strength while feeding. We won't be able to ride them for a day or so, and will have to travel by foot. We need to return to Daniel's village to warn his parents of the horrors that await them within the Achievement Centre.'

Daniel's heart sank like a stone tossed into a well of despair at Mary's remark. 'I'm going to check the horses and then take them outside for some fresh air,' he replied. 'Are you coming with me, Gwendolyn?'

Before she could answer Mary butted in. 'Wait just one minute,

Mr Jones, until I have finished with the plan. Once we are all satisfied there are no Hunter gangs, Over-seers or their walking Triclops machines about then we will head off at dawn. We will have no choice but to return the way we left although we can take a different route out of the city to start with. Is everyone in agreement?'

Daniel and Gwendolyn both nodded silently. They had no choice. Mary had used her stern but wise voice, which showed she would countenance no objections.

Daniel got up and collected his axe and the shield of gold that glistened with the glow of the fire before heading for the exit.

Champion lifted his head when Daniel stroked his white coat.

'Champs, I have a treat for you,' and led him outside for the first time in weeks, as Gwendolyn followed with Orlov and Mary's horse.

The sun had set and the night sky was clear as the stars sparkled in all their glory while a crescent moon glowed against the giant Orb that sat motionless in the heavens.

'How long is it until your father reaches forty?' Gwendolyn enquired sheepishly, not knowing if Daniel would want to talk about it.

'To be truthful I have lost all track of time since my life was turned upside down and I had to go on the run, especially so since we have spent all this time underground. Maybe a week or more, maybe even less.'

The air was still as the horses grazed on the last of the tall late summer grass that grew among the ruins of this once fine city.

'That's more than enough time to get back to your home village and stop your father going to the Achievement Centre.' Gwendolyn hoped her words would give encouragement to Daniel, but he didn't smile.

'You would be right, Gwendolyn, in any normal situation, but our situation isn't normal.' Daniel sat down on a pile of rubble and started to flick a stone around with his foot. 'At this present time we are probably the most wanted fugitives on this planet. Everyone either wants to kill us or worse.'

'What can be worse than that?' asked Gwendolyn.

'Being handed over to the Over-seers to be eaten alive, very slowly and extremely painfully,' was Daniel's reply. No further words were said.

9

THE RETURN HOME

Sharp claws grabbed the flesh of his neck and squeezed tightly as the last breath of life lurched from the lungs. Fangs glistened with stinking saliva as it dripped onto the floor, and with one gaping bite tore at the throat. Blood spurted forth as the vein was ripped open, and raw flesh was torn from the spine before it was consumed.

Daniel awoke with a sudden jolt, his heart beating madly, and once again the beads of sweat on his brow confirmed he had just been summoned from another nightmare. He wiped his brow in the darkness. At his feet was a pile of glowing ash that had once been the fire, which now gave just enough light for Daniel to see the back of his hand. He fumbled around the chalk floor until he touched the rough bark of some twigs, then placed them on top of the ash. He blew a panting breath into the glow and slowly the twigs caught alight. The darkness gave way until he could locate the logs that would once again turn flame into fire. One was added, then two others, and when the fourth log was placed on top the fire was complete.

Daniel didn't need any light to tell him Mary was still asleep. The echo of her snoring was confirmation enough as he stared at Gwendolyn curled up on the ground opposite him. The soft skin of her face looked angelic, but Daniel knew it hid a determined character that could be as deadly as any devil. For some reason he found that mix exciting, although he wouldn't admit it. They had only recently stumbled across each other, but he had never spent so much time with someone from the opposite sex, and the more he did so the more he wanted to.

Mary snorted loudly as she turned onto her side, which caught his attention as the rhythms of her heavy breathing started once again. Daniel looked at Mary's outstretched arm, glancing at the watch on her wrist. She had taught him while they had been hiding underground how to tell the time. There was nothing else to do especially in the first couple of weeks when aboveground swarmed with Over-seers, Hunter gangs and Triclops all looking for their blood. Mary had even started to teach him how to read and write, using the dairy as their only book while chalking words on the walls, but he found it frustrating, and even more so when Gwendolyn tried to help. He knew Gwendolyn was only trying her best for him, but for some reason he felt it made himself look weak in front of her as he struggled with only the most basic words while she could read at will. On a couple of occasions this frustration had turned to anger as he had stormed off into the darkness with only a flaming torch to keep him company. He would return once this irritation had subsided while Mary would always have the right words to say to sooth his battered ego.

'Did you find anything of interest on your exploration? It's good to go off on your own occasionally. If not we would all go stir-crazy down here. Would anyone like some tea? Although I'm afraid we have no milk, or sugar, or even tea, but never mind at least we are still alive.' A smile would follow and everyone would be friends once again.

It was now five in the morning according to Mary's watch, and Daniel decided to scout the outside world to see if at last it would be safe enough to leave the old flint mines, and make the return journey home.

The sun was already on the horizon. Daniel hid behind the

thicket of bushes that concealed the entrance and spent five minutes listening for any danger. Only the birds could be heard as they sang their dawn choruses. Listening intently he could make out some individual birds, but there was one song missing, the crow of a cockerel that Daniel had always awoken to in his home village. He ventured out into the open, darting about the ruins, trying to blend into his surroundings. There was nothing, no danger, just miles of desolate destruction that reached as far as the eye could see. He returned to wake up the others.

Mary as normal took a while to be awoken from her slumber, but Gwendolyn was soon up and about with a smile. The bags were packed as breakfast was missed and after the horses were saddled they were led out into the morning glow of the sun.

'So which way do we take then, Mary?' Daniel asked and she pointed into the opposite direction of the rising sun.

'We will head west until we reach open countryside before heading south.'

The trio started to walk by their horses as they navigated the rough terrain of fallen masonry, loose bricks and overgrown vegetation.

Daniel stopped to take a final look over his shoulder then called out to the others, 'Let's return home.'

* * *

'So what do you think?'

There was no reply, just the sound of lobster shell being cracked open followed by the mumblings of delight as soft white succulent meat was thrust down a gaping mouth to the cavernous belly below.

'So, like I said, do you think she's worth a horse?'

Ogling eyes looked over the forlorn female figure that sat in front with hands tied behind a chair and a gag shoved into her mouth. The claws of the lobster took more effort to crack open. Silence was the only reply forthcoming as Wolf began to get agitated.

'Look – what are you? A trader or some ruddy chief?'

Another loud crack announced the claws had been defeated, soon followed by slurping as the meat was sucked from the carcass.

'If you're not interested there are plenty more traders I could go to in the market.' Wolf nodded at Fat-man. 'Come on, Maxwell. We're wasting our time here. Let's go elsewhere.' And he turned for the door.

'She's a bit battered and bruised.'

These words stopped Wolf in his tracks.

'So you're interested then in doing a swap?'

'I could be, but…' Dell looked down at his flabby gut, then picked up scraps of lobster that clung to his shirt. 'Don't want to waste this, do we? This stuff costs more to barter for than that old nag in front of me.' He looked up, holding Wolf's stare. 'And an old nag is all she is worth.'

Wolf had had enough. 'You must be kidding.'

Dell didn't flinch. 'I never kid, Mr Hunter. So why are you here in the first place? I thought you would have no need to return to the slave market. You should be able to take whatever you want. Of course we fall under the protection of the Over-seers so you have no jurisdiction here. Do you? If you need something from us you have to trade for it, and by the state of this female you have brought with you today you don't have much to barter with. Do you?' Wolf said nothing and Fat-man couldn't help either. 'I have a mule around the back.'

'A mule,' spluttered Fat-man.

Wolf stayed silent

'A mule?' repeated Fat-man. 'What are we going to do with a mule? We need a horse, not a mule.'

He looked at Wolf, searching for a response. Instead, Wolf leaned forward, held out his hand, and said, 'You have a deal.'

'What the hell are you doing?' Fat-man cried out as he followed Wolf around the back of the hut to the trader's pen at the back.

'Getting the best deal possible,' he replied. 'We have visited most of the other slave traders and Dell knew it. No one wanted her. After Mad-dog and his gang had finished with her I'm surprised she was still alive. Not only that, she's no spring chicken. She's closer to receiving her just reward at the Achievement Centre than either me or you, so think about it. What would you do with her if we couldn't trade her? Take her for your wife?'

Fat-man hesitated, then asked, 'So what are we going to do with a mule?'

Wolf smiled. 'You asked the wrong question. I have a horse. The question you should have asked is what are you going to do with a mule?' And then he started to laugh. 'Let's return home.'

10

BLACK SHUCK

The mood was happy although enclosed by nervousness as they walked, and was only broken when they came across a round island overgrown with bushes and trees that broke the straightness of the road.

Mary explained to Daniel that it was called a roundabout and that once thousands of vehicles would travel around it all day. She knew he had no concept of numbers beyond a couple of hundred, and she could tell by the look on his face he though it a crazy idea to spend your time going round in circles.

'If I'm correct this road will carry on and we should come to a river.'

Gwendolyn's heart felt as if it had missed a beat when she heard these words from Mary, but as she carried on talking the mention of a bridge made her relax.

'There should be a bridge and once over the river there should be no other of nature's obstacles until we leave the city.'

Mary paused and Gwendolyn felt uneasy all of a sudden because she knew what Mary had to say next would start with the word 'but'. She felt sick at the prospect of having to cross another expanse of water.

'But of course, if the bridge has been destroyed we will have to go through the heart of the city and that will slow us down, or try to swim across the river.'

Gwendolyn spoke under her breath. 'I hope the bridge is there, I hope the bridge is there, I hope the bridge is there.' She couldn't face another duel with death as they followed the road up its small incline. At the end the bridge came into view.

Mary stopped and Daniel could tell by her expression something was concerning her

'Your mystic senses kicking in Mary?' he enquired.

Mary paused and Gwendolyn felt uneasy again as she knew another 'but' was on the way.

'But there is something else. I don't know what it is but I feel uneasy. I feel as if I'm being watched by something, but I don't know what it is.'

Gwendolyn's hand automatically felt for the bow resting over her back, and she noticed Daniel do the same with his axe.

'So what do you think it is? Do you think Hunters or Over-seers are nearby?'

Mary shook her head while her reply didn't give any answers.

'I don't know. I don't think it's Over-seers. You can normally hear them clanging about in their metal suits, and I don't think it's Hunters because they like the theatre and dramatics of the chase. No. There's something out there watching us and my gut feeling tells me we will find out quite soon what it is.'

Daniel decided to take the lead while, with his axe in hand, he walked next to Champion, firmly holding onto the reins. Mary followed in the middle holding her umbrella as if it was a sword, with her bag slung low over her shoulder so it rested on her arm like a shield. Gwendolyn followed at the rear. She too had taken the bow from her back and kept watch behind to make sure nothing crept up unseen.

The adrenalin was flowing freely through the three tense travellers as they approached the bridge, they stopped, looking on in disbelief.

It was still intact and free of major obstructions, but strewn across its surface were bare bones from many different beasts of all shapes and sizes. The most obvious skulls and the sight that would have unsettled the nerves of even the bravest warrior were the human skulls that mutely told their own sad stories.

Daniel took a step forward, but Champion hesitated and as his rein was given a gentle tug he snorted back his anxiety. Daniel tugged again, and again he snorted his concern. He was only persuaded to move forward by the reassuring stroke of Daniel's hand along his white coat as softly spoken words of encouragement were spoken.

Champion's reaction had spooked Mary's horse too and when Orlov started to snort his displeasure the second warning sign of danger ahead had been signalled.

Daniel couldn't see why the horses were concerned with the bridge crossing. It was only a small bridge which would be crossed within a minute. It looked in good order with no visible damage, and was to his eyes the best built bridge he had ever seen. The bridges back in his home valley were made of wood, and held together with nothing more than rope. In comparison this bridge could take much greater weights. He knew if Duster was here with him now he would stride confidently across it without so much as a snort or a neigh. Slowly they walked to the bridge and when Daniel reached it he stopped, jumped up and down on the tarmac surface as hard as he could, and said delightedly, 'It looks safe, although the bones are a concern, but we don't have time to take a detour so we have no other choice but to cross.'

He had already reached the middle by the time Orlov's hind legs came clattering onto it so now there was no turning back. Champion lifted his head again and swayed his white mane violently, pulling Daniel's arm back. He lost hold of the rein. While trying to calm Champion he took his eye off the road ahead until suddenly his attention was grabbed by the sound of barking.

He turned back to face the road in front and there at the end of the bridge stood a small terrier-like dog, defiantly barking. Soon it was joined by another who came charging out of the burnt remains of a building ahead. It was barking as well soon followed by another, then another, then another.

The dogs made a deafening sound as they barked menacingly, blocking the road off the bridge. The noise made the horses frantic and they started to rear up on their hind legs. Daniel looked behind and was ready to suggest they walk back the way they had come, and find another way, but it was too late. Gwendolyn had her back to him facing the way they had just arrived, and there standing guard against any possible retreat was another line of ravenous dogs growling violently.

The sides of the bridge were too high for the horses to get over although the drop to the river didn't seem too dangerous, but the reality soon sunk in.

They were trapped!

Slowly the trio took steps back until they were huddled in the middle of the bridge trying their best to look calm while showing no fear, but the horses gave the game away with their frantic snorting and neighing.

More dogs came running out of different ruins until the line was so thick there were too many to count. Daniel again looked up to the building to his right from where the first dog had appeared, and there on the roof stood even more dogs, like soldiers on the ramparts of a castle.

Then there was a loud gut wrenching howl and the barking started to die down.

For a second time the howl called out and this time all the dogs respectfully fell silent. They just stood there either side of the bridge in rows five deep while more stood on mounds of rubble ready to join the attack at any moment.

Out of the distance a lone dog came running. Daniel could tell it was a large beast, but he didn't realise how big it was until the other dogs automatically made way for it. There was a gentle breeze that whispered its name, Black Shuck, and from it snarls came: I am the Beast of Beelzebub.

Daniel quickly turned to Mary. 'Take Champion's reins for me. If he becomes too uncontrollable then tie them to the railings.'

Gwendolyn had already reacted to the situation because Mary was looking after Orlov. She had tensioned her bow in one hand with an arrow in the other pointing at the dogs on her side as they slowly, step by step, pushed towards her growling.

Daniel's hands were now free to hold his axe and a game of brinkmanship with the leader of the pack began.

It was a large beasty of a dog with black fur that hung in large tangled clumps from its skinny frame, and its eyes roared with hunger. It started to snarl, revealing large threatening fangs with saliva dripping from the pink flesh of its inner jaws.

Daniel had seen that hungry look before. It was inside the Achievement Centre, just before the Over-seers feasted on the live human flesh. There was only one difference: this time these humans were not going to just lie down in submission. They would fight to the death.

Black Shuck, the wind whispered, as the beast slowly took a pace forward, then another.

Daniel stood his ground.

He could hear Mary muttering to herself and glanced back. She was trying to hold the reins of three startled horses with one hand while at the same time her other hand was thumbing inside the bag that rested against her stomach.

'I know it's in here somewhere. So where is it?'

In the fleeting glance Daniel had lost the moment with the beast, and had to take a step back because it had now crossed onto the bridge followed by its hungry malevolent followers. He could still hear her and wanted to turn around again to find out what she was so intent on finding at a moment like this, but he couldn't.

The dogs were encroaching ever closer. There was no more

standoff, the pack was ready to pounce, and only waited for their leader to make its move.

'Here it is!' exclaimed Mary in triumphant, and she held her hand in the air.

Daniel didn't want to take his eye of the lead dog, but Mary's excited exclamations became too much for his curiosity, and he had to look.

'This is going to even things up a bit.' And with that she looped the horse's reins under her arm so both hands were free, then pulled a small strap from the end of a long slim cylinder.

'Flare,' she shouted. 'Let's see how they like this.'

Daniel had been mystified by many things Mary had said or done since he had first met her, and this was no different. He thought the nickname Mystic Mary suited her well, and now she was up to something again, and whatever it was it not only made him, Gwendolyn, and the horses jump back startled, but also the wild dogs.

There she stood with her back straight and arm outstretched, and in her clenched fist she held the tube as smoke appeared. Red flames came spurting out making a thunderous hissing noise, and as she started to move her arm from side to side, the smoke bellowed continuously until the bridge became engulfed in a cloud as thick as fog.

All sense was lost in a cacophony of sounds. The horse's hooves clattered on the road while the dogs were barking wildly, and above it all Mary could be heard shouting.

'Right, you dogs. Come and have a go if you think you're hard enough.'

Daniel couldn't see a thing through all the red haze. He took five paces to his right and used his sense of hearing to work out the position of the oncoming pack as their paws scuttled across the surface of the road as they hurtled towards him.

He took one step forward then stopped before stretching his left leg out in front then lowered it so his right knee was resting on the ground. With the axe held tight in both hands he swung it low in the blindness of the smoke from right to left until it made contact with the whimpering body of a dog. Standing up he took one more step forward then stopped before stretching his right leg out in front so this time his left knee was resting. The axe was swung low from left to right until once again it made contact, and sent its receiver howling to its doom.

He stood up again and repeated the action, maiming any dog that so dared to get in his way. Again and again he stepped forward and swung his axe low in the swirling smoke, and again and again another whimpering mutt was dispatched.

Now he changed his tack. He took five paces back then five paces to his left so he was roughly back to where he thought he had started, but it was impossible to tell where exactly he was on the bridge through all the smoke, noise, and confusion.

He could still hear the hiss from the flare and Mary saying, 'Take that you brute, and that, and that.' And an image flashed into his head of Mary swiping and stabbing at the approaching dogs with her umbrella.

He knew Gwendolyn would be swiftly dispatching the attackers at her end of the bridge, but he was still concerned they would be overrun by the ravaging pack, and end up exhausted on the floor while their live flesh was ripped from their bones like the Overseers in the Achievement Centre.

Daniel knew these were the most dangerous of all dogs. They were not like the couple of domesticated animals that scavenged for titbits in his village, but dogs which had been living wild for generations. They were constantly hungry and would not give up on any prey until they had eaten.

As a young child he had heard the horror stories told at night when safely in front of the family fire about large packs of dogs. They roamed in the wild looking for anything to eat, and if they couldn't find it they would eat their own dead or dying comrades.

Daniel was determined it wasn't going to be him, or his friends, so took a step forward and lowered his leg, then swung the axe low, and again another body made contact with the sharp metal of his axe head. This time as he tried to stand up his ankle was held down and he could just about see the very same small dog that first appeared on the bridge. It held the bottom of his trouser leg firmly in its jaw, and was shaking its head violently from side to side.

The smoke was starting to lift.

Kicking out his leg hoping to dislodge the little runt was futile because it wasn't going to let go. He kicked out again, but to no effect so in one last desperate act he swung the blunt end of his axe against the mongrel's head before it crashed into his ankle, sending a shock wave of pain up his leg, through his body, and screaming from his mouth.

'Aaahhh!'

The axe dropped to the ground and for a second it was lost in the mists of despair. He clutched his ankle and hobbled about on one foot. The smoke was clearing, and he could see the barrier at the side of the bridge. He was facing towards the river and not the road, for he had lost all direction in the fracas.

He turned just in time to see the Beast of Beelzebub spring towards him. He brought his arm up in defence and its fangs dug into his flesh making Daniel fall backwards, banging his head on the ground. He felt dazed, but didn't have time to dwell on the pain which exploded simultaneously in his left arm and skull.

The beast pounced again, and he just had time to raise both hands and grab it by the front legs as it went this time for his throat. The smell of fear seeped from Daniel's skin as he fought for his life with the giant dog on top of him, snarling wildly in between its attempts to rip the veins from his neck.

They were face to face. The stale breath of the beast punished Daniel's nose, and its saliva frothed lashing into his face.

He tried to roll over but the sword in its scabbard attached to his belt stopped him, so he rocked over to the other side, and there just inches from his face lay his axe. It was so close yet so far. He could not reach it. He could not let go of the dog's legs, not even for a second because if he did his throat would be gouged open.

It was a fight to the death and there could only be one victor.

He rocked to his left again and then to his right trying to build up momentum to aid his bid in throwing the beast off him, but it didn't work. The dog was too big and its muscles too strong for Daniel to overcome.

His strength was starting to fade and the deadly jaws of the beast brushed the flesh of his neck as he strained for a way out.

The breeze was moving on the smoke from the flare when a shadow appeared over the two fighting warriors.

Whack.

'Take that.'

Whack.

'And that.'

Poke.

'And take that in the eye, you nasty animal.'

The sound of horse's hooves galloping on the hard surface of the road echoed in Daniel's ears, and from the corner of his eye he saw a white blur flash past followed by a black blur then a third, and he knew the horses had finally given into their fear caused by the chaos of battle, and had run for safety.

The dog's attention had been taken off Daniel as Mary stood over them, hitting and poking Black Shuck with the sharp point of her umbrella. It was his one chance and with all the power he could muster he rocked from side to side, and then flung the dog off him, and onto its back.

He struggled to his feet, gasping for air, but could not hesitate for a second. His hand was shaking with adrenalin, or fear, which one he couldn't tell, as he struggled to unclip, and pull at the handle of his sword. It came free from its sheath. Stepping forward he swung it wildly at the dog as it was trying to get to its feet. The beast that had only minutes earlier been howling its dominance now whimpered as steel sliced across his gnashing jaws. Injured, its confidence dented, the swish of the approaching blade sent it into a snarling retreat.

The sight of the injured leader stopped the attacking pack as the smell of dog's blood grabbed their attention. The last remnants of smoke had disappeared with the wind to reveal the carnage of dead or dying animals. Some lay still, some crawled injured, but their fate was doomed as their hungry comrades fell on them in a mad frenzy of feeding.

The feeling of warm liquid running down his arm made Daniel look. The blood oozed out of his torn flesh. Pain came flooding back as it overpowered the adrenalin, and he staggered, overwhelmed with the urge to be sick.

Mary had extended her umbrella and used it as a shield while she once again rummaged through the contents of her bag.

'Don't worry, Daniel. I have something for that. I know I do, or is it in one of the other bags strapped to the saddles?'

He turned and looked at Gwendolyn. She had her back to him, and in front of her dogs streamed from the rubble to join the feeding fury as fur was ripped from flesh, then flesh from bone. She had used all her arrows, and now had only her dagger, which she held at arm's length to keep the dogs from attacking.

'Stop fussing, Mary. We need to get out of here now while the dogs are filling their bellies and before they return for us. Go grab Gwendolyn.'

Daniel bent down, picked up his axe, and painfully lifted it over his shoulder. His left arm was paralysed with pain and it was a struggle to replace his sword back in its sheath. It was the first time he had used it in anger. It had saved his life, but he knew if Mary had not come to his rescue he would have been the one the dogs were feeding on, and not their own fallen or injured comrades.

Mary turned her attention to Gwendolyn who refused to move at first as Mary pulled her arm. She wanted to retrieve all her arrows, but the growling from the mutts as they fed stopped her from approaching any animal with an arrow sticking out of it.

'Let go of my arm, Mary. I need to get my arrows back.'

Mary tugged her arm a second time, but with a lot more force on this occasion.

'Don't talk a load of old squit, girl. Do you want to die for the sake of some pieces of wood?'

Mary now used both her hands to grab Gwendolyn's arm, and this time the force of her pulling, and the alarm in her voice made her relent.

'Come on!'

Gwendolyn took some steps back, making sure she kept her arm out and the dagger exposed as a warning.

'Where's Orlov?'

She had only just noticed that the horses had fled, and was ready to berate Mary for not looking after them, when Daniel turned towards her and the wound in his arm came into view. The site of his blood dripping on the ground made her inhale in shock. She held her hand to her mouth as if to hold back a scream, then rushed to his side.

'Quick, Mary. We need something to cover it and stem the flow of blood.'

Mary had already looked through her bag and knew she had nothing, but an idea flashed into her head. 'Give me your dagger, Gwendolyn.'

Gwendolyn looked confused until Mary bent down and lifted the hem of her long dress. Once she had the knife she cut a piece of material from it. She handed it back to Gwendolyn.

'You keep guard while I bandage his arm.'

Mary's hand was shaking as she wrapped the cloth around his arm. When she hurriedly tightened the end Daniel yelped in pain as he tried to say, 'Let's get out of here.'

When he put his left foot forward another pain shot up his leg from his ankle. He had forgotten that he had hit it in error with the blunt end of the axe. He looked down. The bottom of his trouser leg lay in shreds and through the ripped material he could see the flesh of his ankle swelling into a burning pink ball of pain.

Mary could see his dilemma and automatically put her head under his bad arm and started to help him limp forward. Gwendolyn followed by their side, watching the rear, swaying her dagger from side to side as a warning to any animal that felt brave enough to have a second go at them. As they limped past groups of dogs tearing into their meal more joined them from outlying ruins.

To the left was a road which followed the course of the river and Mary led them up it. There was too much gorging going on for them to be bothered by the dogs anymore, and by the time they came to a crossing, the mutts were out of sight.

The area around it was clear with demolished buildings around its rim. The land was covered in the same hard black surface as the roads they had followed with white rectangular boxes painted in regular rows across the surface. Just like the road trees, bushes, and plants were breaking their way through, and feeding on these where Champion, Orlov and Mary's horse.

'Up that hill we will join a road which will lead us out of the city, but more importantly near the old university campus will be the remains of the general hospital. I used to scavenge there for supplies in my youth when I was in the resistance. If we are lucky, and it's a big if, we might find some medicine to clean these wounds, and patch you up properly.'

Mary was pointing into the distance. 'But first Gwendolyn, see if you can round up the horses.'

Mary led Daniel away while Gwendolyn slowly walked towards the horses. She stopped, calling out Orlov's name. She didn't know if he would respond to it. Every time she talked to him she used the name she had given him, and now she hoped the special friendship she felt for him was reciprocated. 'Orlov.'

There was no response. His head stayed down as he nibbled on the green succulent leaves of a low bush.

'Orlov, it's me, Gwendolyn.' Again there was no response, but as she slowly approached she was just glad he hadn't galloped off. 'Orlov, come to Gwendolyn.'

He raised his head and looked straight at her. He snorted his recognition then went back to feeding on the bush. She was only ten steps away and carried on talking to him in a soft voice as she advanced. When she reached his side she started to gently rub the silky black hair down the back of his neck. For a moment she felt so happy because she was reunited with her beloved horse. Orlov didn't resist as she pulled on his stirrup then directed him towards the other two horses.

She approached Mary's first as it was a placid thing and was reassured by the presence of another horse, so she soon had hold of its reins. She wondered if Mary had given it a name and reminded herself to ask her what it was. Champion was more skittish. He had only recently joined the group, and as she approached with the other two he rolled his white mane from side to side, before stepping away.

She called out his name, hoping it would work as it had with Orlov, but every time they neared him he would walk off. Gwendolyn knew she had to be patient. 'At least he hasn't headed for the hills,' she thought, and at the fourth attempt was able to reach up then grab hold of his harness.

She trotted the three horses to the top of hill which Mary and Daniel had now reached and followed them into a large semi-derelict building.

'This used to be such a big building. It was the younger sister of the other cathedral where you found the Golden Shield.' Daniel winced in pain. Normally he loved to hear Mary explain the unknown to him, but at present he just wanted to rest. 'And across the road was another religious building called a synagogue.'

Mary kept on talking, but his mind wandered off towards the dilapidated building that stood in front of them. There wasn't much left. Three sides looked as if they had been totally demolished and it was impossible to make a picture in your mind of what it must have once looked like in all its glory.

Daniel's attention wondered back to Mary who was still talking.

She hadn't noticed that he had not been listening. He nodded his head in agreement to what she was saying as he fought back the pain of his wounded arm and throbbing ankle.

'When I was growing up in the resistance and times were bad I used to think of places like this and wished they had their own secret door where I could be transported away to a peaceful land. Religion is a funny thing really because many people spent their time mocking it, but in the end it's the only one thing that separates us from the animals, and more importantly the only thing that stops people acting like those beasts we encountered on the bridge.'

Mary stopped chatting about the past as she looked at Daniel with concern, then asked, 'We haven't got very far and it could still be another two maybe three hour walk especially in your condition. Do you think you can make it or do you want to stay here while Gwendolyn and I go on?'

Daniel shook his head.

'No. I can manage. By the time you return it will be dark and we will have to stay here the night, and then there's no guarantee you will find anything so we will have wasted most of the day. No. I will come with you. We can strap my leg it will be OK in a day or two, and by then we should be in open countryside and able to ride the horses.'

Mary smiled and Gwendolyn followed suit.

'That's the spirit, Daniel. That's why you are still alive, and that's the reason why we will save your father. Now take a seat. We will rest for half an hour and then make another start. We should be OK from now on, but…'

Mary could see Gwendolyn cringing and decided she had said enough.

11

DANGEROUS BUTCH

'C.A.T. spells "cat".'

The words were spelled out loudly as a withered finger pointed to the page. A large fire kept the souls huddled around it warm as the night sky bristled with stars that wove elegant pictures to the curious minds sitting below.

'And who knows how to spell 'dog'?'

Eager hands shot into the air.

Panting breath came storming in from the darkness. 'Quick! Riders are approaching. Must be Hunters!' A shadow from the trees emerged with sweat on his brow. The assembled crowd quickly rose to their feet as worried parents sent their children scuttling back to their huts.

Last to get to his feet was the oldest person present. His hair was as silver as the floating Orb in the sky above, which continued through to his neatly cut beard.

'I need to go, my friends. I have passed Procedure Four by twenty seasons, and if I'm caught by Hunters I won't get to see another day.' He paused. 'Because we all know what happens when you disobey the Procedures.'

Lifting a shabby brown leather satchel over his shoulder he turned to leave when his arm was pulled back.

'Please don't go. Hide until the Hunters have gone and then return. Everyone in the village loves listening to your amazing stories, and who is going to carry on teaching us all to read and write, and what about your books? Please stay'

Silence was followed by a gentle if tired smile. 'I can't. I need to carry on moving, but I have hopefully left behind a seed. A seed of information, that with a bit of luck will grow into a tree of knowledge which will one day sprout many branches of inquiring minds.'

He turned and walked off into the thicket.

'Please return one day, Butch,' the head of the village called out. 'I promise we will all continue with your classes and to treasure the book.'

'That's what makes me so dangerous,' came the final fading reply from the darkness.

* * *

A hand was waved in the air and the procession of horses came to a stop.

'Looks like a village ahead. We will pay it a visit and see what food there is. We can also camp here for the night.'

Mad-dog lowered the four fingers of his right hand.

'Leyland. You come with me and bring a couple of others.'

A kick to the side sent his horse trotting forward as the path cleared the trees. The moonlight revealed a small village of mud huts assembled around a large fire flaming wildly. Its inhabitants were scuttling back to their homes while an uneasy silence filled the air.

As the four Hunters neared a man approached them with hands raised in submission.

'Hello, newcomers, and what do we owe the honour of this visit from such a distinguished group as you? There has been no need for the presence of Hunters around these parts for many a season.'

Mad-dog said nothing at first as he dismounted, then crouched next to the fire, soaking up the warmth that spat from its flames.

'We were just passing through, but now we are staying the night.'

'My name is Tom and I am head of this village, and if there is anything I can do while you are here then just ask.'

'Yes. You can provide food for thirty men, and now!' shouted Leyland and the friendly smile on Tom's face dropped as he stuttered,

'But we are only a small village. We can't feed that many new people.'

Leyland raised his hand and brought it down hard across Tom's face, as he sat high upon his horse.

'Don't talk back to us. Do as you are told and go. Go now and start preparing.' Tom sheepishly agreed, turned and walked off. 'I should have thrust my knife into him for such insolence,' Leyland remarked, as he dismounted from his own horse and bent down next to Mad-dog.

'Don't stress yourself, Leyland. Take a look at this and tell me what you think.' He pointed to the soil.

Leyland's eyes lit up at the sight of individual letters fingered across the dirt surface. 'Someone has been practising letters and that can mean only one thing.' He stood up. 'I'm going to go after that head man and will slowly slice pieces of flesh from his body until he tells us where Dangerous Butch is.'

Mad-dog grabbed his arm and pulled him back down.

'Don't bother. We've been riding all day and everyone needs to rest. Anyway he could have gone in any direction. We would have to split the gang four ways, and still not find him. No, this is what we are going to do.'

He stood up and stretched, followed by Leyland.

'We will camp here for the night, then in the morning head up the path. We will wait at the river crossing. We know Dangerous Butch travels on foot so it will take him at least three days, and eventually he will need to find food and shelter. We will ambush him then.'

He stretched again. 'Then we will go after those two youngsters and that old lady and once we have them…' A smile spread over Mad-dogs face. 'And once we have them too and handed them over to the Over-seers then there is nothing to stop us going after Wolf and Fat-man.'

Leyland grinned and replied with glee in his voice, 'Because we all know that failure to carry out the command of our masters means only one thing, and that's execution.' They both laughed out loud.

12

THE STARVING SOUL

'Here we are.' Mary stopped and pointed down the road. 'Around that corner is the hospital.'

'What's a hospital?' Daniel asked with his customary air of curiosity.

'It's the place where hopefully we will find the things that we need to patch you up,' she replied, and then nudged her horse forward before stopping. 'Gwendolyn. What's up?'

Gwendolyn looked hesitant and was in no mood to investigate any new derelict building with all the dangers it could hold, especially since she now had no arrows left. She felt defenceless. As long as she could remember she had never ventured outside without her bow and a quiver full of arrows to protect her. She now felt exposed, almost naked, and longed to be underground hidden like a rabbit safely in its burrow.

She was steadying her nerve, ready to overcome the fear, when a rustling sound from the long grass to her side had her hand grabbing for her dagger. She turned and held it out at arms length.

'Come out of there, whoever you are!'

Her heart was beating fast, but the presence of Daniel hobbling to her side with axe in hand gave her renewed confidence, and she took two steps forward.

'Come on out, I said, unless you want me to come in there and cut you to pieces.' She was bluffing, and the beads of sweat rolling down her brow gave the game away. 'This is your last chance,' she shouted in desperation, and took one final step forward.

'Please don't hurt me.' The pitiful reply rustled from the long grass swaying in the cool breeze that carried autumn in its wake. 'Please – I beg you – don't hurt me.'

Two brown eyes appeared through the strands in sunken sockets, and then a skinny frame emerged from the verge.

'Gwendolyn, put that knife away. That poor thing isn't going to hurt anyone. Look at him. He's all skin and bone,' said Mary as she pushed her way through.

'What's your name?' demanded Gwendolyn. It reminded Daniel of the first time they had met, with the abrupt and aggressive manner she had used towards him.

Mary kneeled down with her arms open. 'Leave the poor starving soul alone.' And with that the young stranger nudged into her arms, and started to sob. 'Don't worry. Everything will be OK. Let out all your tears, and then why don't you tell me your name?'

He looked up, wiping his wet face with his sleeve, then again his runny nose before bleating out, 'Jack. My name is Jack Patel.'

'Are we going to get moving?' Gwendolyn asked in a belligerent tone. 'We are sitting ducks out here in the open. Where do you live boy?'

Mary looked up and gave Gwendolyn a stark stare.

A skinny arm was raised into the air and pointed to the distance in the opposite direction of the hospital, and through Jack's sobs they found the answer. 'Over there, underground in the chambers.'

Mary looked in the general direction. 'Do you mean near the old university?' Jack nodded 'What about your parents?' she enquired in her best supportive tone, hoping her concern about their absence wouldn't show.

'They were taken away by some men. I was out with my mum picking berries when she was taken by these men on horses. I ran back to dad and told him what had happened, and when he went to save her they took him too. They tied him to a horse and dragged him away to a place they called the Achievement Centre, and I haven't seen them since.'

Mary couldn't hide her concern anymore and, after a push or two, managed to get to her feet. She whispered quietly to Daniel and Gwendolyn, 'I think Hunters have got them. They must have stumbled across them while they were looking for us. In a way we are responsible for what has happened to him.'

Daniel nodded but Gwendolyn didn't flinch. The mention of underground chambers had pricked her interest.

'So why don't we go find shelter in these chambers. There's plenty of grassland for the horses to graze on, and we can then go scout the area for food and medicine while Daniel rests, and looks after young Jack.'

Mary liked Gwendolyn's idea and turned to face Jack. She held out her hand. 'My young hero. Show us where you live and we will see what we can do for you.'

* * *

The door swung open and John's exhausted body stumbled in. He slumped into his favourite chair in front of the fire and struggled to bring his panting breath under control. The house was empty but more importantly it was quiet. John closed his eyes and could feel his head become heavy as it slowly slipped forward.

Mother walked through the open door and noticed her husband asleep. She walked over and looked at his sun-kissed features, then gently pushed aside some loose locks of hair that dangled down his face. She kissed her finger and pressed it against his cheek, then closed the door behind her as she left.

'Sarah, your father is having a rest so don't go running about the hut,' she called out as she walked across the yard to the barn. 'Have you fed the chickens?'

'I'm doing it now, Mother,' shouted Sarah from inside, but before Mother got the chance to enter and have a look she was distracted by the voice of Badger as he approached.

'Is John back from the cutting grounds yet?'

Mother stopped and turned around. 'Yes, but the poor soul is worn out and having a rest. Once he wakes up he will be starving, so I would leave it until later if you want to speak to him.'

'That's OK. I was just coming over to say that all the plans have been made for your big Achievement Day. The whole village will be there to send you both off to the Achievement Centre and we have organised a feast to eat at the Three-ways.'

Mother stepped forward and gave Badger a hug.

'Thank you so much, and thank you again for looking after Sarah once we have gone. Myself and John are so excited and can't wait to receive our just rewards. It's been so hard with Daniel away, and the Hunters also taking Duster just made his work load twice as hard. He comes home worn out and has aged so much I'm just so glad that in five days we can both go to receive our rewards.'

Badger grinned and hugged Mother tightly.

'Everyone is going to miss you when you are gone, and don't worry too much about Sarah. She will be loved as if she was one of my own children. Anyway Daniel should be back soon from his apprenticeship training and will become head of the family.'

Mother blushed and turned her head. She didn't know when her son would return, or where he was. A pang of pain fell heavy on her heart at the thought of Daniel not being at one of the biggest events in her life, to see her off to the Achievement Centre. This was what everybody worked towards all their lives, to receive their just rewards. There would be no more toiling in the fields. No more worrying. No more heartache at watching loved ones dying from unknown illnesses. If you kept to the Seven Procedures and survived to see out forty seasons then the Over-seers would look after you for the rest of your life in the comfort of the Achievement Centre. Of course there were unanswered questions, but she had kept these to herself. She had wondered over the years why you could never visit your loved ones once they had entered, or why they never returned to visit, but she knew it was heresy to think about such questions, let alone talk about them openly. So she kept her faith in the Seven Procedures.

Sarah came running out the barn laughing as excited hens scuttled behind her, pecking at her out stretched hand. Mother saw her opportunity to change the subject before Badger delved any deeper into Daniel's return.

'Sarah, stop teasing them chickens.' She turned and started to walk towards her as she called out, 'Thank you, Badger, for all your help with the Achievement Day preparations. Both John and I are looking forward to the celebrations. Sarah, follow me into the barn.'

She did as asked, and after Mother had heaved shut the two large doors she sat down on some sacks of grain, then held open her arms.

'Sarah. Give your mum a hug.'

She duly obliged, and as Mother held her daughter with a tight squeeze a tear trickled down her cheek.

'You know I love you? You know that both father and I have always loved you and Daniel, and that although we will be going to the Achievement Centre in five days time to spend the rest of our lives under the care of the Over-seers we will never stop loving both of you.'

Sarah quietly nestled her head on Mother's chest, and then she started to cry too.

'But I don't want you to go. I want you to stay here with me. I want father to stay too.' Her sobbing increased into a flood of tears. 'And I want Daniel home. When is Daniel coming home?'

Mother couldn't hold back her emotions any more as the lone tear that seeped from an eye was joined by another, and then another, until her sobbing matched Sarah's.

'Hopefully soon, my little angel.'

Mother pulled away and fumbled under her long woollen dress

until she found her hanky. She dried her eyes, before gently wiping Sarah's cheeks with it.

'You finish your chores here, and I will go prepare supper for father. The poor soul must be starving.'

13

SECRET CHAMBERS

'Here we are!' Jack exclaimed as he hurried around the grass mound towards a crop of sycamore trees, which followed the line of bushes that bristled in their late summer coat of blackberries.

Jack's three new companions looked confused, but followed him until the lure of the berries had them eagerly picking through the prickly vines in search of the sweet delights that dangled among the spider's webs.

'Here it is the entrance.'

Mary looked up, her cheeks full of berries like a squirrel as juice dribbled from the corners of her mouth. After a large gulp that nearly left her choking she nudged the others. 'You two. It's rude to keep young Jack waiting.'

With that command all three walked around the mound until their attention was taken by a large metal door set into the grass at a forty-five degree angle.

'Gwendolyn, go tie the horses under the trees with sufficient rein to graze.'

Jack pulled at the handle and struggled to lift the door at first, but before Daniel had the chance to offer him a helping hand its rust-encrusted hinges creaked open to reveal a staircase twirling into the dark heart of Mother Earth. By the time Gwendolyn had rejoined the group Jack's head was already disappearing down the stairs.

Mary followed with a hesitant Daniel behind her, and a reluctant Gwendolyn at the rear.

'If I shut the door how are we going to see where we are going?' But just as she spoke her last word Gwendolyn's question was answered. Light filled the dark void, which made her and Daniel jump, while Mary gasped in surprise at the sight of Jack standing by the light switch.

'Lighting!' exclaimed Mary delightedly, and Jack smiled back. He touched the switch again and the darkness returned, followed within seconds by light once again.

'It must be magic!' Daniel shouted in surprise.

'No,' said Mary. 'It's electricity'

'Whatever it is,' said Gwendolyn, 'I'm going to shut the door before we attract every Over-seer, Triclops and Hunter gang in the area,' and with that she heaved on the door until it shut with a loud bang. After a few minutes of silent wonder both Daniel and Gwendolyn were engrossed with the mystery of the light switch, and as Jack made his way down the stairs they both took turns to turn on and off the lights.

'Leave that alone, you two,' Mary called out as she followed young Jack, with a flood of questions desperately seeking answers. 'Where does the power come from?'

Without stopping or looking back Jack replied, 'From the solar panels near the broad. A lot of it is smashed up, but there is enough left intact to keep the lights on.'

She had many more questions to ask but then the stairs ended, and there stretching into the distance was a tunnel with rooms leading off each side. Jack darted through the right hand door followed by Mary, while the sound of clanking footsteps on the metal stairs confirmed the other two weren't far behind. By the time Mary walked into the room Jack was sitting on a long, aged, sofa covered in worn brown leather.

'What do you think of my home?' Jack asked, with open arms expressing his delight at having others to keep him company once again. Opposite where he sat was a large screen television and in front of that on the floor was a games console.

'Wow.'

Mary and Jack turned to Gwendolyn's comment as she pushed her way passed a stunned Daniel who stood silently in the doorway.

'Does any of this stuff work?'

'Most of it. Some I'm repairing but generally I can make most electrical gadgets work,' replied Jack, and he could tell by the expression on Mary's and Gwendolyn's faces that they were impressed, but Daniel just looked confused. It was clear from this Daniel had no idea what any of these new-fangled things that filled the room were.

Mary's eye fell on the armchair. She sat down in it, enjoying its comfort as it eased the aches and pains she had endured over the last few weeks while having to sleep on nothing more comfortable than a hard floor.

'Aaahhh! I could get to use to this very quickly. It reminds me of my own home back in the cellar. Young Jack: how did you end up living down here?'

Gwendolyn sat next to him on the sofa. 'Daniel. Take a seat,' she said, and he did.

Mary smiled warmly and with this prompt Jack's tale flooded out.

'I was born here. There used to be my parents and grandparents, and others too. My granddad worked at the university and these underground chambers were his labs. I was told when the Over-seers first turned up my grandparents and their colleges took refuge down here, and eventually I was born here. Slowly time passed away and so did some of the people who lived here while others left to seek out a new life under the care of the Over-seers, but my parents stayed and we lived happily here until…' Jack's head dropped.

Gwendolyn hesitantly leaned forward and for a second wasn't

sure what to do. She had an urge to hug Jack, but didn't know if this would be the right thing. Her heart felt his agony as she had felt it herself losing her own parents at such a young age. She pulled back, but her instinct told her to put her arms around him to sooth his fears, just like Mary had on so many occasions when she became her new guardian. Gently she placed an arm over his hunched shoulders.

'Now don't worry, Jack. Everything will be all right.'

She could feel her cheeks blush at the white lie she had just said. Jack's lip began to curl and she knew tears were on their way unless quick action was taken. It was obvious that her attempt at making Jack feel better hadn't worked, so she looked at Mary with a pleading gaze, and true to form Mary came to the rescue.

'Jack, look at me. Do you have anything to drink down here?'

An arm was raised and the finger pointed to a sink on the far side of the room.

'Daniel, go get Jack a glass of water. All you have to do is turn the knob and water will come out.' He got up and started to look around the room for a cup.

'Here, Jack. Use this.' Mary had retrieved a hanky from her pocket and handed it over. He took it and wiped a tear away from his cheek.

Mary nodded, then winked at a confused Gwendolyn. Again she nodded while winking as she mouthed silently some words. Gwendolyn, still confused, shrugged her shoulders, but when Mary wrapped her own arms around herself rocking from side to side the penny dropped.

'Oh,' said Gwendolyn, and she leaned forward, wrapping her arms around Jack and gave him a tight hug. 'Like I said, everything will be all right. You will be safe with us.'

Daniel came back holding a green and yellow mug emblazed with a motif of a canary, lion and castle. 'This is great! No more sweating your butt off dragging up a bucketful of water from the well,' he said. He handed over the cup, and sat down as Jack took a deep gulp of water. He had now composed himself so continued with the story.

'My granddad was a scientist working on computers and these laboratories were built underground so that no outside electrical interference would corrupt the experiments. He told us stories about the arrival of the Over-seers and the destruction they caused. My dad was just a boy when he was brought here alongside all the other families. I have lived here all my life and never ventured further than the far fields.'

Jack's head began to droop.

'Have you got any pictures of your family, Jack?' Mary enquired before he had a chance to start crying again.

He jumped up. 'Yes. In the other room.' And with that he disappeared.

Mary leaned forward talking in a low voice.

'I've heard of this place when I was in the resistance. You see we worked in closed cells so if we were ever caught and tortured we couldn't give away too much information. Of course things would slip out so you built up a rough picture of what was happening. I knew we had scientists working in the resistance because they developed the Golden Shield. When the dead Over-seer was found and his body armour was melted down in making the shield it was my unit which had to scavenge about the ruins looking for any gold that we could lay our hands on so it could be mixed with it to make the new alloy. It was also my unit that was looking for the extra solar panels when on that fatal day the Over-seers attacked our headquarters and killed everyone in sight. I never knew what happened after that because I took Gwendolyn in my arms and never looked back, and as they say the rest is history.'

Mary leaned back in her chair, closing her eyes.

'I suppose without our unit to bring these people supplies of food and materiel their numbers must have dwindled until there was only Jack's family left. When his grandparents passed away then there was only three left, and now that the Over-seers have two of them there is only poor little Jack left.'

Mary opened her eyes to the approaching sound of Jack as he excitedly hurried back into the room with an iPad in hand. Flicking his finger across the screen as he sat back down made both Daniel and Gwendolyn gasp in surprise at this new wonderment that skimmed pictures so fast their eyes couldn't keep up.

'These are my grandparents on my dad's side of the family.'

A young couple sat posed holding hands. Their clothes were a brilliant blaze of colours, stunning yellows and vibrant shades of reds, clear blues, and deep purples. The lady was adorned with gold necklaces and her hands were painted with exotic patterns. Jack's granddad's vivid clothes matched that of his wife with the exception of a wonderful turban wrapped in gold lace, while a magnificent jewel-encrusted dagger protruded from his belt.

'This is my other grandmother.' The lady was in a white coat that went all the way to her knees. She was posing next to a work bench with a myriad of glass objects on top that contained fluids in different states of flux. She was holding a glass beaker and it was obvious by the surprised look on her face that the picture was taken while she was working.

'I haven't got any pictures of my other granddad. I think he never made it into the chambers.' He flicked his finger across the screen again. 'These are my parents.'

The couple were younger this time, still in their teens, and sitting on the very same sofa that Jack sat on. His mother had her legs resting on top with a book in hand as she smiled at the camera. His father looked disinterested while he struggled with the controls of a Gameboy.

Mary glanced at Gwendolyn and Daniel, but they were too engrossed in the workings of the iPad, as pictures appeared like magic. They both held out tentative fingers to touch the screen. Their mouths were open, but no words came out until Daniel made another picture appear by a simple flick.

'Wow!' He tapped another picture. 'Wow. It's amazing. Your whole home is amazing.'

Mary rocked herself out of her chair and stood up. 'Daniel, why don't you stay here with Jack, and he can show you more of what life was like in the past, while Gwendolyn and myself go outside and find some food for us all, and some medicine for you.'

Jack looked up. 'We have some things in the medical room at the bottom of the hallway.' His gaze returned to the iPad.

'Well then, Gwendolyn, it's just food we will need to find.'

She looked up too, disappointed. 'Can't I stay here with these two?'

'No. You can't. Now come on. The sooner we get out and about the sooner we will be back. I'm just going to check on what medical supplies there are.'

With that final word Mary walked into the hallway, then down the corridor until she came across a door with a faded handwritten sign on it stating 'Medical Room'. She pushed it open and as she did so a light automatically came on. It was obvious the room had once served a different purpose because in the corner were piles of computer screens covered in years of cobwebs, and what were once desks had now been converted into operating tables. The memories of her own youth in the resistance movement came flooding back, and she wondered if anyone she had known had ever been spread across these tables in agony while people desperately tried to operate on them.

Nearly all the cupboard doors were open with thick layers of dust covering their empty surfaces, but one glass-fronted door was still closed, and took Mary's attention. She opened it and pulled out the red First Aid box. Its weight indicated there were items inside and when she lifted its plastic lid the contents of plasters, bandages and medical wipes were just what she need for Daniel's wounds. A little rummage also revealed some antiseptic cream and a packet of painkillers. She examined the use-by date on the items.

'Five decades out of date, but never mind. They will have to do.'

Walking back down the corridor, Mary could hear her three young companions excitedly chattering to each other, and when she walked into the room they looked as if they had been friends for life, with Jack showing off all the games that could be summoned by tapping the screen.

'Let's patch you up, Daniel.' She sat back down and took hold of his hand. 'Do you still have some water in that cup?' Daniel nodded. 'Good. Take these tablets. They will ease the pain in your ankle. Then go wash your other wounds, and then I will attend to them.'

Daniel did as asked while Gwendolyn took great delight in playing with the iPad.

Looking at Jack's gaunt face she knew her next job would be to find some food for the group. 'Poor little Jack,' she thought. 'Down here all alone for all that time while not knowing what had happened to his parents.' Then again, knowing what happened at the Achievement Centre it was best he didn't. The only comfort she could offer him at the moment was hope.

'This place is great.'

Mary's thoughts were interrupted by Daniel when he sat back down next to her. He held out his wet arm. Mary took hold of it and started to dab it dry.

Daniel flinched. 'That hurts.'

Mary looked unsympathetic. 'Don't be such a wuss. What are you, a man or a mouse?' And then she used the antiseptic wipe over the puncture wounds caused by the fearful fangs of the beast they had encountered on the bridge.

Daniel closed his eyes while his face cringed as he desperately tried to stop the stinging sensation that inflamed his arm from exploding out of his mouth. He wanted to show he was man enough to take the pain, but it was futile.

'That really stings. It really hurts.'

Gwendolyn and Jack tried to hide their amusement while Daniel wiggled on his seat like a squirming worm, but it was no good. They both started to giggle, which seemed to feed off each other. They couldn't hold it back any more because it turned into outright laughter.

'Don't moan, Daniel. Just think you have killed an Over-seer, seen off a gang of Hunters, and destroyed a Triclops and here you are now acting like a five-year-old.'

Soon a bandage covered Daniel's arm.

'Gwendolyn, let's get going.' She sullenly looked at Mary while huffing as she got to her feet.

'I suppose so.'

Silence started to fill the room with only the fading echo of footsteps on the metal stairwell to break the void. Jack looked at the floor while shuffling his legs. The silence was now deafening. Daniel's heart sunk with sadness. Looking at Jack brought home to him what his younger sister would have to face if he couldn't get back to his home village in time to stop his parents walking to their own death up the path from the Three-ways crossing to the Achievement Centre. He leaned forward.

'It's going to be all right, Jack. You can come with us and we will find your parents.' He ruffled Jack's long dark hair. 'Now why don't you show me how you are going to thrash my backside on one of these games of yours?' His faint smile turned into a broad grin.

* * *

The light had faded and a chill wind followed the night as a cloudless sky revealed a glorious display of stars. The rustling of leaves trailed in its wake, and except for the occasional hoot of an owl, or the snort from one of the horses tethered under the protective canopy of an oak tree, there were no other sounds to cover the return of Gwendolyn as she panted for breath like a hunting dog.

'I've had a look around but there was nothing, and without any arrows there was no way for me to get any fresh meat. What about you, Mary?'

Mary looked up from her kneeling position. 'Not too bad. I've picked enough blackberries and raspberries for all of us. I also found an apple tree so we have enough fruit. Other than that, not much else.' She returned her attention to the soil and started digging.

'What are you doing, Mary?'

'Digging,' she replied, 'I was hoping to find some root vegetables. Maybe some wild parsnips, potatoes or turnips, but all I have found is some wild garlic.' She sat back on her behind and huffed. 'It's too dark now to find anything else. Let's take all the fruit and get back underground before the Over-seers start to stir and come calling.'

Gwendolyn agreed and started to pick up handfuls of apples.

'So what are we going to do with Jack?'

Mary held out her arm while trying to push herself up from the ground.

'Here. Give me a hand, can you?'

Gwendolyn responded while asking again in a rather annoyed tone.

'So what are we going to do with him? It's hard enough looking after ourselves without taking in every stray we come across.'

'We took in Daniel,' Mary replied.

'That's different.'

'Why is that, Gwendolyn?'

'You know why Mary.' Gwendolyn's annoyance was turning into exasperation. 'Because if I hadn't slain the Over-seer that day and you hadn't taken him in, he would have died.'

Mary finally straightened her back as she rubbed the dirt off her hands.

'And if we don't take care of Jack what will happen to him?'

There was a short pause as Gwendolyn bowed her head before her shameful tone replied, 'He will probably perish.'

There was another pause before Mary lightened the conversation.

'Everything will be all right. We will take Jack with us back to

Daniel's home village. Maybe with any luck the Achievement Centre nearby is the one his parents have been taken too.'

Gwendolyn didn't want to sound insolent, but she had to ask. 'And what are we going to do then?'

Mary didn't reply at first as she headed off towards the concealed entrance to the secret chamber holding up the rim of her dress which now held all the fruit she had picked. Gwendolyn darted after her trying not to drop any of the apples that nestled in her arms.

'So what are we going to do?'

Again Mary didn't give a direct answer.

'Give me a hand to open this. It's too heavy for me on my own.' Gwendolyn placed her apples on the ground, then heaved at the rusting metal door with its peeling paint until it swung open with a lazy creaking noise. While picking up the apples she made one last stab at getting an answer from Mary, so in her most defiant voice she asked, 'And what are we going to do then?'

Mary was already disappearing down the stairwell with her head just visible when she suddenly stopped, then turned with a motherly expression on her face.

'We are going to do what I have always taught you to do, and what is that?'

Gwendolyn knew the answer, and she also knew this was the end of the conversation. 'Think positive,' she replied.

* * *

Laughter wafted into the air, bouncing off the concrete ceiling, painted white and illuminated by long strip lights that gently hummed.

'I'm getting the hang of this, Jack. Another few games and I tell you this, young man: I will be the new champion.' Daniel laughed again. Jack followed suit, but before he had a chance to mock anymore about Daniel's faltering attempts at beating him at Grand Theft Auto, Mary's head popped around the corner.

'How are we boys? Having fun, I hear?'

Two wide smiles confirmed her prognosis as she entered the room. Walking over to the sink she lifted her skirt hem and dropped the tender, sweet fruit into it. Cristal clear water rushed from the tap when she turned it on.

'Where's Gwendolyn? Is she OK?' Daniel asked as he stood up, concerned at her absence. Looking around the room his heart missed a beat when he realised he couldn't locate his axe or any of the other weapons.

'Relax, Daniel. She is just feeding the horses some apples for their supper. Why don't you and Jack take some water up for them?'

Jack jumped to his feet.

'Yes, please.' Without a second word Jack was running out the door with a bucket fall of sloshing water. Mary waited until she thought the coast was clear.

'So what do you think, Daniel?'

'About what?' he replied, although he suspected Mary's question was leading him towards what to do with Jack. Mary had started looking through the cupboards, opening and closing the doors while mumbling.

'No. That's empty, and that one is empty and this one too.' Then her next response confirmed Daniel's suspicion. 'Young Jack: should he join our merry band of outlaws, or should we leave him here to starve to death?'

Daniel was cornered. What could he say after Mary's leading question? There was no way he could be that heartless and leave Jack to die, but at the same time there was no way they could stay.

'He can come with us, but my first priority is to get back and warn my parents about their fate if they go to the Achievement Centre.'

Mary agreed.

'That's sorted then.' With her mission completed she opened another door then gasped. 'I don't believe it.' Her hand reached in and when it came out it clasped a paper bag. Peering inside brought a smile to her face and her stern demeanour softened. 'Flour. We have some flour! I haven't seen flour in years. I wonder what else we have in here?' She pulled out a green plastic bottle. A quick sniff of the contents confirmed it was olive oil. 'That's OK. I might be able to make some basic pastry or even bread!'

Her delight showed as she started to gently hum a tune and within a minute or two Mary had procured some bowls. 'Let's see if this electric cooker works,' and when she let out a yelp of joy Daniel knew it must do, although he didn't know what a cooker was, and as usual just had to go with the flow.

14

FEEDING TIME

Bang. Bang. Bang.
 The sound carried on the air brought a chill in its wake.
 Bang. Bang. Bang.
 The looming shadow killed the fading sun as it set on the distant horizon.
 BANG. BANG. BANG.
 Silence.
 The vibrating earth that signalled the approaching strides of the Triclops fell silent until the final shock, powerful enough to knock the unsure off their feet, confirmed it had come to rest.
 Wolf pulled up his trousers then tightened the leather belt. Looking behind he kicked soil into the cesspit. After wiping his hands on some straw he walked back to camp to greet the arrival of his masters. By the time he arrived there were silver-suited Overseers standing guard around the Dominator as it barked out instructions next to the entrance of the Triclops that squatted on the ground.
 'Bring prisoners now.'
 Fat-man stood at the entrance of the prison block keeping the door open with his foot while three men and a woman were lead out in chains.

'See? This is what happens to people who don't keep to the Procedures,' sneered Fat-man.

As the final prisoner passed he moved his foot and stuck it out making the last man in the chain gang stumble to the ground. Fellow Hunters laughed at Fat-man's bravado, and he bowed to their clapping.

'Leave him alone, you nasty bully,' screamed a woman at the front as she tried to rush to the man's aid. 'Leave my husband alone.' Her dark brown eyes pierced Fat-man, who for a second felt a pinch of guilt shoot through his soul.

'He should be steadier on his feet,' he replied, then kicked the man on his backside. 'Get up and join your women.' Once again Fat-man's fellow Hunters laughed and clapped. The lead Hunter yanked on the chain just as Prior held out a helping hand, and she gagged for breath.

'Bring prisoners now,' boomed the Dominator and as instructed the chain gang were led up the ramp into the belly of the beast, closely followed by the Over-seers. Once the cargo was loaded the ramp retracted and the door slid shut with a bang.

Wolf walked up to Fat-man. 'That's convenient.'

'Why do you say that?' Fat-man asked.

'Because when Mad-dog returns with his gang looking for some female company we can tell him the Over-seers paid us a visit and took all the prisoners, and he will never know that we exchanged his hostage for your mule at the slave market.'

He slapped Fat-man on the back. 'Let's go for a drink.'

* * *

'Two prisoners are to go in here.'

The Dominator pointed into a steel-clad room crammed with obedient Over-seers standing around two metal tables that stood in the middle. It pressed a button on its arm plate. There was a click and the chains came free, falling to the ground. The four prisoners looked at each other too scared to ask any questions, and then two shrugged their shoulders before meekly walking into the room.

'You are to wait here.' Pointing into another room empty except for a bench to sit on. The remaining two prisoners shuffled towards it with heads held low, then disappeared behind a door as it shut with a hiss.

Clicking now emanated from the Dominator and his fellow silver-suited Over-seers as they reacted excitedly while they followed their leader.

'Undress now and lie on the tables,' the Dominator bellowed, and as instructed the two people started to take off their clothes. Enthusiastic clicking now filled the room echoing off the walls in a frightening manner. The door shut sealing everything inside.

Once the fodder was laid forth on the tables two prongs came whirling from the sides of each table and clasped around the upper and lower half of the helpless bodies. The fear for one was too much and his bowels emptied themselves.

Suddenly the lights went out and a hissing sound filled the air. A violet light illuminated the room, making the flesh turn lustrous while a siren wailed a deadfall din. When it stopped each Over-seers loosened the glove from its wrist and pulled off the protective cover. The action was repeated with the other, and once free, long spindly fingers stretched out in relief. Finally the helmet was removed to reveal the truth of the Over-seers. A hideous creature appeared with skin as tough as worn leather. Its eyes glowed a devil's red. They stared at the live flesh that wiggled on the table in desperation for air, saliva dripped from the protruding fangs that now extended in anticipation. The Dominator raised its hand with claws extended, then in a ceremonial swing of the arm slashed at the human's flesh, tearing away a long strip of living skin which it popped into its mouth, then slowly chewed with delight.

The signal had been given to the others and through the screams of the doomed souls on the table a feeding frenzy began. First the flesh was devoured, then chunks of meat were ripped from the bones, breaking veins that squirted blood around the room, and all the time the human meal cried in dreadful pain as they were devoured alive.

* * *

Daniel pulled up his trousers and tightened his leather belt. He looked behind and wondered what to do next.

'Now, what did Mary tell me?' He looked around the room and then it came to him. 'She said pull the handle down.'

He looked at the door and pressed down on its handle but nothing happened. 'I think this toilet thing is too complicated for me. I much prefer to use a cesspit.' To his side stood the sink and he pressed down on its protruding handle then jumped back in surprise as water gushed out, and splattered over his trousers.

He looked again at the toilet and examined it closely. 'I'm sure Mary said there would be a handle to use, but all I can see is this round silver thing on the top.' Unsure what to do next he pressed down on it then watched in amazement as water gushed down the insides swirling away his bodily fluids. 'Wow. This is fantastic. I wonder where it goes?' He was brought out of his wonderment by the calling of Mary

'Daniel, go get the others. Supper is ready. Hurry up. It will get cold.'

Mary was standing over the table when the three very hungry and excited youngsters came running through the door. She looked up, held open her arms, with a broad smile across her face and said with a cheerful heart, 'Supper is served.'

Everyone hurriedly sat down, noisily pulling out their chairs.

'We have to use our imagination because of the limited supplies we have, but I have managed to rustle up garlic flatbread for starters. And it is flat, I'm afraid,' she said under her breath. 'Next we have apple pie for our main course, but it's a pity we don't have some cream to soften up the crust a bit, and some sugar. It could be a bit bitter to taste, but never mind, and for dessert we have a raspberry, stroke blackberry, fruit salad.'

Mary tried to be confident with her positive take on the meal laid in the middle of the table; she didn't need to worry, for once she said, 'Get stuck in,' no one grumbled as eager hands with knife and forks at the ready dived into the food. 'All we really need now to make this a proper meal is some meat. Maybe a nice piece of roast meat with plenty of crackling to chew on.'

After supper Mary settled down on the sofa while the others washed the dishes. Although the odd spring sprung in the wrong direction, it was the most comfortable thing Mary had rested her backside on since fleeing from her previous home in the cellar. When the others were finished with their chores they settled down and around Mary. There was no fireplace but the room was comfortably warm, and when Jack turned off the main lights leaving just two side lamps to glow with a yellow tint which left the far reaches of the room darkened, it became quite cosy.

'If we were able to stay here this would make a perfect home for all of us, but, and as I say there is always a but… but we can't. Both Daniel and Jack need to find their parents and that means returning to where this all started.' Mary looked at her three silent companions and they all nodded in agreement. 'We also need to find some food because we are now out of supplies, so I suggest we leave in the morning and head first to Hagar's village and seek supplies from her, so I'm glad we are all in agreement. I suggest we get a good night's sleep.'

Gwendolyn now piped up. 'Can we play some more games before we do?'

'No. You can't. You will be up all night.'

Jack now jumped into the conversation. 'My iPad just doesn't play games. Take a look at this.'

He got up from the floor and disappeared out the room only to return a couple of minutes later with something under his arm.

'See? It's an Over-seer's helmet.' He fumbled in his pocket, then pulled out a black lead. 'Here. Give me the iPad.' Daniel picked it up from the floor and passed it over. Jack plugged one end into the iPad and the other into the helmet then sat back down on the floor.

'Like I said my granddad and the others who lived down here

were all computer scientists, so when my dad grew up down here all he and the other children had to play with was computers, and that was the same with me. I never had any friends my own age and as more people died or moved away I spent more and more time taking apart and then rebuilding electronic devices.'

Jack's faced was illuminated as he tapped on the screen.

'I built this interface between the iPad and this helmet, and look what it can do.' He tapped again and the helmet came to life. Every time he tapped a different command there was a counteraction from the helmet.

'I can open it and close it, turn on or off the power, and other things too. It's not just the helmet. There is a room full of old Overseers junk at the end of the hall, brought here by the underground resistance for my granddad and his colleagues to work on. I don't know if they ever did any good. All I know is that in the end there was only my mum, dad, and me left living down here, and now they have gone as well.'

Jack's head dropped and he started to sniffle.

Gwendolyn felt uneasy while Mary wanted to give him a hug, but it was Daniel who was first to react. He jumped up.

'Come with me, Jack. I've got something to show you.' Holding out his hand Jack took hold of it and was helped to his feet. They both walked out the door. When they got to the bottom of the stair case Daniel looked behind it and pulled out the Golden Shield.

Jack's face lit up. 'Wow. That's fantastic.'

'Yes, it is, and it's very probable that your family helped to make it, so when you are sad and missing your parents just take a look at this, and remember they are not far away.'

Daniel wiped Jack's wet cheek with his sleeve.

'I've got a sister about your age. She's called Sarah, and we have a cat called Swipe, and plenty of farmyard animals so you will have plenty of friends to play with soon.' He paused then tried to give a reassuring smile. 'I promise you that.'

They walked back in the room just in time to see Mary and

Gwendolyn tapping at the screen and giggling in delight with the control they now had over the Over-seer's helmet.

'I think Jack is ready for bed now, Mary.'

She looked up. 'OK. You get ready and I will be through in a minute to say goodnight.'

Jack walked into his room and changed into his jimjams. Looking at the bare concrete walls that had been his home all his life he felt happy for the first time since he had seen his father being tied up and lead away by those group of men. He remembered feeling so helpless and wanting to scream out, but he had promised him he would stay hidden behind the rubble. He had already seen his mum being taken away and the thought made his throat feel dry, just like it did that morning when he ran home to warn his dad. A tear trickled down his cheek and although he had promised his dad he would be strong it was no good. He couldn't hold back the tears no matter how hard he tried.

The sound of the door creaking open made him look up and Mary walked in. He quickly jumped into his unmade bed then leaned over his side table to switch on his bed-side lamp. Mary turned off the main light then sat on his bed.

'Everything will be OK, Jack. We will look after you now and we will do our best to find your parents.' Leaning over she gently kissed Jack on the forehead.

'But I miss my mum so much,' he replied. 'I just want my mummy and daddy back.'

Mary affectionately stroked Jack's hair. 'I'm sure your mum is OK. Trust me.'

Jack wiped his weepy eye. 'Do you think so?'

'Of course I do, Jack. What is your mum's name?'

'She's called Prior.'

'I'm sure Prior is all right and is safely with your dad right now.'

Mary gave him a goodnight kiss and turned off the bedside lamp before leaving the room.

15

SWEET REVENGE

The clatter of iron on wood echoed across the river as descending horses carrying their mounts snaked in a line over the bridge. People loaded down with goods for the market strapped across their backs waited impatiently for the Hunters to pass.

Mad-dog held up an arm and all came to a stop.

A mumble of disapproval muttered under baited breath caught his attention. 'What did you say?' The waiting crowd humbly looked down, not daring to make eye contact. 'Get out of our way,' and when he kicked the sides of his horse it darted forward. Adults and children alike scuttled to the sides like crabs desperately trying not to get trampled under the horse's hooves.

A small cart full of cabbages got pushed over in the confusion and its content tumbled into the ditch.

When Mad-dog reached the guard house he jumped off his horse and stormed through its open door. He was confronted by the backs of two Hunters sitting on stools tucking into bowls of steaming stew.

'Why isn't one of you on duty at the bridge?' he screamed out in anger, making them both jump. A bowl dropped to the floor, spilling its piping hot contents over the lap of the expectant recipient, who jumped up cursing his bad luck. He turned in fury ready to cuss at the intruder, but when he saw Mad-dog his open mouth shut in an instant while his gaze sheepishly dropped.

The second Hunter, realising their foolish act, tried to make amends through stuttering breath with a feeble excuse.

'I was only collecting something to eat. There is plenty left if you want some.'

Mad-dog lunged forward and within a second had drawn his dagger. Grabbing the grovelling subordinate by the throat, while pressing the dagger into the side of his neck, Mad-dog said in a low but menacing voice, 'Don't lie to me, you little turd. Get out there and keep an eye on everyone who is crossing the bridge.' Mad-dog let his grip go, shoving his terrified captive against the wall while holding his dagger out at arm's length. 'And if I catch you again not doing your duty I will slit your throat from ear to ear, do you understand?'

They both nodded grudgingly as they scuttled out the door.

Mad-dog picked a bowl from the shelf then filled it with stew from the pot that boiled gently over the open fire, before sitting down on the now vacant stool, just as Leyland walked through the door.

'Can you believe those two idiots?' he commented. Mad-dog, slurping his hot meal, just glanced up in agreement and said no more as Leyland joined him. 'Anyone could have crossed, including the people we are supposed be hunting.' Mad-dog wiped some dribble from his chin.

'I don't think they will have tried to use the bridge in the first place, Leyland. Anyway, we are just chasing shadows when it comes to Dangerous Butch. Seriously, with all the different descriptions of Butch we've managed to force out from people, and look what we have got to go on. All we know is he's a seven foot midget between the ages of twenty to a hundred with either blue or brown eyes, and in some cases supposedly one of each colour.'

'Just like your eyes, Mad-dog. Maybe you are Dangerous Butch,' Leyland joked, but Mad-dog didn't see the funny side.

'Don't you forget, Mad-dog is my name, and also don't forget I'm the boss so less of your lip, or I will gouge your eyes out with my bare hands, and then everyone will be calling you No-eyes.'

Leyland couldn't tell if he was joking so thought it best not to find out, and changed the subject quickly.

'What about the other group we're looking for? Them two youngsters and the old lady?'

Mad-dog lifted the bowl to his lips and drank the dregs of his meal, then tossed it into the bucket full of water in the corner.

'I don't think any woman who has surpassed her age of Achievement by many years will try to sneak over the bridge, especially with three horses and two others in tow. They would stick out like a sore thumb.'

Standing up he stretched his arms before taking a lengthy drink from a leather jug that had been hanging from a hook on the wall. He passed it onto Leyland, who enquired, 'What I can't understand is why anyone would want to risk learning to read. What is the point of it? All you need is a belly full of food, plenty of drink, clothes on your back, and a dry roof over your head. So why is it dangerous?'

'What are you talking about?' enquired Mad-dog, puzzled with the path the conversation was taking. Leyland took a gulp from the jug and continued.

'Why is reading so dangerous that the Over-seers won't allow anyone to learn how too?'

Mad-dog slapped him around the face. 'You stupid fool, Leyland. You're a Hunter so you shouldn't even be thinking such things. We work for the Over-seers hunting down people who don't keep to the Seven Procedures. In return we get all our basic needs provided for through the people's offering via the Tribute huts, and anything else we need we can take in fines from anyone who has broken a sub-law.'

Leyland rubbed his cheek but stayed silent.

'All in all we have a very good life. We don't have to toil in the fields or sweat over a loom, or any other manual work. We never go hungry and people fear our very presence so we have to bow to no one other than our masters, the Over-seers.'

Mad-dog grabbed the jug back and took another drink.

'I don't care why we can't read or write, I don't care to think why the Over-seers deem it such a threat, or why Butch is such a danger to society.' He took another slug from the jug before handing it back to Leyland. 'All I care about is either catching Dangerous Butch, or the three other as yet unnamed fugitives, and if possible catching all of them so we can hand them over to the Over-seers for their own execution.'

Leyland sensed the time was right to talk about a subject that might improve Mad-dog's mood. 'You know what I find a bit suspicious? Wolf's gang. Or should I say what happened to it on their last mission.'

'What do you mean, Leyland?' asked Mad-dog in an inquisitive tone.

'Wolf claims that his small posse was attacked while travelling through the Great Forest by a huge pack of starving wild dogs that were hungry for their flesh. He even gave the impression that the legendary Black Shuck may have led the pack.'

Mad-dog stood silently listening, lost in the point Leyland was trying to make.

'Think about it, Mad-dog.' He still looked perplexed so Leyland decided to come to the point. 'Wolf came back minus two members of his team, but also minus three horses. Now tell me this, horses are the most expensive thing to barter for, with only Hunters and the most successful people able to have one. So how did an old lady and two youngsters get their hands on three horses? Are you thinking what I keep thinking?'

A pleased smile spread over Mad-dog's face and Leyland followed.

'You make a very interesting point, Leyland! If Wolf is lying and somehow aided three of the most wanted criminals in the land then sweet revenge will be mine.'

Leyland stood up and took another drink before offering the jug to Mad-dog who shook his head. He tossed it into the corner just as Mad-dog slapped him on the back.

'Well done, Leyland. You know what this means? If we find these three with just one horse from Wolf's gang then he is in serious trouble.' Mad-dog started to laugh and Leyland as usual followed. 'Forget about Dangerous Butch, Leyland. We have only one purpose now and that is to find these three.'

With that Mad-dog walked out of the guardhouse in a much better mood than when he had walked in.

* * *

'I must say that's the best night's sleep I have had in a very long time, or should I really say the most comfortable. I almost forgot what a bed felt like to sleep in. It's a pity, but we can't stay here any longer. Has everyone got everything?'

Mary looked at her three companions. 'Right. The horses have had a good time grazing plus a feed on apples, and there are enough left to last us for two days at the most, so we will have to hope nothing gets in our way until we reach Hagar's village. With some luck she will be true to her word and we get what we need to carry on the final leg of our journey.'

'What if she's not?' piped up Gwendolyn, and Mary responded with her usual retort.

'Positive thinking, please, that's what I want from all of you. Positive thinking. We take one stage at a time, live by our wits, and most importantly we look out for each other.' She now gave one of her stern looks. 'Is that understood?' They gestured in agreement. 'Right then, Jack will mount with Daniel as he's the most confident rider, while I take the lead trying to take us back the way we came.'

Gwendolyn walked over to Orlov and stroked his shiny black mane as Daniel heaved on the heavy metal door and shut it for the final time. Jack looked on, not sure of his own feelings. One moment he felt scared leaving the only home he had ever known. Then the next excitement raced through his body at the thought of the adventures that lay ahead, only to be filled with sadness once more. Then there was the joy of hope in being reunited with his parents which quickly turned to rage at the thought of his helplessness in their moment of need. All these emotions started to well up within, but Jack was determined not to give in, that he would not cry again in the presence of his new friends.

Daniel walked over and with a quick step up was sitting securely in the saddle strapped to Champion's back. Jack admired the white beauty of Champion, but was brought out of his trance by Daniel's voice.

'Jack. Grab my hand, then put your foot in the stirrup. When I pull you push hard with your other foot. Once you are on top put your arms around my waist and hold on tight.'

Jack smiled back, but now his nerves started to take control of his senses, and he could feel his hand trembling, but he trusted Daniel. He didn't know why because he had only met him the previous day, but something buried deep down in his subconscious told him he could trust these three. Holding out his hand he took Daniel's, placed his foot where instructed and did just as Daniel had asked. In a few thrilling seconds his arms were clasped securely around Daniel's firm waist. Looking across to the other two who had also mounted their horses he wanted to give them a wave, but suddenly Mary nudged her horse making it move forward. Champion did as well so he held on tight and enjoyed the new experience.

The sun was just rising and the birds were in full song. There was a chill in the air but the sky looked clear of heavy cloud indicating the weather would be fair, and would not hinder a good days riding.

* * *

'I just wanted to say thank you to everyone who has supported me through these troubles. To all the kind people who gave me comfort during my period of mourning, to the people who helped in the rebuilding of the storage shed after the savage fire which not only destroyed it, but also caused the death of my husband and his two apprentices in their valiant attempt to save it, and the contents within. Again I must say a big thank you to all of you who have provided enough food from your own supplies to get me through the winter.'

There was silence for a second then a big smile appeared and with arms outstretched the final sentence was said in gleeful joy. 'And finally a very big thank you for making me the new head of the village.'

A loud cheer arose and clapping filled the air as the assembled crowd rejoiced.

'I have laid out a spread of delights in my barn for everyone to enjoy so please do join me, and let us forget about the recent past, and rejoice in our coming future.'

Another loud cheer erupted as Hagar got down from the bale of straw which had been her stage and as she walked confidently to the barn the whole village followed her in celebration.

When she reached the open doors of the barn Hagar stood at the entrance and greeted everyone as they lined up in an orderly queue. They filed towards the tables inside that carried a host of cooked meats, breads, sweet potatoes and succulent fruits. In the rafters sat three people who started to strum on their instruments, and jolly music filled the air.

Hagar greeted everyone with a handshake and a personal thank you as the little ones rushed in between peoples legs, eager to start feeding on the feast of delights.

Finally only Phil the carpenter remained to be greeted. As he passed Hagar asked, 'Where is Widow Fay?'

'Where do you think she is? She's where she spends all her time since the death of her only two sons, and that's at her husband's grave. She's there from dawn to dusk.'

Hagar sighed. 'It's a shame Phil. There weren't enough remains from the ashes of the fire to make two new graves. At least she would have somewhere to mourn their passing.'

Phil gave a half-hearted smile and nodded in agreement.

Hagar stepped out into the middle of the path, then looked to the end of the village where a lonely figure dressed in black was bent over a small heap of earth. She called out, 'Join us.' There was no response. Walking back towards the barn Hagar took hold of Phil's arm. 'Let's join the others. It's a shame about her. She is all on her own now with no heirs to take over when she goes to the Achievement Centre.'

Phil agreed, and answered, 'And with her husband six foot under there's nobody there waiting for her. Poor old Widow Fay. Do you think we should go over there and see if she wants to join us?'

Hagar tugged his arm. 'No. There's no point. I've asked her already and she just ignored me. We've all suffered losses throughout our lives and are very lucky if can get through life in one piece to make it to the Achievement Centre.'

They both walked into the barn and the cheers echoed into the distance to the lonely widow who sat by the mound of earth.

She looked up and used a finger to push aside the black veil that covered her head.

'I swear on my own soul and the soul of my dead husband, and on the souls of my two deceased sons that I will take revenge on you, Hagar, and when I do it will be a sweet revenge.' She looked down on the grave and gently caressed the sun-bleached grass that covered it. 'I know your secret, Hagar, and you will pay for the death of my two sons.'

The black widow bent forward and kissed the earth, then pushing on her knees she got to her feet. Standing in silence she glanced towards the barn, then covered her face fully before turning and walked off between the trees and disappeared into the forest.

16

REGRETS: WE ALL HAVE THEM

'That's it. That's the last of the fruit.'

A combined groan was the reply. Another broken branch was added to the dwindling fire, sending sparks whispering in the chilly air. Mary rocked herself up from the ground, then walked in a circle.

'It will be another two days at least before we reach Hagar's, and it's no good moaning about our lack of food. We've had two days hard riding and I'm as hungry as the rest of you. Fruit isn't the most filling of meals, but at least it's better than eating grass.'

Mary walked over to her horse that was busy nibbling on the very same thing and rummaged through her saddle bag. Discreetly taking out a small black cloth she shoved it into the pocket of her long dress. She turned and it looked as if no one had noticed. The other three were huddled around the fire engrossed in Jack's iPad.

'I'm just going for a walk,' she called out, and got a murmur in reply. They didn't seem too bothered as Mary slunk off through the trees until she found a clearing. Resting against a large boulder she retrieved the cloth, opened it, placed her glasses squarely on her nose then lifted her gaze heavenwards.

The sound of insects calling in the night was Mary's only companion as she admired the beauty of the stars that twinkled so clearly she felt they were within her reach. A light shot across the sky, then another, and Mary chuckled with delight at the shower of meteorites. Although she loved having company occasionally she just needed a little bit of space for herself, to think, to ponder, to daydream and sometimes just to enjoy the wonder of nature. Resting her head her eyes became droopy until too heavy to keep open, then a gentle snore escaped her lips.

The sound of rustling startled Mary out of her slumber. She was still fumbling with her glasses while getting to her feet and had just managed to put them away when Jack's voice called out.

'Daniel. Gwendolyn. Where are you?'

His voice was hesitant, almost scared, and Mary's concern was obvious when she replied. 'Jack, over here. I'm over here. What's up? Is everything all right?'

Out of the trees tumbled Jack in a state of anxiety and the joy on his face when he saw Mary was obvious as he rushed over, wrapping his grateful arms around her waist.

'What's up, Jack?'

He looked up. His big brown eyes were moist with tears. 'I got lost. I wanted to go for a wee and walked into the trees. The more I tried to find my way back the more I got lost. I'm so glad I found you. I thought I was going to lose you.'

Mary stroked his hair while Jack sniffed away his tears.

'Don't you worry, my little friend. Take a seat with me, and let's enjoy the free film the heavens are putting on for us tonight. I suspect you haven't had many opportunities to spend time outside at night?'

Jack agreed. Although he had an extensive knowledge of the universe it was all gleamed from the information stored on various electronic devices, and not from first-hand experience of the real world. Mary once again rested her back against the boulder with Jack sitting next to her. They both looked up and said nothing at first until memories came flooding back to Mary.

'Actually Jack, you are quite lucky in a perverse sort of way to be able to glorify in such a wondrous sight as what is before our very eyes. In my day most boys your age lived in built-up areas, and there was so much light pollution they would be lucky to make out the odd star. In the big cities it was even worse with the air pollution. Smog from all the cars, vans, juggernauts, buses and factories. It was quite terrible, and this pollution was even more dangerous because it attacked not only mother nature, but your very own body. '

Mary glanced at Jack, and got the impression from the intensity of his face that he was listening, but not really taking in what she was saying. She fell silent and it would have been the perfect moment of contemplation if it wasn't for one thing that spoilt the whole mood. No matter how much you tried to ignore it the giant Orb hung in the sky like a silent emblem of the Over-seers. You could almost have forgotten about the hardships of life while engrossed with the majesty of heaven if it wasn't for the sight of this mighty round beast of a living machine.

'Regrets – we all have them, and I suspect my generation's biggest was that they didn't take heed of all the warning signs, and take more care of this beautiful planet. Never mind, young Jack. I doubt you have any regrets.'

Mary was ready to close her eyes and listen to the ensemble that nature provided when she was drawn back to Jack. 'What's the matter?'

He was sniffling and now looked sullen.

'You can tell me. I promise I won't tell anyone else.'

It took another three of four reassuring prompts before Jack started to relent.

'I have my own regret! I wished I had never done it.' Then Jack fell silent and said no more.

'Done what?' Mary enquired, but Jack sat still with his head bowed while his bottom lip quivered. 'Done what, my little friend?'

Mary lifted up Jack's chin with her finger and smiled that gentle reassuring smile that gave confidence with every wrinkle on her aged face. But Jack said nothing.

'You know what, Jack?' Mary was hoping for a spoken reply, but Jack stayed tight-lipped. 'Even though we have only known each other for a few days I feel as if we have a special bond because we come from a different world, a different time and place to everyone else around us. And do you know why?'

This time there was a small response. Words uttered in a low tone, but ones that brought Jack out of his silence. 'Why's that then?'

'Because, my young friend, you are the only person, other than me, who has lived in the modern world.' Mary paused for a second, re-examining the sentence in her head, then realised how foolish it sounded. 'What I should have said is we are the only ones to have experienced the past. The way life was before the Over-seers arrived. How it was like to be the master of electricity and how to use it lavishly as a work horse for your own convenience. The luxury of having running water from the tap, with flushing toilets too. Computers, iPads, televisions, sound system, gaming machines. I could go on and on, but only you and I have experienced such things. I have taught Gwendolyn about them with books, but she's never known what these things were like in real life. Then there is Daniel. He has a lot more experience of life than you do, Jack, but his experiences are totally alien to you and me.'

Mary chortled. 'Alien! I'm talking as if Daniel is an Over-seer, but he's not. He has just had an altered perception of life compared to you and me.'

Mary put her arms around Jack and pulled him close to her chest. He snuggled in. There was a pause and a slight breeze could be heard rustling through the trees.

'That's something else they would have struggled with in the past: all that noise pollution. The constant hum of motor vehicles roaring past, and air planes, and helicopters above as well, and alarms going off. Then you would have music blaring out.'

Mary had to stop to catch her breath.

'Then again the Over-seers may not have been humanities saviours, but looking back you could make an argument to say they were the planet's saviours.' Mary sighed. 'Anyway. That's enough of my rantings about the past. Why don't you tell me what's bothering you?'

Jack enjoyed the comforting feeling of having his hair stroked by Mary, and he could faintly hear her heart beating as he nestled in her embrace. It reminded him of his grandmother, who would always do the same thing, especially when he had been told off by his parents. He would go running to her open and forgiving arms. Whatever he told his granny he could do no wrong, so Jack always felt safe in telling the truth no matter how naughty his parents thought he had been.

'I didn't mean to do it.'

Mary looked down.

'What was that, Jack?'

'I didn't mean to do it. I was only playing and thought it was a bit of fun. One day I found some old memory sticks full of files. I was bored so I uploaded them onto a computer. They were encrypted and I found the challenge of finding out what was such a secret a fun thing to do. It took me a while but I done it. They were files on research that had been carried out by my grandparents and others concerning the Over-seers. One file was all about decoding how they communicate. I was fascinated and this is why I adapted the iPad so I could use it to communicate with the Over-seers helmet.'

Jack stopped unsure if he should carry on, but Mary hugged him even tighter so he felt secure enough to continue.

'When it worked I started to use the iPad on other bits and pieces of Over-seers' equipment. It was just all piled in a heap and was considered junk, but to me it was just a big pile of toys. It must be how they found us. Why they sent the Hunters. I think I must have set off some tracker signal or something, and that's why they come looking. If it wasn't for me my parents would still be safe.'

Jack started to sob. Mary had a revelation. She had always wondered how the Triclops had found them so quickly at the cathedral when Daniel got his hands on the Golden Shield, just in time to save their lives. She was convinced it had been looking for them, but then again was it looking for something else? Like Jack said, a signal he had inadvertently set off? There was no point pondering and Mary knew it. What had happened had happened and it served nobody's purpose to dwell on it. All Mary was concerned about was the present, in helping Jack and Daniel's parents, and to do that she had to keep their spirits up even if she had her own doubts about the chances of success. She always talked about positive thinking, even though there were times when deep down she struggled to keep her own fears under control. It had always been a great responsibility bringing up Gwendolyn in such terrible circumstances on her own, and now she had another two to look after. It was at moments like this that Mary wished she had someone who could look after her for a change, someone she could snuggle against, someone who would stroke her hair while reassuring her that everything would be all right, someone to protect her. There had been people in her youth when she was part of the resistance movement who she could have gladly let herself go to, but it was never a good idea to get close to someone because they could so easily be dead by the end of the day. She preferred not to get on first name terms with fellow resistance fighters, but rather just give them a number, Mr One or Mr Two, Miss Three or Mrs Four. It may have seemed a cold way to treat people, but it was a lot better than having the warmth of someone's love taken away from you by the cold crushing death-grip of an Over-seer.

A vision of someone's face appeared in Mary's mind. It was someone she once knew, just a number, not a name, but she still remembered the number. It was Mr Forty-Two. A special number for a special person. She did wish she had had the time to find out their name, but she never did. She never saw him again after that fatal attack on the resistance headquarters, the day she escaped with Gwendolyn, fleeing from the destruction, fleeing from the dead, fleeing from the hopeless situation.

'Regrets. We all have them,' thought Mary, but this wasn't the time or place to dwell on them. Her emotions were threatening to bubble out into the open. Giving Jack one final hug she exclaimed, 'Don't blame yourself, Jack. You did nothing wrong and nor did your parents. All they wanted, and what most people want, is to be left alone, to get on with your own lives without interference from others, and as long as you hurt no one else, their family, or their property, then that is how it should be. Human history is littered with people and organisations that have exploited the common person for their own gain, and that's why we aren't going to let those jumped-up alien Nazis get away with it!'

A sudden rush of enthusiasm lifted Mary's spirit, sending her scrambling to her feet. She held Jack's hand tightly, leading him back through the trees. By the time they came across the clearing Jack had dried his face while Mary was already planning to break camp.

Daniel and Gwendolyn were still engrossed in a game and had shamelessly not even noticed either Mary's or Jack's departure, or even their return. They were hooked on the iPad.

'It's lucky it's only me and not a bunch of marauding Hunters because you two would be in a right of pickle by now,' Mary called out, as she picked up a duffle bag and attached it to her saddle.

Even then they didn't acknowledged her so once she had finished she crept over to the fire. With a finger to her lips she looked at Jack and smiled. He returned the gesture and watched in anticipation. Daniel and Gwendolyn had their backs to her facing the fire while the iPad sung a ditty of electronic notes in response to the constant tapping of the screen which masked Mary's silent approach. They sat close to each other with heads bowed. Light from the screen illuminated their faces. When Mary was within a hair's breadth of them she bent down, and then with the loudest voice she could muster shouted out, 'Boo!'

Gwendolyn screamed in fright and Daniel followed suit. For a second or two she tussled among the leaves on the ground with searching hands, desperate to find her bow and arrow, while the look of surprise on Daniel's face sent Mary into a fit of rapture. Jack's boyish laughter wafted across.

Daniel was annoyed and it showed in the tone of his voice. 'What did you do that for?' He wasn't so irritated at what Mary had done, but in the fact that both he and Gwendolyn had been so lax, and had got caught out so easily by her prank.

Gwendolyn was even more infuriated because it brought home to her how defenceless she was without any arrows to use. The maddened look on her face just made Mary laugh even more as she walked back to her horse.

'I hope that taught you two to be on your guard at all times. We have to be very careful, and getting lost in a make-believe world isn't going to save your skins if you get caught.'

Jack went over to Gwendolyn and held out his hand. She was now in a huff and grudgingly handed back the iPad.

'Right, you lot. There has been a change of plan. We aren't going to stay the night, but are going to push on to Hagar's village. We will have to romp our way there.'

'What does that mean?' a puzzled Daniel asked.

'It's an old army term. It means we will travel at speed for a while, then take a walking rest. Then we keep on repeating it, taking only occasional breaks for a quick respite to take in water.'

Daniel began to kick dirt onto the fire and once it was extinguished he covered it completely so leaving no trace of their existence. Gwendolyn followed behind with a big branch sweeping the ground with it like a brush. The group were becoming seasoned campaigners in hiding their existence and once everything had been packed away Mary gathered the group into a huddle. It was virtually pitch black under the canopy of trees giving added emphasis to Mary's final words before they carried on with the next leg of their journey.

'Whatever regrets we may have had in the past there is one thing I don't regret, and that's having you three in my life. I couldn't wish for three better people to be friends with, and I'm convinced we will be all right.'

As the group walked off through the trees leading their horses Mary just hoped her tone had been positive enough to hide the doubt that rumbled deep within.

17

I KNOW NOTHING

Slowly the branch was pulled to the side and Daniel peered through the gap in the bush.

'What do you see?' Gwendolyn asked in a hurried voice. 'Is it all clear?'

He leaned to the side. 'Here. Take a peek yourself. It looks safe to me. I can't see anything that would indicate any Hunters over there, or Over-seers.'

Gwendolyn leaned forward and studied the scene in front of her, but as she pulled back she cried out loud.

'Be quiet,' said Daniel. 'What is the matter with you?'

Gwendolyn was tugging at her long pony tail, and the grimace on her face showed her discomfort.

'I've got my hair caught on the prickles of this bush, and nearly pulled out a whole strand of it. Here. You have a look and see what you can do.'

Daniel put down his axe next to his Golden Shield and started to fumble with her hair.

'It's no good. I can't seem to untangle it. I have an idea!' He let go and pulled the dagger from the sheath attached to Gwendolyn's belt as she struggled to pull herself free.

Gwendolyn looked startled. 'You're not going to do what I think you are? Are you?'

Daniel grinned. 'Don't worry. I'm only going to cut your ponytail off so you can free yourself.'

'No, you're not!' Gwendolyn exploded.

'Keep your voice down girl. The whole village will hear us.'

'I don't care if they do. You are not cutting my hair.'

'What do you think we should do then? Wait here until some stranger walks past and we can seek their help?' Daniel asked in a sarcastic tone.

'Cut the branch off,' replied Gwendolyn getting more desperate by the minute. 'When we get back to Mary she will be able to untangle it.'

Gwendolyn gave Daniel a hard silent stare, then exploded again. 'At least she's got the patience for it.'

'OK. Keep your voice down. I just don't understand you girls. What is so special about hair anyway?' Daniel tutted as he started to cut the thick base of the branch. 'I'm starving. All we have had to eat over the last four days are apples and we even ran out of them two days ago.'

'Shut up, Daniel, and cut the branch. I want to get back to the others.' Once he had finished they stooped low and hurried back through the trees. 'Are we going in the right direction?' Gwendolyn queried in hushed tones to a rather bemused Daniel. 'What are you sniggering at?' she snapped again.

Daniel stopped and straightened up. 'You should take a look at yourself. You look like a walking tree with all that in your hair.' Gwendolyn punched him on the arm, and hard too.

Daniel rubbed it. 'Why did you do that for?'

'Why do you think?' she snarled in reply.

Daniel knew from previous experience he wouldn't win an argument with Gwendolyn so instead pointed to the distance. 'Look. I can see Champion.'

Gwendolyn peered through the trees and there in the shadows, clear as the sun on a cloudless day, was the brilliant white form of Daniel's horse. She darted forward, leaving him in her wake as she rushed back.

When she came out into the small clearing young Jack was first to notice, and he started to giggle. Mary, who was sitting on the remains of a very large tree that had once stood mighty in the forest but now lay prostrate across the ground, stood and turned to see what Jack had found so amusing.

'What wonderful camouflage you have used. I doubt anyone would have seen you skulking about the trees with all that in your hair.'

Gwendolyn wasn't amused at Mary's light-hearted remarks, and sat down on the trunk in a huff. 'Can you just get this thing untangled without butchering my hair?'

Mary joined her then put her arm around Gwendolyn's shoulder before pulling her towards her in a hug. 'Of course I can.'

Before Daniel had come bursting into her life she would have buried her head in Mary's arms and may have shed a tear or two, but now for some reason she couldn't allow herself to even if she wanted. Instead she felt miserable and it showed on her face.

When Daniel appeared he immediately reported on their scouting mission to Mary and she seemed pleased with the news.

'That's great. We are all tired and hungry, and we are all becoming as grouchy as the grumbles in our bellies. '

Pausing while she studied the tangled mess that was Gwendolyn's hair the hunger in her belly forced Mary to take action. She grabbed Gwendolyn's matted ponytail with one hand and the stem of the branch that stuck out from her head, and gave it one almighty pull. Gwendolyn cried out.

Mary stood up and threw the branch away.

'Now that problem is solved let us go and solve another problem.' She rubbed her belly. 'Because I know one thing: just a sort walk from here should hopefully be somewhere where we can get some food. Now the last time we passed through this village we all know what happened.'

'What happened?' Jack asked and the other three looked at each other without saying a word. Not wanting to alarm him Mary didn't know what to say so Daniel took the lead.

'Nothing this didn't sort out,' and he held his axe triumphantly in the air.

Gwendolyn looked over to her horse. Hanging from its saddle was her bow and empty quiver. She felt insecure. Without any arrows it was of no use at all. Dread descended over her soul and she started to have second thoughts about entering the village to seek food. 'If only I had some arrows I could have hunted down some rats,' she thought, and the image of rat and cat soup boiling in a pot full of potatoes appeared like magic, making her mouth salivate.

The horses were led to the edge of the village and tied to a tree while Mary crouched down behind a bush. Peering out, her eyes settled on Hagar's home. The sun was setting and the night was carried on a chill wind, so she knew with just another hour of waiting everyone in the village would be tucked up in the warmth of their huts with fires blazing. Their path would then be clear.

* * *

The door swung open and daylight flooded into the darkness of the guards' hut. Against one wall, resting on wooden blocks, was a bed of straw and on top of this with his back to the entrance lay Mad-dog. The sound of snoring rose and fell with his heaving chest.

Leyland walked over and nudged him. 'Wake up, Mad-dog.' There was a grunt but no movement so he pushed even harder. Suddenly Mad-dog jumped to his feet, startling Leyland. He held a dagger in his outstretched hand.

'Don't you ever come sneaking up behind me again. Do you understand? I could have cut your heart out!'

Leyland hesitated, stuttering his response. 'OK. But I've got something you will be interested in.'

'What is it?' Mad-dog asked in a demanding tone as he sat back down while brushing strands of straw from his brown shirt.

'Come in here,' called out Leyland. In shuffled a woman dressed all in black with her head covered by a scarf.

Mad-dog looked up. 'What would I want with her?'

'Not her. It's the information she's got that will interest you, Mad-dog.'

There was silence in the room. The clatter of carts and people rumbling over the wooden bridge outside as they carried out their daily routines filled the void.

'What is it, woman?' barked Mad-dog

She didn't reply at first, and true to his name her refusal to reveal the information without bartering for something in return sent a mad rage through his still sleepy head, sending him to his feet like a rabid dog.

'What have you got to tell me, woman?' Saliva spat from his snarling jaws.

She looked at him with a steely glare, then spoke in a soft, but questioning voice. 'I hear that you Hunters are looking for some people?'

Mad-dog looked her straight in the eyes. 'We're always looking for people. That's our job.'

'I also hear that if anyone can help you find these people there is an award?'

Leyland could see Mad-dog was getting annoyed and tried to hurry the woman. He raised his fist. 'Come on, or have I got to beat it out of you?'

Her head turned slowly towards him. She said nothing, and gradually he dropped his hand to his side. Turning back to Mad-dog she asked, 'I hear that you will go to the Achievement Centre as an award for helping Hunters in finding anyone who has broken the Seven Procedures?'

Mad-dog looked disinterested and didn't reply.

'I also hear the Over-seers seek three people, a young man and a girl?' She paused as if to emphasise the importance of the information she had to give. 'And a woman who has passed her day of Achievement by many years.'

Excitement spread over Leyland's face with the eagerness of a puppy looking to its master for an award. 'See, Mad-dog! I told you!'

Taking three steps forward his large frame towered over her, as Mad-dog responded with an inquisitive tone tinged with a hint of menace. 'Let us hear what she has to say first.'

She looked Mad-dog squarely in the face before asking her final question. 'So if I tell you what I know can I go straight to the Achievement Centre as a reward?'

Mad-dog gave her the signal when he nodded silently. She started to tell him what she knew.

'I have seen them as they passed through my village.'

'How recently was this?' Mad-dog enquired, and when he was told he burst out laughing. 'You're telling me they passed through your village over two full cycles of the moon ago! What good is that information? They could have reached the end of the world by now.'

He turned as if he was going to move away, then in a flash turned back grabbing the woman by the throat which lifted her off her feet. Taken by surprise she gasped for air as his grip tightened. Taking three more steps with her feet still dangling from the floor he pushed her with such force into the wooden side of the hut that she was left dazed, and could no longer fight for breath.

The whiskers on Mad-dogs chin brushed her face as he squeezed ever tighter on the defenceless woman's throat. Whispering into her ear he asked, 'So tell me why I shouldn't end your life right now for wasting my time?' Gurgling noises was all he could hear. 'Quickly woman! Have you got anything else to tell me?'

All she could do was to nod her head as the fear flooded from her eyes. Mad-dog loosened his hold just enough to let her talk, but not enough to let her think she would live.

'A woman in my village helped them on their way. She will be able to tell you where they have gone.' She gasped for more breath. 'Her name is Hagar. She is the head of our village.'

The grip slackened again just enough to give her hope.

'It's only half a day's ride away from here down river. You will know when you are there because the village meeting tree standing at its centre is just a burnt-out shell.'

Mad-dog threw her to the ground where she slumped like a quivering wreck while sobbing profusely.

'Leyland, let's go.' But when he tried to walk away he was impeded by the woman, who had grabbed him by the ankle as she begged through her sobs.

'Please let me go to the Achievement Centre.' The begging became louder. 'Please let me go. My husband is dead as well as my two sons, burnt to death in a terrible fire.'

He kicked out his leg trying to dislodged the grieving widow, but it only made her hold on more tightly as he tried to walk out the door. 'Leyland – can you get this damn woman off me, now?'

'Please let me go. I deserve it. I have always kept to the Seven Procedures. Please let me go.'

Leyland put his arms around her waist and yanked with all the might his runt of a body would allow. Pulling for a second time she finally let go after a thundering fist crashed into her skull.

Mad-dog rubbed his knuckles. 'If what you say is true and we capture these fugitives you can go to the Achievement Centre.' He headed out the door before stopping. Looking back he asked, 'These three people: did they have horses with them?' She nodded. 'And was one of them a pure black stallion, by any chance?' She nodded again. A big grin spread over Mad-dog's face. 'Come on, Leyland. We have a date with destiny, while at the same time I think Wolf has a date with the hangman.'

* * *

The fire had now settled down into a gentle glow of rhythmic flaring yellows that radiated from the inner core of burning red wood with the caring warmth of a cloudless sky on a bright summer's day. The night had settled down, covering the sun with its sleeping blanket so waking the stars from their slumber. A chill wind came galloping in, chasing nature with its shivering touch, keeping both man and beast alike tucked away from its cold strokes.

Hagar settled down in her favourite chair. She adjusted the pillow from behind her lower back and then stretched out her legs so her shoeless feet could soak up all the heat the fire now freely gave. Resting her head, she closed her eyes and pondered on how recent events had so unexpectedly changed her life for the better. How fortunate the arrival of the three strangers had been in helping to gain her freedom from her brutish husband Jeff. Especially that fit young man with his axe. A joyful shudder shot down her spine and she gently altered her sitting position.

'I wonder where they are,' she thought. 'I hope they are safe.' She smiled. She shouldn't be smiling in theory, but mourning the death of her husband instead, but she was glad that Daniel had chopped his head off. She was also delighted that Gwendolyn had shot his two thuggish apprentices dead with her arrows. She was now free from Jeff's violent servitude and was no longer a slave to his every immoral whim. For a second a sad thought shot into her heart for Mrs Fay because she had now lost her only two sons. With her husband having also passed away the grieving widow was now so lonely.

'So should I be,' thought Hagar. 'I haven't got any children either, although Jeff had always blamed me for being barren, but maybe if he had treated me with more gentleness my body would have been more receiving.'

A loud spat came jumping from the fire and Hagar opened her eyes. She starred at the flames that danced so provocatively while holding her gaze in a trance-like state. Although she felt guilt for Mrs Fay it couldn't stop the over-whelming feeling of happiness she now enjoyed. With all three of their bodies being burnt to an unrecognisable cinder in the grain store fire, and everyone thinking it was just a horrible accident, all of Jeff's deceitful crimes committed against his fellow villages and the Over-seers had disappeared with the last of the smoke from the smouldering remains. And to top it all off her friends had rallied around to rebuild the store and then made her head of the village.

There was a gentle knock at the door.

Hagar pushed herself free of the chair and walked over. It was darker in this part of her home so she picked up a half worn candle fixed by its own wax to a clay tile. Lifting the door latch she pulled it towards her just enough so she could hold the candle in the gap while taking a look at the unknown visitor.

Hagar exhaled, then opened the door with welcoming arms. 'Talk about a coincidence! Come on in. You must be cold.'

In walked Mary, followed by Gwendolyn with Jack, who was holding her hand tightly. Daniel covered the rear, looking behind, checking no other people had seen their entry in the village as he hurried the others along before shutting the wooden door quietly behind him, and finally bolting it.

The room offered a welcome warmth that was matched by Hagar's hug as she pulled Mary towards her, while they exchanged kisses on both cheeks. Next she leaned towards Gwendolyn who flinched as she pulled away, unsure of the etiquette, and feeling strange that someone would want to offer such open friendship after she had very nearly shot her with an arrow. Hagar sensed her unease and turned her attention to Jack instead.

'So who do we have here?' Jack had no qualms in responding likewise, as his hair was being ruffled.

'My name is Jack Patel.'

'Hello, Mr Patel. Or may I just call you Jack?' He smiled and nodded. 'Jack, any friend of these three is a friend of mine.' Hagar held out her hand to Jack, who reacted by shaking it enthusiastically. Next her attention turned to Daniel. She cusped his forearm and gently rubbed it. 'And how is my young warrior?' she asked as she flirtatiously gave him a single kiss on his right cheek. He blushed and said sheepishly, 'All right.'

Gwendolyn didn't realize it but she was scowling towards Hagar, forcing Mary to secretly nudge her arm. Gwendolyn looked at Mary who quietly nodded towards Hagar, while vividly smiling. It forced a smile from Gwendolyn. Mary showed her approval by nodding again in agreement.

Hagar turned towards the fire. 'Sit down and warm yourself. Are you hungry by any chance?' By everyone's response Hagar knew they hadn't eaten for days and hastened to make some sandwiches of sliced ham with creamy cheese made from thick-cut bread smothered with dark sweet pickle sauce.

Over the next few hours Hagar was told the full story in dramatic detail of their travels after they had left her. How they had reached the great cathedral and found the Golden Shield. How Daniel had used it to destroy the mighty Triclops by reflecting its deadly ray back to the terrifying monster, making it tumble to the ground. How they had hidden for many weeks in the old underground flint mines while above Over-seers and Hunters searched for them. By the time they had finished in explaining their return to save Daniel's mother and father, Jack had fallen asleep with his head resting on Gwendolyn's knee while she sat on the floor resting her back on the side of Mary's chair. Although Hagar took great delight in what she had heard there was one thing she was finding very hard to understand, and now asked for the third time the same questions.

'So you are telling me that the Over-seers are not from this world? You are also telling me that there is no life of luxury under the care of the Over-seers when you reach your fortieth season? I'm also to believe that the Achievement Centres are nothing more than feeding stations for the Over-seers? She looked perplexed, almost confused, but the insistence of the other three was slowly bringing her around to the truth. 'And finally the Over-seers feed on us alive? Tearing our flesh away and eating us like an uncooked joint of meat?'

Hagar was shaking her head slowly from side to side as she tutted in disgust. 'I thought it had to be too good to be true. All this daily chanting with the Seven Procedures about the Over-seers being our saviours and the glories to come.'

She looked into the fire that had now died down to a heap of ash with chunks of glowing red hot embers.

'Life has taught me at great expense that not all promises made are kept by the people who make them.'

Gwendolyn yawned, making Mary follow suit, and when she did it a second time Daniel started to yawn as well.

Hagar was perplexed, still in disbelief.

'You say your horses are tied up in the trees? You can stable them in the barn and you are welcome to sleep there as well. I only have one bed here, but there's plenty of hay in the barn to sleep on. It's nice and dry and I've got some blankets that will keep you warm. I will stock you with supplies, but it would be best if you left at first light before any of the other villagers are awake so you don't get seen.'

Mary was first to her feet. 'Thank you, Hagar for your hospitality and your help. We really do appreciate it.'

Hagar got up next and put her arms around Mary. 'No. It should be me thanking you because if you hadn't told me the truth I would have happily gone off to the Achievement Centre on my fortieth birthday none the wiser. Although I still have some years left before I need to worry about it. The knowledge you now have must make you some of the most dangerous people for the Over-seers. Whoever has this knowledge is basically a dead person!'

Then it dawned on Hagar that she was now in danger. If the Over-seers knew that she knew the truth about them they would execute her on the spot. 'I don't know what to do with this information you have given me.'

Gwendolyn stopped stroking Jack's jet black hair and joined in the conversation. 'I suggest you keep your mouth shut until it's your turn to go to the Achievement, and then go on the run.'

Daniel now stood up and leaned over to her. 'Here, Gwendolyn. Let me wake young Jack.' After a bit of vigorous shaking he picked Jack up, still half asleep, leaving him unsteady on his feet while he rubbed his eyes, groaning that he wanted to go back to sleep. Gwendolyn got up and was first at the door.

'Give me a hand in getting the horses to the barn.' She disappeared, followed by Mary, while Daniel held Jack's hand. Just as he was going to leave Hagar stopped him and lent in close. Her breath touched his ear and Daniel could smell the sweet aroma of scent on her neck.

'If there is anything you need.' She paused while her nose rubbed against his lobe. 'Or want during the night please don't hesitate in coming to me.' She paused again. 'My door will be unbolted and left on the latch.'

Daniel could feel his heart race while his cheeks started to flush. In that moment Gwendolyn's head appeared around the door.

'Come here with me, Daniel,' and with that she grabbed his belt and led him out the door.

The horses were collected and as they walked towards the barn Mary suddenly stopped. 'Did you hear that?' She looked concerned.

'Sounds like thunder to me,' replied Daniel, but she wasn't convinced.

'We would have seen a flash of lightning before we heard it. Quick. Help me to my knees.' She held out a hand. Placing her ear to the ground she hushed the others into silence. One of the horses snorted. Holding her hand out once again she got to her feet with Daniel's help.

'It's not a Triclops.'

'Look! I saw a flash of light up the path,' exclaimed Gwendolyn. 'Is it lightning?'

'No, it's worse, a lot worse. It's a large posse of horses and they're heading our way, which can only mean one thing – Hunters! Quick! They will be here any minute. It's no good hiding in the barn. We need to get back into the woods.'

The thundering racket came storming towards them with every hurried second of panic as confused horses were dragged by their reins from one direction to the next.

'Not this way. Back the way we came. No stop. I can see torches over there. Let's go through the village. No – it will take too long to reach the woods on the other side. Quick. Head for the side. Stop. There's too much thicket on that side. We can't get through. Turn around. Run to the other side.' Mary's instructions became as confusing as the commotion from the galloping horsemen who burst from the wooded path and charged into the village with flaming torches that flared like prophetic lights at the gates of hell.

Daniel lurched towards Champion and quickly untied the Golden Shield. Once secured to his arm he grappled with his trusted axe, then shouted out to the others, 'Take the horses. I will try to hold them off as long as I can.'

'Not without me you're not,' said Gwendolyn. 'I may have no arrows but I know how to use these.' In each hand she held a dagger. Mary grabbed Jack's arm as tears of fear rolled down his cheeks. Franticly she tried to coax the horses into the trees, but they could sense the danger. Stubbornly they cantered with swaying heads, sending tempered steam from their flaring nostrils.

The lead rider screamed to his comrades as he charged towards Daniel with a sword in hand.

'We have them! Take them dead or alive.' With sword raised above his head, swinging with great force, it came lashing down, clanking against Daniel's shield. In a flash he had passed, heading to his next target.

Mary knew she was next.

'Hold these and don't let go.' She thrust the horse's reins into Jack's hands. The fear in his eyes turned to panic, but he did as he was told, holding on with all his might. There were just seconds left before the sharp edge of a blade came slicing its way towards her skull. With horse breath bearing down on her neck Mary turned to face her demon. With a thrust of her arm she pulled out her umbrella, then flicked it wide open waving it wildly, clipping the horse's nose. It reared up high on its hind legs, startled, sending its rider crashing to the ground.

He lay still at first, then groggily raised his body to his knees. Before he had a chance to get to his feet, Mary had picked up a small rock and sent it hammering across the back of his head. He slumped forward and lay unconscious.

Mary gave a thumbs up to Jack, but her triumph was short-lived when her attention was drawn to the sound of what seemed a never-ending stampede of man and beast.

Daniel had two men on horses taking turns to find a way through his defensive shield. When a third on foot tried to join the fray Gwendolyn let fly one of her daggers which pierced the horseman's back just below the shoulder. He let out a colossal cry of pain. Desperately trying to reach the dagger that protruded from his flesh was futile while still mounted so he struggled off his horse. But fate often deals a deadly hand, and just when he thought he had hold of the dagger's handle the other Hunter's horse knocked him backwards. He stumbled to the ground, landing on his back. The dagger squished through his body, leaving its tip projecting from his chest as he gasped his last breath.

Daniel saw for a fleeting second his attacking foes' distraction at their colleague's fate, so swung his axe low while holding his shield high. Its sharp edge sliced its way through the cartilage of an unprotected knee, sending its owner crashing to the dirt, where he rolled about screaming in excruciating pain. Daniel ran at him with his shield for protection and went crashing into him. Daniel fell, but got to his feet first. Using his shield once again he swung sideways, knocking his attacker out cold.

He could sense the presence of someone behind him, so swung around with his axe raised ready to deal a deadly blow. Startled at Gwendolyn's scream he stepped back.

'It's me, Daniel, only me.'

They didn't have time to ponder on what could nearly have happened. Mary had called out to them warning of another attacker as she came scrambling over to them. She was trying to make a distraction by opening and shutting her umbrella while squawking at the top of her voice like a flightless bird in distress.

The attacker's horse took fright at Mary's antics just as

Gwendolyn let fly her final dagger, aiming for the rider's chest, but the horse had reared on its hind legs and so took the full force of the blow across its powerful shoulder. Its skin split and blood began to pour from the wound. Its rider had managed to stay on, but as the horse's hoof touched down the pain was too much to endure and its leg gave way. Leaning sideways the horse came crashing to the ground, crushing its master under its hefty body as he yelled a dreadful cry of pain. The sound of breaking human bones echoed throughout the village.

Mary had reached them, panting for breath.

'Let's run for it. There are too many of them.' As they all turned they stopped dead in their tracks. There stood Jack, still holding onto the horse's reins, but behind him stood a thin, gaunt looking man with one hand smothering Jack's mouth. The other was holding a cut-throat razor pressed under poor Jack's chin.

'Put the weapons down, boy, or I promise you this child will have bled to death by the time you reach me.'

Daniel looked at Gwendolyn who held open her empty palms, indicating she had no other knives to use. They both looked towards Mary for guidance. She said nothing at first, but calmly retracted the hood of the umbrella, tied it shut before dropping it to her feet. Then as she slowly raised her hands she turned silently towards Daniel and gave him the nod. Gwendolyn followed suit. There was nothing he could do. The axe was first to hit the ground, then the shield, then he joined the others in raising his hands above his head.

Within seconds the surrounding gang fell on their prey in a frenzy of excitement, hurriedly binding their captives' hands so that they posed no further threat. A sense of doom shrouded Daniel's heart with the realization of their hopeless situation.

Mad-dog got to his feet. Rubbing the back of his sore head, his fingers squelched with the seeping warm blood that had soaked the strands of his long matted hair.

'Well done, Leyland. I can always rely on you to sort out the situation.'

Leyland smirked and tightened his grip around Jack's throat. 'Should I slit it now or will he hang with the others?'

Someone shouted out, 'Quarter them.'

Leyland's smile turned into a broad grin.

'Yes. Let's tie each of their limbs to a different horse and enjoy the splendour of watching them being torn to pieces.'

Someone else cried out again, 'Quarter them,' and more joined in the chorus. 'Quarter them, quarter them, quarter them.' The noise became ever louder until silenced by a strong, but feminine response.

'What are you Hunters doing in my village?'

The assembled men began to part and through them, with the grace of a dolphin cutting a wave, walked Hagar. Her long hair, which had been braided into a tight bun earlier, now flowed freely down her back. She wore an elegant nightdress, taut at the waist, so enhancing the shape of her ample bosom, tantalisingly revealed by two untied buttons.

She walked over to Mad-dog and stopped just a foot away. 'I take it you must be the leader of this motley crew?'

'And who's asking the question?' Mad-dog replied with glee.

'I am Hagar, leader of this village.'

Mad-dog smiled. 'So you are the one who has been aiding these fugitives? You should be quartered alongside these other four for helping them evade justice.'

Hagar held her nerve. 'I know nothing of what you speak.' She paused, and just as Mad-dog was going to reply she repeated her words with added authority. 'I know nothing of what you speak, and if you have any evidence then show it to me now. I have always followed the Seven Procedures as set down by our saviours, and have always been a loyal servant of the Over-seers. I am under their protection and so should these four be until the Over-seers say otherwise. So I will have no executions in this village.'

Mad-dog was left momentarily silenced, then came back for the counter attack.

'We have information from the widow Fay that says otherwise.' His eyes narrowed.

Hagar gave him a gentle disarming smile. 'You are a leader of a mighty Hunter gang. I would say you have got to this position of power by being able to distinguish who is telling the truth and who is not. You can either believe the words of a very sad, lonely and, I must add, deranged widow, or you can believe the words from a respected leader of a loyal village. What is it to be?'

As he hesitated she went in with the fatal blow. Learning forward so that her delicate perfume could work its charm with the hairs of Mad-dog's nostrils, she whispered in a low sensual tone, 'A man with just half your presence would at least let these four live until they have faced the Over-seers.'

As she pulled away Hagar could see the desire twinkling in his eyes with the brightness of the stars in the heavens above.

Mad-dog looked over to his men. 'Tag them and bag them, men. We are taking them back to camp with us.' A sigh of disappointment groaned from his men's lips.

Hagar turned and walked off towards her hut without looking at Mary, Daniel, Gwendolyn or Jack as they were being tethered to horses while having their heads covered with sacks.

Leyland came over and using his knife he cut a chunk of cloth from the shirt of the dead Hunter and handed it over.

'Here. Use this for your head wound. What are we going to do with his body?' he asked, but Mad-dog didn't look too bothered.

'Leyland, if he is clever enough to get killed then he is clever enough to bury himself.'

Mad-dog got onto his horse, clutching the reins in one hand while holding the screwed up cloth against the back of his skull.

'Men, we head back to camp with these fugitives, and by the time we have finished torturing them they will have wished their bones had been flayed around this village.' A loud cheer went up from his men.

18

THE BEST DAY OF OUR LIVES

The cockerel crowed.

John opened one eye, before pulling his sheepskin rug back over his head.

The cockerel crowed once more and then again. It was no good. His sleepy head, which only moments earlier had been in a deep slumber, started to stir with thoughts. Opening both eyes the back of Mother's head came into focus. She was still fast asleep, breathing softly. He wanted to give her a cuddly, but decided she deserved a lie in. Gently he pulled the warmth of his cover away and got to his feet while brushing flotsam off his night clothes.

After relieving himself behind the barn, he opened its doors to check all the animals inside were safe. All was well, and once they had all received their morning feed he returned to his hut. The fire was out, but rummaging through the ash he found some red embers and used them, with the help of some kindling, to bring a flame to life. Once logs had been added the fire was powerful enough to boil water. John added some herbs to the pot and when it had brewed he poured himself a cup of tea. He sat down in his favourite chair in front of the fire.

He took a careful sip from his clay mug just as Sarah came bundling through the bedroom door. 'Happy Achievement Day, daddy.' Before John had a chance to take a second sip she had plopped herself on his knees and gave him a big hug. He struggled to place his drink on the floor without spilling it, but once he had he wrapped his arms around her lovingly.

'I love you, my little darling. You know you're my pride and joy?' She smiled and buried her head in his arms. 'Badger and his family are going to take great care of you until the day, hopefully soon, when Daniel returns to become head of the family.'

John gently flattened Sarah's dishevelled hair and gave her a kiss. 'Why don't we make Mother breakfast in bed before the start of the Seven Procedures?'

Mother was woken up with a kiss. She stretched out her arms and wrapped them around John's neck, then pulled him close. 'Happy Achievement Day,' she smiled, before kissing him. Their intimate moment was interrupted by Sarah as she came walking in carrying a rather large wooden tray laden with treats.

'Thank you, Sarah. Now let's leave Mother to enjoy her breakfast while we get the early morning chores out of the way.'

They left the room. Mother's smile dropped just as John returned.

'I've just forgotten to get...' He didn't finish the sentence. 'What's up my darling? You look sad.'

Glumly she raised her gaze towards him and replied, 'It's Daniel. I just wish he was here with us today.'

John had tried his best to lift his wife's spirits since Daniel had so unexpectedly disappeared, but he had that sinking feeling that he hadn't succeeded.

'I know. I miss him too, but he will be OK. And you know why? Because we brought him up with love, so he knows the difference between good and evil, and more importantly, we taught him from an early age to stand on his own two feet. Wherever he is I know he will be OK.'

John held out his hand and Mother took it. He pulled her up towards him and hugged her tightly. 'This should be the best day of our lives. Today we have to worry no more because we have pleased the Over-seers, and now they will look after us for the rest of our lives.'

Standing taller than Mother he stroked her long hair while she buried her head in his arms just like Sarah had done earlier in the day.

'I have no choice. I have to go today as instructed by the Procedures, but you don't.' John drew away, then kissed Mother's lips. 'You don't have to go yet. You still have a season before your fortieth day. If you want you can stay here until Daniel returns. I will wait for you in the centre and you can join me later.'

Mother's glum expression changed.

'You're right; Daniel is a big boy now and he can look after himself. I can't be without you, John. I want us to go into the Achievement Centre side-by-side just like we have spent most of our life outside it.' She grabbed John's head with both hands and slapped a passionate kiss on his lips. 'Come on hubby, get the Daily Procedures meeting out the way so the celebrations can begin.'

* * *

Badger heaved another load onto the back of his cart.

'Dad, we need to get to the meeting. The Seven Procedures will start any minute.'

He turned around. 'Go on without me, son. I've got too much to do today making preparations for the celebrations at the Three-ways.'

'Mummy, dad's not coming to the meeting.'

Badger held a finger to his mouth. 'Shut you up, boy. You will get me into trouble. Don't let the whole village know.' He paused. 'And definitely don't let your mum know or she will tear my head off.' He bent over and held open his palm. In the centre of it was a small but juicy red apple. 'Now you can have this if you don't tell anyone I'm not coming.' His boy snatched it out of his hand while nodding enthusiastically.

Badger stroked his beard with its two-tone colouring of grey whiskers interwoven with black hair, then smiled a toothless grin. 'And if anyone asks where I am you tell them you don't know.' Badger held out his other hand and this time there was a sweet bun on his open palm. 'And if nobody finds out, this little treat will be waiting for you at the Three-ways.'

In the distance came the sound of banging as wood hit wood.

'Now get you off, my son. That's the call for everyone to head to the well.' His boy darted off to the centre of the village and Badger returned to loading the cart. He had managed to borrow a horse for a couple of days from someone he knew from River-mouth, so there could be two carts to take the honoured guests, and all the food everyone had gladly provided towards today's feast. By the time the final cheer went up from the assembled crowd, followed by a long succession of clapping, Badger had finished all the preparations.

Discreetly he darted behind a row of huts and then joined somewhere in the middle of the crowd as they dispersed from the meeting. Looking through the bodies he saw the long red flaming hair of his daughter Eudora. Pushing his way towards her his wife came into view alongside his other children.

He sidled up to his wife.

'That was a very moving moment, I thought.' He winked at his boy, then put his arm around his wife's arm.

'Yes, it was,' she replied, then said no more. Badger felt confident no one had noticed his absence. He knew he had taken a big risk in not reciting the Seven Procedures as required, but he felt it was a risk worth taking for his best friend John.

'Let's get home, finish our chores for the morning, then round up the whole village and head for the Three-ways.' The children cheered and ran off home.

* * *

'Where's Sarah?' John called out.

'She's with the Badger's family,' Mother replied from the bedroom. As John walked through a tingle of pride went shivering down his back as he admired her. She was sitting on a stool brushing her hair. She was wearing her best dress, a favourite of John's that showed off every curve of her perfectly petite body. He had bartered for it from a visiting trader at River-mouth. It had taken a full three months' worth of timber in exchange, but he had never begrudged a single day's labour to purchase it for her. It was a gift to celebrate her thirtieth season just after Sarah's birth, and it looked as good on her now as it did then.

'I love you.' John couldn't help himself. The words just seemed to spill out from his thoughts, but he didn't care. He didn't care if the whole world knew how much he loved her.

Mother got up from her stool. 'Here. Hold your chin up,' she said, and when he did as he was told she started to brush his beard. 'Would you have known all those many years ago when we were just children ourselves that we would spend the rest of our lives together?' John could only shrug his shoulders as Mother pulled away at a particular knotted section of whiskers. 'Other than my father, and Daniel, you have been the only man in my life.' She tugged again sending John's face into a grimace. 'And you are right. This is the best day of our lives. We have had to toil hard over the years and lost many dear people along the way. We have had to endure harsh winters and hard times, but there have been plenty of moments of joy along the way as well. We are also lucky to have two children who survived into childhood. So I'm thankful, but what I'm most grateful for is having you by my side every step of the way.'

She gave John a quick peck on the lips. 'There. You are all done.'

He was ready to return the peck with a full blown smooch when there was a loud knock at the door. He hesitated, wanting to kiss Mother first, but soon a second knock came rattling at the door, followed a few seconds later by a third. Mother walked out the room leaving John to tut at his own missed moment. He followed after her, and as she opened the door deafening cheers greeted them.

Soon helping hands had taken hold of Mother's arms as she was lead to her awaiting carriage. With a quick lift she was sitting on the back of the cart with her legs dangling down the open back. John was slapped on the back by many congratulating hands as he walked through the assembled crowd. With a jump and a push he sat by her side, then wrapped his arm around Mother's waist, before planting a big kiss on her cheek. The crowed reacted with a joyful chorus of merriment and applauding.

Badger tugged at his horse's reins and the cart began to move forward. As it left the village the crowd snaked behind it to the sound of beating drums accompanied by graceful ditties played on wooden flutes.

When the Three-ways came into view the little children ran ahead screaming with excitement, and by the time Eudora had arrived at the back of the procession, leading the second cart, rugs had been laid out across the grass, and people were dancing around the Tribute hut.

Strangers began to emerge along the path in joyous mood. Some walked on their own after travelling many days to reach this point, while others who lived closer arrived with family and friends who would see them off on their own big day at the Achievement Centre.

Friendly banter and greetings were exchanged, as well as food and drink, among all who were amassed at the Three-ways. After much dancing John collapsed onto some rugs placed conveniently in the shade of a large over hanging tree. He panted for breath and looked over to the throng of dancers, and in the middle of them stood Mother gyrating her body while holding Sarah's outstretched arms. He smiled.

Ready to close his eyes, the moment was stolen by the sound of one almighty low pitched blast of a horn that echoed throughout the land. A strong sudden beat of the heart sent his pulse racing with adrenaline. He tingled to a sudden point of sheer excitement. Shuffling to his tired feet a helping hand was extended by his best friend Badger. Once up Badger hugged him closely and John returned the affection.

'I'm going to miss you both, and don't worry about Sarah. My family will take great care of her until Daniel's return.' He let John go.

'You only have the one season to go, Badger, before you reach your fortieth and your chance to enter the Achievement Centre.' John paused. 'And when you do I will be there waiting for you.'

'You better not scoff all the food before I arrive,' Badger joked.

Once again a colossal horn blast indicated that everyone on their Achievement Day had to now assemble at the rock guarding the third path which indicated the no passing point.

He joined Mother. They held hands and walked through the throng of fellow villagers who called out their best wishes. Tears of joy started to roll down Mother's face. John struggled to hide his feelings as his eyes welled up with moisture. By the time they had reached the rock it was no good fighting the emotion, and a single tear burst down his cheek. He wiped it quickly. There were so many people assembled it was impossible to count their numbers, but then the third and final blast sent a thrill of enthusiasm down everyone's spine as a good proportion of these stepped forward, passed the stone and went up the path.

There was a deafening roar of approval from those left behind, and it only started to die down once the last person walking up the dirt path had turned the corner and disappeared among the throng of trees. The sound of birds twittering their sunset calls now took over. People talked in hushed tones in reverence for this most important of experiences, the most exceptional of days.

One and all stopped in confusion when the path came to an abrupt halt. In front of them was a cliff face of smooth grey coloured stone. No one knew what to do next. They looked at each other with enquiring faces, but as no one had ever experienced this moment before the whole group were perplexed.

Mother squeezed John's hand. He acknowledged her concern just as the sound of rumbling emanated from behind the cliff. Slowly a gap appeared and it increased in size as the two halves of the wall started to spread apart. The gasps of awe were soon drowned out by the increasing vibrations that followed the ever increasing black hole which appeared in front of the cluster of people.

Then two silver-suited Over-seers appeared standing silently, each with an arm raised, pointing into the darkness. By instinct the fodder began to move forward and the first bodies began to vanish within the black void.

John and Mother were the last to enter as they took one last look at the surroundings that had been home for all of their lives. As they did so the sunlight slowly began to fade while the walls started to close. When all was consumed in darkness John and Mother both said in hushed unison, 'I love you.'

19

BROTHERLY LOVE

The cockerel crowed.

Wolf opened one eye, then pulled his sheepskin rug back over his head.

The cockerel crowed once more, and then again. It was no good. His sleepy head, which only moments earlier had been in a deep slumber, started to stir with thoughts. Opening both eyes the rough texture of a mud wall came into focus. A spider was elegantly lowering itself down, and with a quick swipe of his hand it could have been crushed, but Wolf decided to let it carry on with its journey. He pulled the warmth of his rug away and got to his feet.

After relieving himself behind his hut he was just walking back though the door when the sound of horses approaching caught his attention. Wolf suspected it could only be Mad-dog and his gang. His pulse suddenly increased with anxiety. He waited at the door in anticipation and it wasn't long before Mad-dog appeared at the head of his troop. Behind him rode his men, before the sight of four strangers with their heads covered in sacks, tethered by ropes as they were dragged on foot, came into view. Leyland came next with some more men riding behind him. At the back of the procession came the sight that sent a shot of doom though Wolf's heart: three horses without riders. One he didn't recognise. It was pure white and looked as if it could run with the wind, but the other two he did know. They were the two horses that once belonged to his gang, and which were taken by the deadly trio they had previously encountered. His eyes shot across the middle of the cavalcade to the prisoners. Although there were now four, including one who by his size could only be a child, his instinct told him that the other three hooded detainees must be the fugitives sought by the Overseers.

As Mad-dog slowly passed by he looked down without uttering a word. The grin across his face told Wolf all he needed to know. It was up to Leyland to cock a sentence in triumphant as he passed by.

'Why don't you tell that forgetful side kick of yours…' He spat out the remainder of the discourse with vile glee, '… that we have found his horse?' He started to snigger and although Wolf had been trying to look cool about the whole situation his dislike for Leyland showed in his steely stare as the anger flushed in his cheeks.

Wolf could take no more so walked back into his hut slamming the door behind him. He was still walking about in deep thought around the single room that consisted of his home when the door swung open. In rushed Fat-man, his face all reddened, and panting with obvious fear. He was almost hyperventilating by the time he sat down on a stool, gasping as he poured some water from the leather jug into a wooden cup.

'What are we going to do? We told everyone we had been attacked by a rabid gang of wild dogs that had overwhelmed us, and that they had attacked Ginger and poor old One-eye, killing them and the horses!' Fat-man took a nervous gulp of water, then another before finishing off the rest with his final swig. 'Now Mad-dog has got our horses!'

He glanced at Wolf looking for reassurance, but his reply only sent Fat-man into a frantic panic.

'I'm afraid it's worse than that, Maxwell, my friend. Mad-dog also has captive the three fugitives that took the horses in the first place.'

Wolf stopped and sat down on the edge of his bed while Fat-man refilled the cup with a shaky hand that spilt water over the table top. He drank again, wiping the dribble from his chin.

Wolf reached under the bed and pulled out his drinking bottle. He took a sip then slowly let the liquid seep down his throat. He coughed before holding out his arm. 'Try this stuff. It might calm your nerves.'

Fat-man took it in gratitude before taking a deep breath, then filled his mouth until his cheeks bulged like a squirrel with a face full of nuts. He swallowed it in one gulp, making him cough just like Wolf had.

'The horses aren't the problem because we could just say they must have escaped in the confusion. My main concern is that Mad-dog will get the truth out of his prisoners.' He paused, holding out a hand, and Fat-man handed back the bottle. 'And we both know he will torture them until he gets the information he needs. He will use it to get back at me.'

Wolf took a quick nip then passed it back.

'I don't know why Mad-dog has always had it in for me. Ever since we were children we have been fighting. In fact the very first memory I have was when my father split up a fight between Mad-dog and myself.'

Fat-man coughed again after taking another swig, then answered Wolf's question.

'I know. It's because he has always come out second best to you. Like you said, your father broke up the fight. You were recognised by him as his son, but Mad-dog never was. He was the bastard of the litter. You may or may not be half-brothers, although there's never been any brotherly love between the two of you, and Mad-dog has had to carry that label all his life.'

After taking a third drink he gave Wolf a turn with the bottle as he carried on with his views.

'Then there's your success as a Hunter. You were always the Overseers' most successful, thus the most valued.'

Wolf smiled before refreshing his throat with some more liquid. His complexion began to glow matching Fat-man's, and the mood between the two friends began to lighten as quick as the drink flowed.

'That's not my fault, Maxwell. If Mad-dog wants to go galloping around the countryside like his name suggests, with a massive posse so every wraith and stray can hear them coming that's his problem. Not only that, he has to spend half his time looking to feed his men and sorting out petty squabbles. No, our four man unit was a lot more successful, that was until we bumped into those three who turned up today.'

The bottle was nearly empty. Fat-man held it up next to his ear and gently shook the contents.

'I guess there is just a mouthful left. Here, you finish it off.' It was passed to Wolf and, as he sucked the last dregs from the bottom, Fat-man's final comment on the lifelong animosity between the two rivals hit a raw nerve.

'Of course there was always Julia.' Wolf's glance told Fat-man not to go there, but he did anyway. 'You did steal Mad-dog's betrothed.'

Wolf threw the empty container on the floor in a fit of rage and jumped to his feet. 'No, I didn't. You can't help who you fall in love with, and it's even harder to deny when that love is returned.'

Fat-man looked stunned, and leant back on his stool, expecting a furious fist to come flying his way. Wolf stood silently with his back to him as he stared at the wall. He was taking in deep breaths. Then as quick as the rage had appeared it had subsided. He sat back on the edge of his bed with his head lowered. A hesitant silence filled the room before Fat-man broke it with another question.

'Do you miss her?'

Wolf looked up. 'Of course I miss her, but it's not only that, it's the guilt.' He lowered his head again. 'If she hadn't been carrying our child they wouldn't have both died during labour. If we hadn't loved each other so much she would be with us now although married to Mad-dog. I feel as if it's my fault she is no longer here.

It's the same guilt I have carried all my life over the death of my own mother when she died giving birth to me.'

Fat-man lent over and rested his hand on Wolf's back. 'Don't put yourself down so much, Wolf. What sort of life would it have been for Julia, forced to live with a violent lunatic like Mad-dog? At the end of the day that is what separates you two. You are both ruthless Hunters, but you have some capacity to feel guilt, an emotion which makes us human, and one that just about keeps us from going over the top. Mad-dog on the other hand doesn't. That's why his cruelty knows no bounds.'

Wolf got up again and went to the door. He opened it and looked out across to the prison block. The flurry of activity after Mad-dog's arrival with the stabling of horses and the feeding of hungry bodies had now died down as his men had retired to their beds after their overnight travels.

'You know what we need, Wolf? We need a change in our luck. I don't know how but we do. Maybe a lightning strike hitting the prison block which destroys all who are inside, because at the end of the day if they are dead then they can't give away any information.'

Wolf stood silently pondering as life outside went on its daily routine. Another Hunter gang was just starting to stir, making ready for their own expedition. Three empty carts were being harnessed to horses at the entrance to the stables. Soon they would be heading out to the surrounding Tribute huts scattered about the countryside to collect the weekly offerings given by the populace as instructed in the Seven Procedures. Chickens scurried about the yards pecking the ground for crumbs to eat, and a skinny dog lay about in the dirt, soaking up the rays of the sun as it headed higher into the midday sky. Laughter came wafting over from some women who were bent over a large wooden trough next to the well. They were scrubbing clothes with large round stones. Over at the cookhouse more women were gingerly standing under its wooden structure, scraping leftovers from plates into the pigs' slop bucket as a roaring fire that sent sparks floating in the air heated up the clay ovens. The door to Mad-dog's hut was closed with a neck scarf tied to its handle, indicating he was sleeping and not to be disturbed

'How long do you think we have before Mad-dog gets to work on his prisoners?'

Wolf turned around to answer Fat-man's question. 'I think he will want to get straight into it once he has rested. He is too impatient. If the shoe was on the other foot I would have made him sweat for two or three days. Right, Maxwell. Let's get something to eat, then I want you to meet me at the prison block once the sun has set, and bring an unlit torch with you. I have a plan.'

He turned and, for the first time that morning, he grinned.

* * *

Darkness suddenly became light as the sack cloth was unceremoniously pulled from Daniel's head. While he tried to focus his vision a knife blade was thrust between his tied wrists and the rope that had bound them together was cut loose. Without time to react he was shoved into a dingy, dark cell. The door closed behind with a bang. Still disorientated, he heard the scared voice of Jack.

'Where are we?'

The only light that penetrated the tiny room was through a square hole in the top of the door secured with two metal bars.

'I don't know, Jack. Are the other two in here?' Daniel's question was answered when he could hear Mary's defiant tone on the other side of the door. He looked through the hole into a larger room which had no windows to the outside world. The walls were illuminated by small flickering flames that shone from candles perched on various shelves attached to the mud brick walls. In its centre stood a solid oak table with four chairs seated around it, and against one wall was a bed for the night watchman. At the far end of the room was a stout-looking door. It was closed, and the two large bolts securely locked.

'Are you OK, Mary?' he called out, as she remonstrated with the guard. Mary looked over. Her silver hair, which she always tried so hard to keep in a tidy bun, was now a mess of loose strands. Her hands were free, and as the guard tried to push her into another cell she was determined not to follow his instructions without a fight.

'Look here, young man. I am old enough to be your mother, so would you manhandle her in such a rough way?'

The guard retorted with laughter. 'You're having a laugh. You're old enough to be my grandmother.' And with that he gave her one almighty push. She stumbled into her confinement with the door slammed behind her before she had the chance to rebuke him any further.

'Leave her alone, you gutless bully,' Daniel shouted out. 'If you want somebody to push about I dare you to open this door and face me like a man.'

The guard ignored his taunts while his attention turned to Gwendolyn, who now stood alone and helpless with her hands still tied. A sack covered her head.

'Now, let's take a look at this young lady, shall we? I hope you are more attractive than that old boot I just had to deal with.'

'Hey, who are you calling an old boot?' called out Mary as she struggled to see through the hole in her door.

Again the guard ignored what was said. The long shiny hair of his final captive that flowed from beneath the covering had his interest perked, and he wanted to see what delight there was hidden away. Licking his lips he ripped off the sack and let out a joyful sigh.

'My. We have a little beauty here, don't we now?'

He rubbed the short whiskers on his chin before suddenly lurching forward. Grabbing Gwendolyn's arms he took her by surprise as he pulled her close to him.

'Right, girly. Why don't you show what a cooperative prisoner you are going to be by giving me a little kiss?'

He suddenly pressed his lips against hers and his stale breath entered her surprised mouth.

Daniel grabbed the bars of his door and rattled it in anger. 'Leave her alone, you coward. You just wait until I get out of here. You will wish you hadn't seen us.'

The guard coiled back in pain, pressing his fingers against his lip. 'You bit me.' He grabbed his knife and held it out.

Gwendolyn started to panic and pleaded, 'Please don't hurt me. I didn't want to do it, but you forced me to.'

The guard grabbed her hands, then with a quick swish of the knife had cut her bonds before shoving her into another empty cell. He kicked the door shut and bolted it. Still rubbing his sore lip he sat down at the table to continue with his breakfast that had been so unexpectedly interrupted by the arrival of Mad-dog's gang.

'What's going to happen to us?'

Jack's question took Daniel's attention away from the guard room and back to the cell that now imprisoned them. The smell of stale urine wafted under his nostrils. 'Jack, everything will be OK.' He could feel Jack's arms wrap around his waist. 'We will get out of here, don't you worry.'

The darkness of the cell started to close in with only a small shaft of light to keep the fear away. Daniel knew his words were said more in hope than fact. He wanted to keep young Jack's spirit up, but his own dread started to work its darkness into a sense of hopeless doom. Pressing his back against the door he slid his way down until his backside rested on the floor.

'Jack, come sit next to me.'

The darkness now engulfed them both as Jack snuggled alongside while Daniel gave him a brotherly hug.

* * *

His eyes were still closed but the rush of blood to his loins awoke his imagination. The picture of his last female encounter flashed into his memory. Mad-dog opened his eyes. The greying darkness of the room told him that night was fast approaching, and that his tired body, worn out by a night's riding, had now been refreshed by a good day's sleep. He lumbered into an upright position before finally standing while trying to shake the grogginess from his head. He lent over a bowl and splashed water over his face. Its coldness brought relief. Drying his face with his sleeve he headed for the door, and when he got outside barked for Leyland's attention.

Leyland was sitting under the thatched roof of the cookhouse located next to the prison block, slurping hot soup while simultaneously stuffing bread into his mouth. His head lifted at his master's call. He picked up his plate to drink the dregs of his meal before clambering to his feet. He tore another large piece from the loaf, cramming it into his mouth as he scuttled across the yard.

'There you are, Leyland. Where is that woman we picked up?' You know the one we brought back here. The one whose hut we burnt down with her husband still inside.'

Leyland shrugged his shoulders, while small pieces of soggy chewed bread came spitting out of his mouth when he replied. 'I've heard the Over-seers paid a visit when we were away and took a load of people away in the Triclops with them. She probably got taken then.'

Mad-dog shook his head. 'It's a pity. I could use some female company right now.' Then he smirked. 'But I know where we can get some. Are you interested in some too?'

Leyland nodded gleefully.

'Good. Come follow me. Let's pay a visit to the prison block.'

They rushed over and went through the first door, then turned up the passageway past the armoury to reach the final door that now blocked their progress. It was locked so Mad-dog gave it a thunderous knock with his knuckles. They waited in silence. He rattled the door until a reply came from the other side.

'All right. Hold on. I'm now coming,' the guard said as he got up from the bed, muttering under his voice that he had just got to sleep. A small slit in the door opened. 'It's you, Mad-dog. Give me a moment.'

The slit closed, followed by the sound of two bolts being slid across the door, and then it opened. The two new arrivals walked in.

'We are here to interrogate one of the prisoners. Which cell is the young girl in?' The guard pointed to the third door. 'Good. You can go now and take a break.' As the guard left the room his arm was suddenly grabbed by Mad-dog. 'And take your time. We will let you know when we are finished, so don't return until then.' The guard felt the hold tightened to the point where it became painful. 'Do you understand?'

The guard agreed and when the grip was released he shot out the door, shutting it behind him. Leyland was already at the third cell unlocking the bolts. He disappeared into the darkness, quickly returning, pulling Gwendolyn painfully out with him by the hair.

'That hurts! Let go. Please let go.'

Shouting arose through another cell door. 'Let her go or I swear I will get you.'

Mad-dog walked over and put his head right up to the bars of this door as Daniel continued to protest.

'And what are you going to do about it, boy?' He spat in Daniel's face, then slid shut the cover over the opening. 'Get the girl onto the bed and tie her hands down.' Mad-dog picked up some rope from the floor, then tossed it to Leyland. The door behind kept rattling with Daniel's anger. Mad-dog turned back to the door and opened the hatch once more. Daniels teeth came snarling up to the bars with raging protest.

'If you touch her, I swear I will not rest until I have sliced your guts from your belly.'

Mad-dog's enjoyment at Daniel's helplessness was revealed in his reply. 'I tell you what, boy. I'm going to let you watch while my lieutenant and I have our way with your girlfriend. In a way it's quite stirring to think I will be causing you so much pain while we're having so much pleasure.'

Mary now joined in. She couldn't see fully what was going on, but by all the commotion she knew something dreadful was going to happen. She started to kick the door, but her actions soon had her panting for breath.

Leyland was struggling to force Gwendolyn down onto the bed until Mad-dog took a swing with his foot, catching her on the back of her calf, which made her slump to the floor. He grabbed her legs and the two of them swung Gwendolyn onto the bed. She fought back violently trying to scratch and bite in her defence, but within the minute one wrist had already been tied above her head to the corner of the bed, and then within the second her other wrist was incapacitated as well. She kicked ferociously with her legs, her only means of defence, and it took both men a fair few minutes struggle with a leg each to get them tied down too. She screamed for her life while Daniel repeatedly, and hopelessly, tried to force open the door that caged him by ramming his shoulders against it. A rag was stuffed into Gwendolyn's mouth to muffle her screams, then her two dominators looked voraciously over her slender body.

Mad-dog pulled at the belt of her trousers and with a quick yank had pulled them down to her knees. Leyland ripped at the buttons of her shirt until it was half open, revealing her soft unmarked skin. They were ready to devour their pleasure when they were distracted by the opening of a door.

* * *

The door to Wolf's hut slowly creaked open. Casually his head appeared looking to the left, then to the right. There was nobody about so he walked out closing it behind him. He strolled up the track, and just as he was going to cross over to the outer door of the prison block, it too opened. Out walked the guard. He quickly scuttled away without acknowledging Wolf.

Crossing over, Wolf reached the door, and in the shadows of the overhanging thatched roof of the prison block stood Fat-man with the unlit torch in his hand.

'So, what's the plan, Wolf?'

Wolf joined him in the shadows. 'You see the cookhouse with that big fire?' Fat-man looked over and nodded. 'If a rogue spark was to cause that roof to catch fire it would quickly spread to the roof of the prison block, and everyone locked within the cells would perish with the building.' He paused. 'And so would all our problems, so we are going to torch the roof, but first I need to take care of whoever is inside because if they smell smoke they will call out the fire crews who would extinguish my plan before it had time to take hold.'

Fat-man seemed pleased as Wolf continued. 'I've just seen the guard leave so somebody else must be in there. Hopefully it will be Mad-dog, and I can, as they say, kill two birds with one stone or, in this case, four or five.' Fat-man let out a small chuckle of approval. 'You wait here Maxwell, and warn me if anyone comes.'

Wolf disappeared through the first door, and as he sneaked up the passageway past the armoury he could hear a noisy commotion coming from the cell block. He reached the second door and gave it a push. The door opened.

Walking into the room he was greeted by the sight of Mad-dog and Leyland tearing off the clothes of a young lady while she was tied to a bed. Tears were streaming down her face. Behind them came the sound of captives kicking and banging at the cell doors.

Mad-dog glared at the distraction that had temporarily taken his attention away from his desires. 'I thought you had locked the door Leyland.'

Leyland looked behind. 'I thought you had, Mad-dog?' Leyland jumped to his feet and approached Wolf. 'Look here, Wolf. If you want to have a go with the girl you are going to have to wait your turn, and also ask for Mad-dog's permission first.'

Wolf looked at the vulnerable girl. Her eyes were almost drowning in their own tears, pleading for help. For a minute the world seemed to stop. All sound, all movement, just those big, watery, desperate eyes pleading for a saviour. They stabbed at his heart and old memories of loved ones lost made his gut wrench with fury.

Wolf looked back at Leyland before calmly turning to shut the door. After he had bolted it he returned his gaze to Leyland. 'Leyland, have I ever shown you what a useless prick you are?'

Leyland looked confused at Wolf's question, and was left in a shocked daze as Wolf's forehead came crashing onto the bridge of his nose. He staggered back a couple of feet. His nose felt numb for a second, before red hot pain exploded across his face as blood started to spurt from his snout. He brought his hands up to stem it, but within a few seconds they were diverted to his loins as Wolf sent, with a lunging kick, one of his hard leather boots hurtling between Leyland's legs. It clanged into his manhood, and Leyland slumped to his knees. One final swift kick to his head sent Leyland crashing to the floor where he lay unconscious.

Wolf didn't have time to enjoy his moment. Mad-dog charged at him like a demented animal and went crashing into him. They both flew over the table and ended up on the floor. Wolf was winded, giving Mad-dog the advantage, which he took with both hands. He leapt up, grabbing a chair, and brought it smashing down across Wolf's stricken body. The chair shattered. Wolf's body erupted in pain, sending out a spurt of anguish from his mouth.

Mad-dog picked up a broken chair leg and brought it down with all his rage, hitting Wolf in the side of his body. Wolf squirmed on the floor and tried to drag himself up, but another lash from the wooden leg sent him flat to his face. He crawled along the floor as Mad-dog went in for the kill. He lashed out, hitting Wolf again and again. As Wolf crawled to a pitiful stop Mad-dog screamed with joy. He knew just one more bludgeon across Wolf's skull would kill him. Taking some steps back until he had plenty of room to swing his last fatal blow he slowly brought the broken chair leg up above his head, taking his time to savour the moment he had waited for all his life.

With all the potency he could muster he brought down the leg of the chair, but then it fell from his open palm, where it clattered harmlessly to the floor. Mad-dog shrieked in agony. Someone had grabbed hold of his head from behind, with the fingers of one hand digging into the inner reaches of his left ear, while the other hand was scratching its way desperately towards his right eye socket.

Mary was tiptoeing, straining her neck so she could just about peek over the lip of the hole in her door. Much of the room was out of her sight and she had been unable to see most of what had been unfolding in the room, but what she could see now were Daniel's arms protruding. He had hold of the head of that frightful man that had captured them at Hagar's village. She called out words of encouragement. 'Go on, Daniel. Rip his head off.'

Mad-dog was desperately trying to release Daniel's grip from his head, but his recent sparring match with Wolf had drained his energy. He pulled at Daniel's hands, but they held firm. It felt as if his brain was being pulled out through his ear, then suddenly his right eye squelched as Daniel dug his fingers deep into the socket. As Mad-dog used all his weight to pull free he stumbled forward leaving his eye behind in Daniel's hand.

'My eye! My eye! I can't see. Where is my eye?' he cried out in blindness, as he fell over Wolf's inert body. His head hit the corner of the solid oak table and he crashed to the floor where he lay motionless.

Daniel squeezed Mad-dog's eye-ball hard in the palm of his hand until its sack burst, sending squirts of liquid dribbling to the floor. He tossed the remains of it across the room where it landed on Leyland's face. He slumped back onto the floor of his cell in a state of shock. He could feel the stickiness of his fingers, and once the adrenaline began to subside he started to feel pangs of guilt at what he had just done. His heart was racing as fast as a horse could gallop with the wind behind it. He had to take deep gulps of breath to satisfy his lungs. Young Jack asked if there was anything he could do, but Daniel was left speechless.

Wolf groaned then tried to raise his aching body. The first

attempt failed. The second attempt got him to his knees. He slowly shuffled to the bed, then took a moment to focus his thoughts. A third attempt managed to get him seated on the edge of the bed.

He looked at the girl who lay in front of him and thought, 'I don't even know your name.' She was paralysed with fear, unable to move, and was totally at his mercy.

He took in some deep breaths of air and could feel his heart beat slowly calm down. He took hold of Gwendolyn's trousers and pulled them back up to her waist. Then he lent forward and did up the buttons of her shirt, so once again her modesty would be covered.

Wolf took another deep breath.

'Now listen to me young lady. You have two choices. You can either do as I say and you will live.' He paused as if to emphasis his next point. 'Or you won't, and you will stay here and die. Do you understand?'

Gwendolyn's eyes were a flood of emotions and she blinked them in agreement.

'OK. Now if I let you go I don't won't any biting, screaming, scratching, kicking or hitting. Is that agreed?'

Gwendolyn blinked again.

Wolf took the rag out of her mouth, and she started to sob uncontrollably. He used it to dab dry one cheek as tears kept on pouring down, then dabbed the other cheek. Slowly, with painful fingers, he untied Gwendolyn's bonds and as soon as she was free she curled up into a ball.

There came a pounding on the door and Wolf recognised the voice of Fat-man. 'What's going on in there? Are you all right, Wolf? Somebody open this door!'

Wolf tried to stand up but the excruciating pain sent his head into a spin, and he had to hold onto the table. He felt sick and for a moment he thought he was going to faint. Holding his rib cage he slowly hobbled to the door and pulled back the bolts.

When Fat-man pushed open the door he was shocked at the bloody sight that greeted him.

'What has been going on in here? It looks like a war zone!'

Wolf didn't have the energy to explain. He sat down on a chair and with a croaky voice asked Fat-man to check on whether the other two were still alive, and if so to tie their hands and feet and gag them both. He did as instructed. He checked their pulse, and when he started to gather up all the rope Wolf then knew that Mad-dog and Leyland were regrettably still alive. His final instruction to Fat-man, before he slumped forward onto the table, resting his weary and sore head, was for him to release the fellow prisoners.

Mary was first out and she rushed to Gwendolyn's aid. She scooped her up in her arms and rocked her gently from side to side, just as she had done when Gwendolyn was just a little child, and she needed reassurance after being hurt. Gently she stroked her hair and whispered a sweet lullaby to calm her frightened soul. Gradually the flow of tears subsided until there were no more to shed, and once her face was dabbed dry Mary helped Gwendolyn to her feet.

When Daniel was released he asked Gwendolyn if she was OK, and a small if hesitant smile appeared. He headed to a bowl standing on a tall pedestal in the corner. Next to it stood a large black leather jug that sloshed with water. He poured some into the bowl and used a towel hanging from a hook on the pedestal to wash the slime of Mad-dog's eye that was already drying fast into a think gooey paste all over his hand. He washed it again and again, and then again, each time scrubbing harder until he was sure there was no residue left.

Mary now attended to Wolf. She asked Daniel to fill up a beaker of water which he brought over, and she forced him to drink it. Wolf was splattered in blood, none of which seemed to have come from any visible wound on him, although she couldn't be so sure about any internal wounds. His face was already swelling, and bruising. Mary lightly pressed the different bones of his body and came to the conclusion that he didn't have any broken ones, but maybe some fractured ribs that should heal with time.

Fat-man was relieved to hear this news but he needed to find out what was going to happen next. 'What are we going to do now, Wolf?'

Wolf lifted his head and indicated he wanted another cup of water which was given to him. Once he gulped it down he slowly straitened his back while gently rotating his joint muscles. 'There's a change of plan, my friend. I'm going to have to take these four to the stables so they can get their horses and flee. I'm going to flee as well. I can't stay here anymore, but you can.'

Fat-man was perplexed.

'I will leave you bound and gagged alongside these two, and when the guard returns you can tell everyone that you heard a commotion, went to investigate, then tried to come to Mad-dog's aid, but I attacked you and left you here with these two.'

Fat-man's face dropped, and he wasn't pleased with this new plan. 'No, I don't want us to part. I will come with you.'

Wolf tried to get to his feet, but needed a helping hand before he was steady enough to stand. 'No, my friend. There's no need for both of us to get into trouble. Once Mad-dog is patched up you can ask to join his gang, telling him you want to seek your revenge for what I did to you and my fellow Hunters. He will jump at the chance to have your knowledge and loyalty. No. You must stay behind.'

Fat-man's head dropped slightly with disappointment. He lifted up his wrist and then held them together behind his back. Daniel bound them securely, but before he could start on his feet Fat-man had two last requests for Wolf. 'Before you go can you do me two things?'

'Sure. What are they?'

'Can you punch me as hard as you can on my face? These two won't take that story seriously if they don't see some blood and bruises on me.'

Wolf recoiled at his request, but Daniel had no problem, and without warning he pulled back his arm, then sent in a thunderous blow against his cheek. Fat-man dropped to his knees. When he lifted his head small droplets of warm blood were dribbling from his nose, and the right side of his face looked red. He spat out a mouthful of bloody saliva, and the remains of a rotten black tooth fell onto the floor.

'Thanks. That tooth had been giving me gip for weeks.'

Just before Daniel was going to stuff a rag in his mouth Wolf asked what Fat-man's final request was.

With a warming gentle grin, he said, 'Take good care of yourself my friend, because the next time I see you I don't want it to be on a gallows.'

Wolf smiled back in agreement. Daniel finished binding and gagging Fat-man, then he and the other three looked towards Wolf for his next suggestion.

'We need to get out of here and fast. First we need to stop at the armoury next door to get some weapons before sneaking over to the stables located at the far end on the camp, and then get the hell out of here.'

No more instructions were needed, especially now Leyland was starting to come around. As the others followed Wolf while he headed out the door Gwendolyn held back so she was last to leave. She waited just long enough for Leyland to open his eyes so he could see she was standing over him, then she gave him the hardest kick in his groin she could muster. Muffled cries of pain mixed with the tears in his eyes. Gwendolyn left the room.

Wolf opened the door to the armoury and invited the others to help themselves. Daniel clapped when he saw the Golden Shield and his axe, and grabbed them both.

Gwendolyn was even happier when she saw the rows of arrows that could restock her quiver that rested against the wall with her trusted bow. She stuffed in as many as it could carry, then put some more behind her back, secured by her belt. Now she felt safe again, knowing that if anyone came near her she could defend herself.

Mary was soon loaded down with all her duffle bags, but they were now mostly empty. 'We need some food. Are there any supplies we can get before we go?'

Wolf shook his head. 'We can't risk it. In fact we haven't got time. I expect the guard to return any minute, and when he does, the whole camp will be after us. We will have to worry about that when we come to it. Now follow me.'

Jack suddenly saw his prized iPad on a shelf and took it, stuffing it into one of Mary's bags. Wolf got to the outer door. He opened it slightly and peered through the gap.

'It looks all clear for now. What you four need to do is keep to the shadows. Keep close to the back of the buildings until you get to the end of the camp. I will walk down the track as if nothing is wrong, and once I have opened the stable doors and given you the all clear, you can then run across the track and into the stables.'

He pulled the door wide open, picked up the unlit torch that Fatman had brought before walking into the fresh air. The other four sneaked away, keeping to the shadows as instructed. Wolf strolled confidently, if painfully, to the cookhouse fire and used it to light the torch, then strolled through the middle of the camp.

The night was chilly and most people were in the great hall. Merriment and laughter came forth from the biggest building in the camp. Someone popped out of the hall to relieve their bladder in the gutter, then called out to Wolf when they noticed him walking on his own.

'Are you coming in, Wolf?'

He carried on walking and replied, 'No. I'm just doing my rounds, checking everything is OK. You go back in. It's cold out here. I might come in later.'

When Wolf reached the two large doors of the stables he put the torch on the ground and pulled open a door. Picking up the flame he leaned into the building quickly to check no one else was present, then waved the torch from side to side to indicate to the others all was clear. They soon came scuttling across the track, and into the cover afforded by the barn. Wolf closed the door. His flaming torch could only light up part of the barn, but it was clear to see there were many horses housed within its long and extended frame.

Wolf walked down the centre aisle, pulling back the latches on each and every gate opening the doors as he did so.

'Find your horses and get mounted, except for the lad. I will need your help.'

It seemed to take for an eternity to find, then saddle their horses, but Wolf took great delight when he came across Mad-dog's beast.

'Hello, my big beauty. I think I will add an insult to his injury by taking you with me.' The horse snorted. 'Lead your horses to the main door.'

Everyone did as asked. It took Mary three attempts to get on hers while Daniel gave Jack a lift up so he could catch a ride with Gwendolyn. Wolf managed, after suffering repeated spasms of pain, to get in the saddle of Mad-dog's horse with a helping hand from Daniel.

Once on top Wolf threw his torch into a large bale of bedding straw, and instructed the others to hold their nerve until the barn had caught alight. Then he told Daniel that once the building was full of smoke, and all the other horses were ready to stampede with fright; he was to open both the large doors so every horse in the building could get out, causing chaos in the process. Then they would make their escape.

First smoke began to arise from the pile of straw which the horses' sensitive nostrils soon picked up. They started to neigh and scrape their hoofs along the dirt. Then a flame burst into life. A horse nearest to it started to jostle for space away from the danger. More flames appeared and soon they had reached the rafters where they spread with frightening ease in every direction. Now the smoke became a choking cloud and Wolf shouted out the order.

Daniel quickly pushed open one door and before he had a chance to open the second he was nearly trampled underfoot by terrified horses that tried to bustle their way into the open. It took some effort but he managed to open the second door as he was knocked to and fro. Now the horses stampeded *en masse* and he just managed to jump on to Champion before he too joined the startled masses.

By the time someone else came out of the great hall and noticed the flames lighting up the night sky as they whipped ever higher from the stable roof, the renegades had long disappeared into the night.

20

THE OVERLORD

The metallic door slid sideways with a quiet hiss, followed by the clank of metal boots as they marched in unison across the shiny floor. They stopped in a straight line. The room was bathed in violet light as a suffocating atmosphere suffused the three black-suited Dominators.

In unison they bowed, resting on one knee as the glare of their red eyes paid respectful homage by looking at the floor. The leathery, spindly fingers of one hand were clenched to their chest in deference.

No sound was heard until the door closed behind them.

In harmony the Dominators' dutiful retort began. 'We serve our race for their survival so that they may honour our ancestors as our ancestors honoured us by our survival.'

Silence followed and nothing moved until the reply was received. 'May our ancestors be pleased by the words you now speak.'

Three helmetless heads rose together so that they could face their master.

In front of them seated on a high-backed chair made of pure clear crystal with two ample arm rests sat the Over-lord, his rank marked by the dark red colour of his metal suit.

The senior Dominator, whose age gave it its authority, stood up to make its report. 'All the Achievers are now stored in the centre. We count seventy arrivals, forty-six females, twenty-four males. The females will be scanned for impurities. Two hundred seventy-four others await shipment to the Orb.'

The Dominator bowed his head.

'Our ancestors will be pleased with your words. Make ready the shipment for I depart in one cycle. Then you may prepare for the feast.'

The Over-lord stood up and hissed their dismissal.

The two remaining Dominators still kneeling now raised themselves. All three bowed their heads before turning. As they stomped towards the door it opened, then closed once the last Dominator had left the room.

* * *

The darkness became stifling. The air felt cool but laborious to breathe as shuffling shoes on the dirt floor indicated that restless people were now becoming anxious. The odd quiet whisper began to rise in concern, then as quickly as the darkness had engulfed the chamber, it was dispelled as if by magic from light that came beaming from the rock above.

Gasps of astonishment leapt from open mouths as they contemplated the wonder of how the sun could penetrate so far underground. Someone clapped, then others too, until the whole group's excitement echoed off the cavernous walls.

No one noticed as a door slid open and out walked a black-suited Over-seer. 'Silence!' Slowly the clapping faded as all eyes now turned towards it. 'I am the Dominator. You will follow my commands at all times.'

Without saying another word it pointed through the open door, and people began to file in one at a time. In front lay a long passage with multiple doors on either side that stretched into the distance, with silver-suited Over-seers standing guard. As people shuffled along a door would open and instruction given with a silently raised arm that pointed groups of individuals into each room.

Mother held tightly onto John's hand, but his attention was taken with admiring all the metal that clad all four walls. After they had entered their designated room the heavy metal door slid shut behind them. They were not alone, for the room contained many other strangers. Some were walking in boredom around the confined space, while others sat on long benches that were attached to each side of the room, and ran its whole length.

People started to mingle and introduce themselves.

One woman was sitting on her own looking lost in her own thoughts. John nudged Mother, who noticed straight away her loneliness, but there was something else that made her different from the others. It took a moment but Mother realised that she looked too young to have reached her Achievement Day. She sat down beside her.

'Hello.' She gazed at Mother but said nothing. 'Have you been here long?'

She didn't reply at first. She opened her mouth as if she going to say something, but never answered.

'My husband and I are on our Achievement Day. What about you?'

This sparked a response.

'I don't know where my husband is. We were brought here together but he got put into another room, and I haven't seen him since.'

Mother smiled kindly. 'Don't worry. He should be all right. What is his name?'

'Raj. His name is Raj, and my name is Prior. Prior Patel. We were brought here for punishment because we lived in the desolate lands from the East.'

Her lip began to tremble. Mother had seen this emotion on many occasions before and knew exactly what was going to happen next. When the first tear began to dribble down Prior's cheek Mother instinctively put an arm around her so she could cry on her shoulder.

'Don't worry. Your husband will be all right.'

Through mumbled words Mother could make out a name.

'Jack. We've lost our son Jack. He was left behind when we were captured.'

The sobbing increased and John thought a comforting word from him might help so he sat down too.

'Your son will be OK. We unexpectedly lost a son recently called Daniel, but boys are quick learners when it comes to survival, and I'm sure wherever our sons are at the moment they are keeping their heads down, and more importantly out of trouble.'

Prior wiped her cheek and sniffled away her fears, and as Mother gave her a hanky to use a voice was heard from the walls.

'This is the Dominator. All females are to place their hand within the box on the wall.' Gradually they formed an orderly queue and did as they were told. The first one put her hand in, then a voice said.

'You are free from impurities. The Over-lord has selected you for special pleasures on the Orb.' The wall suddenly parted revealing another passage way. 'Enter.'

She did as instructed, then the next woman placed her hand in the box. 'You have failed. Stay here.'

One by one every woman did as instructed. Some were told to stay and some went forward through the door. Prior's tears had stopped by the time she had reached the box and Mother patted her on the back. 'Good luck.'

'You are free from impurities. The Over-lord has selected you for special pleasures on the Orb.'

John was still sitting down, joined by most of the other men as they waited to see who would go forward and who wouldn't. Mother was last. She turned and blew John a kiss just before she put her hand in the box. She felt a sharp nip to her thumb then the voice said.

'You are free from impurities. The Over-lord has selected you for special pleasures on the Orb.' When Mother redrew her hand she noticed a drop of blood on her thumb. She instinctively sucked it dry. 'Walk through the door.' Mother looked around her trying to figure out where the voice was coming from.

'But I don't want to go to the Orb. I want to stay here with my husband.'

John jumped to his feet and stood protectively behind her.

'This is your final warning. Walk through the door. The Over-lord has selected you for special pleasures on the Orb.'

John now joined in. 'You heard my wife. She doesn't want to go to the Orb no matter how many pleasures you promise her.'

The far door opened with a swish and in walked four Over-seers. They barged their way through. The first one to reach John held a grey rod in its hand and when he raised his arm he pressed it into John's back. Sparks began to fly and John let out a horrendous scream of pain that filled the room with fear. Mother tried to come to his aid, but two Over-seers took hold of her arms and dragged her through the wall opening. It promptly shut.

John was wriggling on the floor suffering excruciating torture from the grey rod that the Over-seer was still pressing hard into his body, while the fourth Over-seer stood guard over his comrade. The punishment seemed to be never ending. Blood started to drip from John's nose, and his eyes convulsed with his arching body as it wriggled on the floor like a helpless worm that had been cut in two by a shovel.

The Over-seers eventually withdrew through the same door they had entered, leaving the whiff of burnt flesh behind them as John lay paralysed, helpless to stop his body twitching with discomfort while saliva dribbled from his mouth like a teething baby.

21

WHAT NOW?

The steam flared with every gallop. Heat was rising from the beast's flesh. The sound of panting matched the beat of the hooves as animal and rider alike struggled to keep up the pace. Wolf pulled up his mount resting on its back while he let the pain pulsing in his ribs subside to a more bearable level. The others slowed next to him and everyone took a breather.

'You look in pain, Wolf. We need to rest.' Mary started to look though all the duffle bags while mumbling as usual. 'I think I have just a little bit left somewhere.' One by one she checked every inch and corner until she found what she needed. 'Take this bark and chew, then suck on it. It will help to ease the pain.' Popping it into his mouth he did as instructed, and then lowered himself onto the ground.

'We should be all right here for a while.' He led his new horse into a clearing where there was plenty of long green grass for it to feed on, then slowly sat down resting his back against the trunk of a tree. He chewed the foul-tasting bark while wishing he had brought his drinking bottle, and longing for it to be full with his favourite liquor.

The others followed suit. Sitting down in a circle in whatever position they found comfortable they discussed all the options.

'I think we will be OK for a day or two before we have to worry about any Hunters finding us. A large troop went out on Tribute hut collections so will be out of camp for at least four days. It will take Mad-dog and Leyland a few days to recover and for the rest of his gang to round up all the stray horses, but after that we will have every Hunter gang in the land baying for my blood.' Wolf closed his eyes and rested his head while he let a spasm of pain subside.

'What about the Over-seers?' Daniel asked, keen to get back to his home village without encountering any further hold-ups.

'Mad-dog isn't foolish enough to tell them what happened until he has us all in captivity again, or should I say until we are all dead because he won't want us blabbering. If he told the Over-seers that he had captured you lot only to lose you again, aided by a fellow Hunter, then that would be seen as failure. Over-seers are as ruthless with punishing failure as they are generous with rewarding success. Obviously we still have to keep out of their way, but at the moment they will be none the wiser of our situation.'

Wolf's hand suddenly touched his ribcage as he cringed with pain. Mary leaned over to him. 'Let me take a look.' She started to untie the buttons of his shirt until his tattooed chest was revealed for all to see. It was heavily bruised down one side.

'That will need to be bandaged in case you have broken any ribs.' And she ripped off the undergarment of her dress to use as material. 'I will need to go scavenge for some plants that will aid you in healing and control the pain, but it will be difficult to find them in the dark. Daniel, you get a fire going and make a torch, and you can then come with me to light my way. Gwendolyn, you help Wolf to get his coat and shirt off, then use this cloth for his ribcage.' Mary stared at Gwendolyn. 'And be gentle with him. Don't rough handle him like he's some rat or cat you have caught for supper and needs to be skinned. I will get the water bottles readied so we can also get something to drink while Daniel gets some wood ready for the fire.'

Mary rocked herself forward unto her knees, then using the help of a tree she got to her feet. Daniel sprung up like a Jack-in-the-box and immediately started to pick up dry broken branches for the fire. By the time he returned with arms full of wood Wolf was sitting naked from the waist up while Gwendolyn was gently rubbing his solid muscular frame with its hairy chest as she asked, 'What about here? Does it hurt? Or what about when I press here?' She didn't notice Daniel's arrival.

Daniel felt a pang of jealousy and dropped the branches at her side, distracting her from the task at hand.

'Daniel, get the fire going. We must be off. Time is of the essence,' called out Mary. 'Jack, you can come help me as well.'

With the help of his new-fangled lighter a fire soon burst into flame while an improvised torch was made ready. Then they disappeared into the trees with Jack in tow.

Suddenly Gwendolyn could sense she was alone with Wolf. Her heart missed a beat. It felt as if it had jumped into her mouth. She was trying to show no emotion, but her heart was starting to say something different. Now she was confused and didn't know what to do next. She wanted to show her gratitude to Wolf for saving her, but she felt hesitant. It was the first time she had ever touched the bare flesh of a man, and it had sent a warm tingle down her spine just as it did the first time she saw Daniel's toned, naked body. Her lack of social interaction now came back to haunt her. The confusion increased and the only way she could think of showing Wolf how she felt was to do what she had seen Mary do on occasions when she greeted people. In an instant Gwendolyn leaned forward and without warning she kissed Wolf, before recoiling, shocked at her own action. Her cheeks began to blush so she looked down, hoping to hide her emotions behind the long strands of her hair. Her heart rate exploded. Gwendolyn liked Daniel a lot, but wasn't sure at the moment if it was only like a brotherly love. Wolf on the hand was different because he was older, and her feelings towards him at this point felt different too. She wanted to touch his skin again, to be caring towards him, to kiss him again, but now she felt awkward and made an excuse to get up.

'I'm just going to check all the duffle bags to see if there is any food in them.' She knew it was a lie, but it was all she could think of in that mad moment. She tried to play it out as long as possible so she didn't have to face Wolf, and then started to fuss over the horses, rubbing down their coats with a brush from the bag. She was trying to kill time, to do anything other the face further embarrassment. When the other three came walking back she at long last started to relax.

Daniel smiled at Gwendolyn but he could sense something. What it was he didn't know, but his instinct told him it involved Wolf. He glared at him as he approached and said in a gruff voice. 'Here. This is for you,' and dropped a water bottle at his feet making no effect to bring it closer. Wolf was forced to lean forward sending more pain to shoot through his body.

Mary could also sense the hostility between the two, and used Jack to try and ease the situation.

'Why don't you, Jack, show Wolf what an iPad is? He hasn't seen one before and he will be amazed at what it can do.' Jack got very excited and sat himself down by Wolf's side while he showed off what could be done with his magic machine.

Slowly the tension eased. It would have helped if there were some food to eat, but at least they were safe, with a large fire to keep them warm, plenty of long grass to make comfortable bedding, and once some plants had been added to a boiling pot of water, something resembling tea had been brewed. Although it wasn't the tastiest drink and left a bitter aftertaste, at least it half-filled their bellies.

With blankets wrapped around them Mary asked Wolf, 'So what are your next plans?'

He shrugged. 'I don't know. I hadn't planned on being here. I had planned on…' He hesitated, deciding it was better to withhold the truth. 'I planned on spending my dying days as a Hunter, but that has totally disappeared. I have broken the Hunters' code and the punishment is death, and that's only after painful retribution. I will be tortured ceaselessly, day and night without break, until I beg for death as a release. Then I will face the Hunters' Smile as I am publicly humiliated slowly dieing at the hands of the hangman.'

'What is the Hunters' Smile?' Daniel asked, curious about its double meaning.

'It's where every Hunter in the area will pay you a visit while your body is strung up in public like a turkey, and with a knife they cut a smile into your flesh until you whole body is covered from top to toe in your own blood.'

'Where will you go?' piped up Gwendolyn.

Wolf shook his head. 'I don't know. I hadn't thought of that either. I have always been a Hunter like my father. I have lived in the same camp all my life and have no family. My only friends were other Hunters, all of who are now my sworn and deadly enemies.'

'I know!' exclaimed Jack, in an excited voice. 'You can come with us. We are going back to Daniel's village to save his father and my parents too.'

Mary nodded in agreement, while Daniel had a scowl on his face, and Gwendolyn just blushed. Mary looked at Daniel hoping for his approval because without it Wolf was on his own like an injured animal in the wild.

Daniel said nothing at first. He knew it was the right thing to do, but for some reason he felt that Wolf was encroaching on his territory. On the other hand he had been in exactly the same situation. He had gone stumbling into Mary's and Gwendolyn's world and turned it upside down, but they still helped him without hesitation. He nodded at Mary then held out his arm towards Wolf. Wolf stretched his out too and they both shook hands.

'That's sorted, then,' Daniel said, as he added some more branches to the fire. 'I suggest we try to all get a good night's sleep, then at first light we will head back to my home village to warn my father of his fate in the Achievement Centre.'

Everyone hankered down for the night around the fire as it

crackled away sending sparks gently floating into the clear sky above. The stars twinkled in their silent beauty while the Orb reflected their light making it shine as bright as a full moon.

Daniel looked into the heavens. It reminded him of when he would camp for the night at the cutting grounds with his father, and how they used to sit by the fire talking about life with all the questions that it posed. He became transfixed on the Orb with its majestic beauty and wondered what horrors were going on within its dark heart. The image of Mother appeared in his reflections and a smile came to his face at the thought of seeing her again tomorrow. As his eyes began to get heavy anxiety began to creep into his belly. Would he get back in time to warn father? This thought now started to take hold, increasing the stress he felt, so he turned over onto his side hoping it would change his contemplations. Looking at the fire as the flames danced their final goodbyes his eyelids finally shut and he fell asleep.

* * *

'Aaarrrr... Give me more drink and the stronger the better.' A leather bottle was handed over and the contents gulped without stopping for air. It was thrown back. 'Fill it up now. I can still feel the dreadful pain.'

Although Mad-dog's wounds had been attended to and his missing eye covered up with a patch, puss was already leaking through. 'Give me more drink and now.'

The guard came scuttling over with another jug. Mad-dog snatched it without saying thank you.

'Can I have a swig this time?' Leyland asked with difficulty. His face was badly swollen black and blue. His eye lid was almost shut, but not enough to hide his badly bloodshot eyes that were as red as an Over-seer's. It was painful to walk. Just the thought of taking a step sent tears flooding from his eyes. His shirt was covered in his own blood, and the dry remains of Mad-dog's eyeball clung to it after it had slid off his face when he first came around. His lips had blown up three times their normal size making him look like a freak.

Once again Mad-dog had his fill before he tossed it to Leyland, who struggled to drink it with most dribbling down his neck. 'What are we going to do now?'

Mad-dog stomped around the cell block. 'Why did you let this happen?' he pointed to the guard. 'This is your fault.'

The guard looked perplexed. 'But you told me to leave, Mad-dog.'

'Don't talk back to me!' screamed Mad-dog, with such forcefulness his head went light and he had to hold onto the edge of the oak table that was still stained with his own blood. 'You should never leave any prisoners unattended no matter what the circumstances.'

The guard didn't like the tone of where Mad-dog was leading his accusations. 'Look, Mad-dog, you told me to take a break because you and Leyland wanted to interrogate a prisoner. I'm not going to be your scapegoat because they all got away under your watch.'

Mad-dog shuffled closer to the guard. 'What did you say?'

'You heard me, Mad-dog. I'm not going to be your scapegoat.'

Mad-dog stood silently for a second as if he was savouring his next moment. 'Oh yes, you are going to be the scapegoat.' And with that final sentence Mad-dog thrust his serrated dagger deep into the belly of the guard, twisted it to the left, then to the right before pulling up towards the guard's chest. His blood splattered Mad-dog's already bloodstained shirt, and when he pulled out the dagger it was entangled with the guard's entrails. Gurgling noises seeped from the guard's mouth as the shock of what had just happened was too much for his body to bear, and it slumped to the floor, dead.

Mad-dog calmly walked to the door and ordered Fat-man to come in. He did as instructed holding a rag to stem the blood still seeping from his mouth. His face, like Leyland's, was also swollen, but not as painfully bad.

'Fat-man. I'm going to give you a chance to seek revenge on what

Wolf did to us today, and to the dishonour he has brought on the good name of all Hunters. We are all going to agree that Wolf and this guard were in league together in helping the prisoners' escape, and that they jumped us one at a time before gagging us.'

Leyland nodded without hesitation, and Fat-man knew there was no other choice but to agree with Mad-dog.

'Good. Now that's sorted you can join my gang and help me track down this traitor.' He slapped Fat-man on the back. 'Congratulations. You have just become a member. Now let's go outside and check out the remains of the stable block, then see about rounding up the horses.'

22

THE TRUTH AND NOTHING BUT THE TRUTH

The pulsating bursts of energy that burnt their way through every nerve ending and sinew began to subside. The flesh that tingled with red hot fire making the hairs of the body painfully sensitive to every whisper of movement in the air began to ease. The thick blues and yellows that had so violently seared the vision began to settle. John at last began to feel human again.

He felt his heart beat once more. He thought it had stopped and that he was going to die. Now lying motionless on the cold metallic floor the incessant ringing in his ears slowly faded. Dribble was seeping from his open mouth like a teething baby. Slowly, very slowly, he achingly opened one eye, and tried to ask for help as the words mumbled from his mouth.

All the others remaining in the room sat still on the benches like scared rabbits caught in the glare of light on a dark night making no effect to come to his aid. No one spoke.

With a quiet swish the wall moved and a door appeared. An Over-seer stood pointing into the distance as a voice echoed from the walls ordering instructions.

'You are to dispose of all your clothes and personal items in the hatch, then head to the feeding chamber at once.'

One by one people rose to their feet and started to remove their clothing. It was embarrassing for most standing with all they now possessed bundled in their arms trying to hide their modesty.

One by one they queued at the hatch that had opened in the wall. From its dark heart could be felt the warm air of a furnace while the rumble of the inferno could be heard deep below.

One by one they passed John still helpless on the floor as they said good bye to the past and sent their belongings hurtling into oblivion.

One by one without saying a word they meekly went through the open door and up the passage way until the door slid shut behind them, leaving John still prostrate in his distress; the only one left in the room.

* * *

'So you are telling me the truth and nothing but the truth?'

Daniel nodded as he continued to sharpen the edge of his axe with a large round, smooth stone.

'So the Over-seers are nothing more than monsters that feed of live human flesh? They farm us just like we use chickens, letting us roam free until we are ready for the pot?'

Daniel grimaced. Wolf was shaking his head from side to side in utter disbelief.

'I saw it with my own eyes in the Achievement Centre. I stumbled across it by mistake, and when I was nearly caught they came after me. I killed one by slicing through its armour on the back of its neck with this little beauty.' He brought the axe head up to his face and kissed it. 'They're not invulnerable. They have certain weak spots like the joints of their armour, or the slit in their helmet which they see through. Gwendolyn killed one with an arrow by shooting it straight between the eyes!'

Wolf still couldn't believe it as he kept asking the same questions over again. 'So you are really telling me the whole truth and nothing but the truth? No wonder the Over-seers want your blood so much.' He paused as if embarrassed, but he had to ask the next question.

'You know in all the confusion last night at the prison block and with our escape I never got to ask your name.'

'Daniel. Daniel Jones. That's my name.' Daniel carried on sharpening, leaving Wolf with many more questions than he had answers to.

'So I know the old lady is called Mary, and lucky for her she never made it to the Achievement Centre, but what about her daughter?'

Daniel looked up. 'Gwendolyn's not her daughter. Well, she is, but she isn't. It's a long story, and Mary will have to explain it to you one day because it involves so many things I had never heard off, and probably you haven't either.'

'Like what?' Wolf asked, a bit peeved that Daniel could think his own experience of life wouldn't have taught him everything that needed to be known.

'She was in this thing called the underground resistance that tried to defeat the Over-seers when they first arrived, with things called guns and bombs. And when she was a child in the time before their arrival, people lived in big cities made of concrete, and drove cars, talked over great distances with objects called phones, and they had square boxes called computers and televisions. Don't ask what good these were, or what they were used for, but they did, and it was all powered by this special magic called electricity.'

Wolf knew Daniel was right as he continued talking strange words which he could not correspond too. He was lost and trying to find a way out of the situation without admitting he was wrong. He looked over to Mary asleep under a blanket, resting her head on a mound of leaves as a pillow, with Jack snuggled up to her for warmth.

'What about the young boy?' he asked, distracting Daniel and so changing the conversation.

'Young Jack we picked up recently. He was living in the desolate lands in the East. He was born there, living with his mother and father when they were captured by Hunters who were there looking for us. I don't hold out much hope of finding them, but we felt it was our responsibility to look after him. After all, if we weren't there his parents would still be with him.'

Wolf agreed. 'They must have been the couple brought into our camp not so long ago, but they were taken away by the Over-seers in a Triclops. They would have been taken to the Achievement Centre at the Three-ways I suspect.'

Daniel raised his eyebrows. 'That's what I mean. Now you know what goes on in there you can see what I'm saying.'

Wolf frowned. 'Are you going to tell him?'

Daniel shook his head. 'No. The only thing Jack has in his life at the moment is hope. Take that away and he will be left devastated. No. We will wait until later today when we get back to my home village. I will explain to my dad the whole horrible situation, and see what he says.'

Daniel now smiled while the tone of his voice lightened. 'Because there is one thing I know about my dad, and that is whatever the problem he will find a solution for it.'

Daniel lent sideways, picking some dead branches from the pile, then added them to the fire, and just as it started to flare into life Gwendolyn came charging out of the trees. 'Look, look at what I have got!' She held out her arm and held up four dead wood pigeons. 'Breakfast!'

She immediately sat down next to Daniel without making eye contact with Wolf, and started to pull away at the bird's plumage. Handfuls of grey feathers fell to the ground while others were caught by the light early morning breeze that was slowly warming up with the rising sun, helping to banish the first frost of autumn that now covered the ground with its crisp white breath. They drifted away, dancing on the current.

'There's something else you need to know, Wolf. See my Golden Shield?' Daniel lent on his elbow and picked it up as it glistened. 'This shield has the power to deflect back any deadly ray a Triclops can throw at it, so destroying the beast in the process. I know because I've done it.'

Wolf couldn't help but be impressed, but again didn't want to show it. He leaned forward and tried to rock himself onto his feet, but the pain kept him from succeeding.

'I think we better wake up the other two. We need to get moving.'

Daniel picked up a bird and started to gut it, giving Gwendolyn an excuse to leave.

'Wake up, wake up,' she said, slowly rocking Mary's body as she lay gently snoring in her dreams. Jack's eyes opened at once and he started to his feet. Mary took another few encouraging nudges that grew with intensity before she finally stretched out her arms yawning.

'Morning all,' Mary said in a positive tone that refreshed everyone's spirits. 'It looks like we are going to have a beautiful day to day. I hope you all got a good night's sleep?'

Gwendolyn gave her a helping hand to get her to her feet as she brushed leaves from her clothes. Then she pointed to the pigeons and smiled without saying a word. Mary gave her a big hug and said, 'Well done, my little angel. I knew once you had some more arrows you would be back to your old self, and we could fill our bellies once more.'

Daniel piped up, 'Take a look at this as well, Mary.' He pulled back his blanket and underneath it was a heap of fruit. 'Apples, pears, raspberries and blackberries. I picked all these at first light when everyone was still in the land of sleep. There's more than enough to last us until we get to my village. Once we are there we won't have to worry about scavenging anymore. There will be plenty of delights.' He grinned. 'And for you, Mary, a lovely little treat you have dreamed about for years: fresh, hot bread baked that day with as many lashings of butter as you want.'

Mary clapped excitedly. 'I can't wait to meet your family. I think our fortunes are about to change.' Mary didn't like to lie. It wasn't in her nature. She had too with young Jack, but what the others didn't know was that she had also been with Daniel. It's wasn't a dark lie as far as she was concerned, more of a good-natured white lie, but still it was a lie. She had felt something strange the last couple of days about his father, a premonition about his current fate. She had sensed something was wrong, but didn't want to get Daniel worried, especially after they had been captured. Then again she could have been wrong, that Daniel's father was safe, but again she had nearly always been right. Everyone that now sat around the open camp fire had all suffered some negative experience recently in their life, and she felt it only right to keep with the positive mood until the truth was known.

The birds were boiled with added fresh mint that grew nearby, washed down with fresh water from a stream that bubbled up from under the ground. Breakfast was finished off with mouthfuls of sweet succulent fruit.

Once finished the fire was covered over with dirt. Leaves were sprinkled on top to hide away any signs of their presence, then branches used to mess the ground so covering all tracks. The horses were led to the stream so they could quench their own thirst.

'This should lead to a larger stream further up, and if we join it and keep to it; it will lead us back to my home,' Daniel stated as he pointed in the direction.

'The chalk stream bed should also mask the horse's hoofs, so making it harder for Hunters to track us,' Wolf added, as he was given a helping hand by Daniel to mount Mad-dog's horse.

Once all the riders were safely up Daniel gently nudged the white of Champion's belly with his heel, and took the lead at walking pace through the rush of the water, while the others followed him.

* * *

John rubbed his palms. The stress was starting to show. It had built up over the time he had spent on his own in the empty room. The ringing in his ears had finally stopped alongside the occasional twitch. The helplessness he felt was starting to turn into anger. The boredom was frustrating enough, but being cooped up with no means of communicating with Mother was beginning to turn him stir crazy.

He longed to be outside again, to be free, to breathe in the fresh air, and feel the breeze on his face, to be able to look at the sky with its constantly changing features, and to hear the birds.

How long he had been sitting on the bench since he was able to pull his body off the floor; he had no idea. It could have been hours or it could have been days. Time had merged into one long constant with no end in sight. He banged his fist against the top of the long bench, and jumped to his feet in anger letting out an almighty cry as he paced around the room like a caged lion.

Suddenly the wall moved and a doorway appeared. Standing at its entrance was an Over-seer pointing in. John rushed towards him, but his path was blocked by oncoming people. One after another they kept coming into the room as instructed.

He shouted out to the Over-seer, 'Where is my wife? Why can't we leave? I want the truth and nothing but the truth.'

The Over-seer ignored him. John began to push his way through the oncoming tide of human ignorance until his hand grabbed the Over-seer's shoulder. 'Tell me the truth.'

Without further warning the beast, who showed no emotion while encased within its silver helmet, raised its hand and took hold of John's arm. Clasping it so tight he fell painfully to one knee. A Dominator now approached. Standing over John it simply prodded him with his rod that had earlier caused him such devastating pain, and once again his body convulsed uncontrollably. This time the punishment lasted just long enough to allow John to slowly crawl back on his hands and knees into his confinement, and when the door slid shut behind him he collapsed.

The new arrivals stood perplexed in silence with no one offering to help, just as the previous people had, until a large jovial chap gave John a hand to sit back on the bench.

'What's up with you, my dear fellow?' John was struggling to breathe. 'You should know the truth by now. We are all here to receive out lovely rewards after forty loyal seasons of hard work, and loyalty to the Over-seers through following the Seven Procedures.'

John shook his head from side to side, still unable to talk.

'Don't be so silly. You must have done something wrong to have upset the Over-seers. They're our saviours, here to help us, and to reward us.'

Somebody let out a cheer in agreement which was followed by someone else clapping. This became infectious as the whole room erupted into cheers and clapping. A woman became over-excited and shouted out with almost religious belief: 'We give thanks to the Over-seers.' The others repeated it until the chant became deafening.

'We give thanks, we give thanks, we give thanks to the Over-seers. We give thanks, we give thanks, we give thanks to the Over-seers. We give thanks, we give thanks, we give thanks to the Over-seers.'

On and on it went with the crowd, whipping themselves into a frenzy of joyous praise. The anger building up within John turned into rage, which burst through his body, giving him the strength to stagger to his feet. The room felt as if it was spinning as everyone bar John were jumping up and down, clapping, and singing out their relentless homage.

'Listen to me. Listen to me!' cried out John, but nobody took any notice. 'Listen to me, you fools, just listen to me.' Again he cried out in anguish, but it was futile.

In desperation he turned back to where the door had once been, and rushed at it with all his might, crashing into it, trying to force his way through. He tried again and again and then again until his shoulders hurt too much and couldn't take any further beatings. In one last futile act of desperation he started to bang on the walls with his fists, crying out,

'Tell us the truth and nothing but the truth.' Every time the crowd sung John banged violently on the door until his stamina gave way. He slumped on the floor in defeat.

23

THE POUCH

The waft of human waste assailed the nostrils.

'Here we are.'

Daniel bent down and pulled away a branch. Excitement tingled in every hair, and the eagerness to return home was in his voice.

'Across the stream, on the other side of the stink-pit, at the far end of the meadow, is my village. My home is the double hut opposite the biggest barn you can see. If you wait here I will go and find my family.'

Mary put her hand on his shoulder. 'I don't think that would be a wise move. We need to bring your father to us. If you suddenly turn up after all this time it will attract the attention of everyone who knows you, and there could be a lot of awkward questions.'

Daniel got to his feet, disappointed at having to wait, and it showed as he helped Mary to hers before they walked back through the trees to where the others were waiting. Jack was eating a pear while Gwendolyn polished off some blackberries. Wolf was pacing about, and was the first to notice their arrival.

'So what do you think?'

Mary was in deep thought and it was a minute or two before she seemed to have made up her mind. 'Somebody needs to go into the village on their own and bring back Daniel's father. He can't do it, and I can't either because it would cause too much of a stir.'

'That's true. I bet no one has ever seen such an old lady as you.'

Mary glanced at Wolf. 'Less of your cheek. You're not that old that I can't put you over my knee.'

'I can't do it,' he replied, embarrassed by the way his cheeks flushed like a little boy who had just been told off. 'No one will willingly talk to a Hunter, plus it will get everybody in the village curious as to why I'm there.'

'I will do it for you!' exclaimed an excited Jack, as he wiped the remains of pear juice from around his mouth.

'Thank you, young man, but we need someone a bit older.' Mary looked at Gwendolyn who carried on eating obliviously. 'Gwendolyn. You will need to do it.'

Her heart jumped into her mouth when she heard those words, and her worst fear came rushing to the surface. The thought of meeting, and then having to deal with more strangers was something she had been dreading, and was desperately trying to think of a way out.

She stuttered, 'but, but...' then got interrupted.

'There are no buts. You will have to go to the double hut opposite the largest barn, knock on the door, find Daniel's father John, and then persuade him to come over here.' Mary took hold of her hand.

'But, but...' Mary wasn't going to except any excuses and was walking her towards the edge of the woods before she had the chance to protest. 'But what do I say? What if he doesn't believe me? What do I say?'

Mary gently squeezed her hand and gave Gwendolyn one of her reassuring smiles. 'Don't worry about it. He will come.'

Before Gwendolyn knew it she was splashing her way through the stream that meandered its way around the edge of the meadow. She looked behind, taking one last peek as Mary disappeared back into the trees. With every step her anxiety increased. She had only recently got used to Daniel after spending nearly all her life on her own with just Mary as company. Jack and Wolf's sudden appearance was still taking her time to get used to, and now she had to walk into a large village full of strangers.

Her palms were clammy while her throat felt dry. Looking down she studied the wild plants that grew among the grass, bleached dry by the long hot summer. Some were in flower, their last petals of the year before they hunkered down for the oncoming winter, while others were seeding.

Suddenly the call of a cockerel caught her attention, and when she looked up she was only steps away from the large barn where an albino cockerel was standing on top of a pile of logs, flapping its white feathered wings. People, mostly women and children were hurrying about engrossed in their day to day chores, not noticing her arrival.

She scadaggled across the dirt track, hoping not to gain their attention, then softly knocked on the wooden door of Daniel's home. There was no reply. She knocked again, and when again there was still no reply her pulse shot into panic mode. She knocked for a third time, but harder on this occasion, and then on the fourth attempt she gave the door one almighty knock.

'Can I help you?'

The voice from behind made her jump, and she instinctively reached to her side for her bow, then realised she had left all her weapons with the others. Panic set in. The first instinct was to run, but she had no choice other than to follow the next one, and that was to turn around and face whoever it was. She turned in apprehension.

'Can I help you? Who are you looking for?'

She was trying her best not to look nervous and to fight her urge to run. She wasn't sure how to react in such a situation because she had never experienced it before. 'I…' she hesitated. 'I'm looking…' she hesitated again, then just blurted it out: 'I'm looking for John.'

A semi-toothless grin appeared from behind the long beard that was more grey hair than black. 'He's not here. Who is looking for him?'

'I am,' Gwendolyn replied, confused that he should need to ask such an obvious question.

'No. I mean what's your name?'

Fear spread into hesitation, but this time she was ready to give in to her fear, and make a run for it back to the woods, especially when the stranger held out his hand.

'Hi, I'm Badger. I'm looking after John's place for him until his son returns.' Badger was still holding out his hand in friendship, surprised that she didn't return the compliment. 'I'm a friend of the family. Like I said, I'm looking after the place, and Sarah, until Daniel returns.'

Gwendolyn felt herself relax just a tiny bit. Instinctively she held her hand out to Badger who took hold of hers, and then shook it while smiling enthusiastically.

'I'm afraid John has reached his Achievement Day and has gone to the Achievement Centre. What a lucky man. In fact his wife has also gone with him although she still has a season to go.'

Badger winked at Gwendolyn. 'But don't tell anyone what I just told you.' He winked again and let go of Gwendolyn's hand.

She stood frozen to the spot, not knowing what to do next because she had all the information she required and now wanted to rush back to Daniel to tell him the bad news, but for some reason she didn't know the polite way of ending the situation without looking suspicious.

'I've never seen you around these parts before. I think I wouldn't forget such an angelic-looking face. You must be from River-mouth?'

Once again Gwendolyn was stumped for words, so decided that saying nothing, and just nodding her head would be the best option.

'So are you a friend of Daniels?' She nodded. 'That's good. How is he doing?' She nodded again. Badger winked again. 'So are you Daniel's girlfriend?'

She wanted to laugh out loud at such a preposterous remark, but fear kept her mouth shut; she just nodded once again.

'Daniel is a lucky lad indeed to have such an attractive young lady, but then again you are lucky to know so such a good fellow.' Badger winked for the final time. 'And from such a good family too. You can't go wrong there, you know!' He then raised his bushy eyebrows. Gwendolyn replied with a final silent nod.

'Right. I must get back to the barn and feed the livestock. Do you know when Daniel will return?'

Gwendolyn now found the courage at last to answer the question. 'Soon. He will be here very soon.' And with a courteous look she darted past Badger and off into the distance.

Badger turned around and walked back to John's barn, watching as the strange young lady he had just encountered ran off across the track and over the meadow towards the cesspit, as he jokingly mumbled to himself, 'My! She was a strange creature, but then again all women are. Maybe she was just desperate to relieve herself.' And with that last thought he disappeared back into the barn.

Gwendolyn was dreading having to tell Daniel the news. When she came bursting through the trees she was gasping for air. Without saying anything Mary picked up there was something wrong, for she knew that Gwendolyn should not have returned so quickly if Daniel's father was there, and she sensed that Daniel knew that too.

'He's not there, is he?' Daniel hastily questioned. 'He's already gone to the Centre, hasn't he?' Gwendolyn was now panting, leaning forward, resting her hands on her knees, and when she raised her head in response to Daniel's question her apologetic look confirmed his suspicions.

'Damn.' Daniel kicked out at the ground, sending a plume of dirt into the air, which spooked the horses as they jostled to get out of the way of his anger.

He turned and walked off, picking up his axe, and then headed to the nearest tree. The stress that had been building up within him the closer he got home now burst out into the open. He swung his axe at the base of a tree, sending chips of bark flying in all directions. Again and again he swung his axe at the base of the innocent tree as he released all his energy. One axe swing after another, with each one followed by a gut-wrenching roar that came from the belly, but was felt by his heart.

Both Mary and Gwendolyn went to his aid, but Wolf stood in their way with an outstretched arm.

'Believe me, it's best to leave him alone until he has exorcised all his anger.'

Mary tried to push pass, but Wolf was insistent. He grabbed her arm and pulled her back. She wasn't too pleased with Wolf and swung at him with her umbrella, hitting him on the shoulder, but Wolf knew what he was doing.

'Leave the lad alone. If he doesn't get the rage out of him it will fester within him, slowly growing until it consumes him. By then he will have lost his self-control, and the beast inside will take him over.'

Mary succumbed, and watched helplessly with the others as Daniel continuously swung his axe at the tree. Finally the sound of snapping wood indicated it was on its last legs. Then without further warning it came crashing to the ground, bouncing a couple of times before it came to rest. Birds startled by all the commotion left their perches, flying in all directions. By the time the noise had settled down Daniel was slumped on his knees. His shirt was sodden wet while his head was bowed. He let go of the axe and said nothing.

No one dared say a word until Gwendolyn felt she had to tell Daniel the whole truth. 'There's more, Daniel.' He didn't respond. 'Your mother decided to go with your father into the Achievement Centre.'

It took a few silent seconds before a roar of anguish shattered the silence as Daniel got to his feet. 'I'm going after them now!' he screamed, as he stormed towards the stream.

Mary went after him trying to stop him, but he wouldn't listen. She held his arm, but he tugged it free. Gwendolyn jumped in his way, but he just pushed her to the ground. Young Jack tried to grapple his waist, begging with him to stay, but Daniel just brushed off his pleas. Wolf finally ran up from behind and wrapped his arms around Daniel's chest in a tight bear hug, absorbing all his fury.

'Listen to them. You aren't going to do any good to anyone by charging off to the Achievement Centre. All you are going to do is get yourself caught, and then executed.'

Daniel violently tried to release himself, but Wolf held tight, hoping his words would persuade Daniel to calm down.

'Look, you have to control your hatred, and turn your wrath against the Over-seers by using your brains, because just using brawn is going to not only get you killed, but also your friends. Is that what you really want?'

Mary now joined the conversation, standing in front of him, while Wolf held his grip. 'Look, Daniel. There is always ways to do things if only we stay calm, and think about it. Don't you agree?'

Slowly Daniel began to think rather than just act. He started to control his anger, taking in deep breaths until his madly beating heart began to subside. Mary's positive outlook on life always had a calming effect whenever she spoke, and now it started to work its magic on Daniel.

'We aren't going to give up on your family, or on young Jack's. They are all in the Achievement Centre, and if we all work together we will get them out.'

Wolf could sense that Daniel was now settled enough to let him go without him charging about like a bull in a barn full of boisterous chickens. His arms dropped to the side. Daniel stood still, then without saying a word walked over, picked up his axe, and sat down on the trunk of the fallen tree.

Mary started to pace about in deep thought, rubbing her chin, and talking to herself as if she had an imaginary friend. Gwendolyn walked over and sat down next to Daniel. She didn't say anything, but thought her presence would at least reassure him that he wasn't alone. Wolf attended to the horses while Jack found a patch of sunlight piercing through the trees which he could use to charge up the solar panel attachment he had once made for his iPad.

Suddenly Mary stopped. 'Eureka!' she called out. 'I have it.'

She beckoned them towards her. They gathered around.

'I will go into the Achievement Centre after them! I'm way past the time when I should have gone, and when the next lot of poor ignorant souls go in, I will go in with them, and get everyone out.'

She held open her arms as if expecting a round of applause, but Wolf asked the obvious question. 'And how are you going to get them out once you are in there?'

Mary had a cagey expression. 'I haven't thought about that bit yet. I was just going to wing it once I was inside, and hope something would turn up.'

'You would have a better chance if the two of us were inside,' Wolf said, 'but I don't know how we could both get in there. Then again I don't plan on staying around.'

Wolf felt heartless. He just wanted to get as far away as possible and leave the others to themselves, but he couldn't stop thinking about the kindness Mary had shown towards him. Something deep down in his soul told him he would end up taking part in this crazy plan.

'You would have a better chance if there were four of us in there, and I know a way we could do it.' All eyes turned to Daniel.

'And how would that be, Daniel?' Mary asked, not convinced he had thought it through. 'You and Gwendolyn just can't walk in there claiming you are on your Achievement Day.'

'But we can crawl in there the same way I did when my younger sister first discovered the entrance to the tunnel. It's too small for Mary to crawl in, and Wolf would find it a struggle too, but if you two could get in from the front by just walking in with all the other Achievers then we could meet you inside by the back way.'

Mary stood contemplating Daniel's suggestion, before shaking her head in disagreement. 'But the problem is what we do once we get inside. There are going to be plenty of internal doors that control the airflow between what humans can breathe, and what the Over-seers need. Then we need to make an escape. A group of adults can't crawl back out. We would need to open the door from the inside, and come back the way we went in.'

Jack started to bounce up and down in excitement and held up his hand. 'Me. Me. What about me?'

'Calm down, Jack. You will have to stay here and look after the horses.' Mary ruffled his dark hair affectionately.

'No. You don't understand. Me, I can open the doors inside with this!' Jack help up his arm, holding his iPad. 'Like I said before I have adapted it to be able to communicate in the same way as Over-seers do. I can open and close things with just simple commands by using the interface that's in your duffle bag.'

Wolf bent down and looked Jack sternly in the eyes. 'No. It's too dangerous for you.'

Jack stuck his chest out and suddenly he seemed to mature in stature. 'I will die out here on my own without you, so if you are going to die in the Achievement Centre trying to save my parents then I want to die with you.' Everyone was taken aback by his brave statement. 'Anyway, as I see it you're stuck without me. None of you are intelligent enough to work the system, and, as you both clearly said just a little while ago to Daniel, we need to use brains and not brawn if we are to rescue the others.' Jack gave them a defiant nod, expanding his chest out as far as he could like a peacock on parade.

'That's sorted then. We are all in this together,' Mary said, as she started to stroke her chin once again as her mind went into a whirl of thought. 'The only problem is timing. We need to keep track of time once we are inside. If only we had another watch for Gwendolyn to use.'

Wolf looked confused. 'A watch? What is a watch?'

Mary held up her arm, pulled back her sleeve, and pointed to the small round glass-covered metal box that was strapped to her wrist. 'A watch is one of these little things that will tell you what the time of day it is.'

'That's not a problem. Back in my home my father has a secret pouch hidden away and in it is one of those watch things.'

Daniel knew this was the excuse he needed to return home. Although he had learnt to trust Gwendolyn, and knew she wouldn't lie to him, he still wanted to go and double check for himself that his parents had truly gone. He knew the fire was always kept alight, even if it was just warm hot embers, and that if the ash was cold then they had gone for good.

'I will have to go now. I will sneak in and then out again and bring the pouch back here, but I will need to go now because the sun is way past its mid-point, and soon the three blasts of the horn that calls all Achievers will be bellowing its doom across the land.'

No one objected, and without a further word Daniel disappeared into the trees.

Not wanting to be seen by anyone else in the village he took the long route back to the hut, skirting the edge of the tree line that encircled the community he had called home all his life. A tinge of sadness swept over him. He had longed to return to his family and friends ever since he was forced to go on the run after stumbling on the truth about the Achievement Centre. Longing to see Sarah again pounded on his soul, and the urge to take the risk became ever more powerful with each step he took.

Finally he was as close as he could get before he needed to break cover. The hope of seeing Mother still lifted his spirits. There was still the chance that Gwendolyn had been wrong. Daniel looked up at the sky. Dull clouds had come rolling in, matching the feeling in his stomach. It was hard to make out the full position of the sun, but he knew this was now the best time to make the final dash as most people would be resting after enjoying their lunch. The thought of a hot cooked meal of stewed meat in a pot full of vegetables, with plenty of fresh bread to soak up the gravy, made Daniel's mouth water. He sniffed the air. There was a whiff of cooking carried on the breeze. 'I hope Mother is there. I hope Gwendolyn is wrong. Please let her be wrong.' The thoughts kept going around and around in his head until they sent his skull spinning, and his legs running.

Daniel sprinted into the open. He ran in a straight line, not looking to the left or the right. His whole focus was to get to his home without anyone noticing. If someone called out his name he had decided to ignore it, and carry on running. He didn't have time to stop and chat. His breath became louder as air was sucked into the lungs in an increasing panic to find out the truth.

Then it was there! The wooden door that guarded the entrance to his home, and before he had a chance to stop he went crashing through before stumbling to the floor.

There was no sound inside. There was no Sarah humming, no father whistling while he beavered away, and more importantly no mother exclaiming with excited joy that her son had returned home. Daniel rubbed some grit from his eye as the sight of the extinguished fire with its heap of ash sunk the last hope of a family reunion like an exploding torpedo.

He quickly crawled over and touched the cold ash. It sent a chill of realisation down his spine. The fire never went cold. It was always lit or kept ticking over. In all the seasons he had lived Daniel had never known the beating heart of the home to go out. There were always enough hot embers left in the morning to reignite into flames, but this pile of slag was cold. Without thinking he thrust his whole hand deep into the heap desperately trying to feel for any warmth. There was none. Hope now quickly turned to anger as he swept away the grey residue, and when there was no more to check his frustration turned to rage.

'You fools. You have gone to the Achievement Centre.' Daniel banged his fist on the floor and then again. He kept hitting the floor each time with greater force until his wrist started to ache. Droplets of sadness splattered onto the ash.

Daniel pushed himself up and wiped his cheeks with his sleeve. Next he checked the bedroom. Again the disappointment cut him. A large web had been spun across one corner of the archway indicating no one had dusted for days. The spider at its heart sat motionless waiting patiently for its next meal to wander by.

He tore at the web, breaking its beautiful symmetric strands into useless threads, and now held the spider in the palm of his hand. He slowly closed his fingers until his tightened grip could end the spider's existence. Daniel now held the power of life or death over this creature just like the Over-seers did over his parents. Just one more squeeze, that's all he had to do.

Then just as the power became intoxicating something inside of Daniel told him it was wrong. He could hear Mother's voice. He could feel its warmth, its love. Daniel opened his palm and studied the immobile creature. Father's words of wisdom spoke to him. 'Remember, Daniel, everything in life has its own purpose that is as important with equal measure, no matter how small it may be. We must respect all wildlife and make sure it survives if we want to survive ourselves.'

Daniel looked at the broken web with a tingle of guilt. He dropped the spider on the floor and it scuttled away without further ado.

'Focus. You must focus, Daniel. Why am I here? I'm here to save my parents, and to do that I need to retrieve the pouch.' He shot over to the sideboard and picked up a knife. Once on his knees, and with vigorous energy, the floor area was cleared from around the hearthstone. With a push from the knife it was raised enough for Daniel to lean under and grab the soft leather pouch hidden underneath.

The stone landed with a dull thud when he let it go. Once at the door he discreetly opened it and scanned the track that ran through the village. In the distance he could see Sarah running towards Badger's house. His instinct wanted to shout out to her, to call for her, to let her know he was safe. He had so many questions he wanted to ask her. For a second hesitation had the upper hand until his focus took hold, and once she had ran into Badger's hut Daniel darted out of his.

He ran at full pelt clasping the pouch and not daring to take a look back. This time he was going to take the most direct route he could back to the others, heading straight across the meadow and past the stink-pit. Splashing his way through the stream at the bottom slowed his speed, and only once he had passed this did Daniel risk one final glance behind.

He came panting back to the small enclosure where the others had been waiting. He was breathing heavily as he held out the pouch at arms-length.

'Here you go, Mary. You should find what you need in here.'

Daniel sat down, resting his back against a tree. Gwendolyn and Jack joined him while Mary stood over them with her umbrella in hand. 'Well done, Daniel. Did anyone see you?'

'I don't think so.'

Mary held out her hand. 'Wolf, can you help me to my knees so I can explain my plan?'

He did as asked and then followed suit, leaning in with the others as Mary used the metal tip of her umbrella to draw pictures in a patch of bare earth she had scrapped clean while waiting for Daniel's return.

'I can only guess at what the layout must be like inside the Achievement Centre, but with what we know about the Over-seers there must be separate levels, or rooms, where both they can breathe and humans as well.'

She started to draw square boxes in the dirt. 'The first room must be where people enter the centre so it will be filled with oxygen.'

Wolf agreed. 'I've been in there. It's a large chamber entered through a big enough entrance to let, and then contain, quite a lot of people. The Over-seers are always helmeted, and in full uniform. At the opposite end is a smaller door that will only allow single file traffic through it.'

Mary then drew three boxes in a row with another two on either side.

'My theory is that you enter here then must be led to a waiting chamber.' She was leading with her umbrella tip going from one box to the next. 'At the other end of the centre is where the Over-seers must live so they can breathe without the need for wearing suits or helmets. The fifth box must be the feeding chamber. You are led into there, where according to Daniel you can breathe until the air vents are closed. The oxygen is then replaced so the Over-seers are free to remove their helmets, and feed on the live human flesh as its poor owner is very slowly suffocated.'

Mary leaned over and grabbed Wolf's hood, pulling it over his head. 'Do you think the Over-seers will say anything if you go in hooded up?'

Wolf pulled it off, brushing his hands over his cropped head. 'I doubt it very much.'

'Good. Then us two can go in the front way. We will mingle with the other Achievers, and walk in with them while these three crawl in the back way through the tunnel. They can bring all the weapons with them, and once inside Jack can use his thingy-me-jig to open the doors. We will need an hour at least to persuade whoever is inside the dangers they face. It will be harder than we think because after a lifetime of being brainwashed by the Seven Procedures people aren't going to be too believing when two strangers turn up and tell them they had been fed a lie all their life. That's why we need two watches to synchronise our actions inside. Then we can lead everyone out through the front while you, Daniel and Gwendolyn, can protect our rear.'

Daniel's disbelieving tone of voice showed he wasn't convinced, and by the look of the others neither were they.

'That sounds simple enough, Mary, but even if we do get out the Over-seers aren't just going to let us go. What do we do then?'

Mary grinned. 'Good question, Daniel.' She started to rummage through the deep pocket of her skirt before pulling out a lighter. Flicking the ball a small flame appeared. Wolf was intrigued. He held out a finger and touched the light that slowly danced on top of the clear rectangle case full of liquid. Instantly he recoiled, swearing at the same time before thrusting the burnt tip of his finger into his mouth.

'I'm going to give you a quick chemistry lesson. We humans breathe air which is mainly made up of oxygen, and the resistance concluded the Over-seers breathe something made up with a mixture of gases including hydrogen. Now, when you add the two together in the right mixture, then add a third element, namely fire, what do you get?'

Jack suddenly threw his arms in the air shouting out, 'Boom! You get an explosion.'

'Well done, Jack. Well done indeed.'

The others kept silent until Daniel asked the next obvious question. 'So who is going to stay behind and light the flame? Because whoever it is they are going to go boom at the same time.' He looked around the group as everyone went silent. Mary piped up.

'There can only be one person, and that's me.'

Gwendolyn wasn't too pleased and she let it be known. 'No, you can't go. I will do it.'

Mary knew this wasn't an option and looked towards Wolf for support, but he took her actions in the wrong way.

'Don't look at me, you crazy old bat. I'm not going to do it. I'm not even keen on going into the Achievement Centre. I don't want to be here in the first place. In fact I must be as crazy as you still to be around, and once this is all over I'm on my way out.'

Gwendolyn leaned over and grabbed the lighter out of Mary's hand and then jumped to her feet. 'You're not going to do it. There must be another way.'

Mary held out her hand. 'Give it to me, Gwendolyn. There is no other way. I am the oldest here. I have lived most of my life, and you lot still have yours to live. It's the most obvious conclusion.' Her head dropped and the silence overwhelmed the rustling of leaves, the only other sound that could be heard. Then she lifted her gaze, which beamed with a sense of joy. 'And it's not only that. I want this chance to finally get my own back. I have had enough of hiding like a rat in the sewer. I'm fed up with spending all my life on the run, but most of all I want to make those gits pay for what they have done, not just to humanity, but to me personally, to my family. As far as I know I'm the last in my line and if I can go out with a bang then I will.'

A tear rolled down Gwendolyn's cheek as she turned and with all her might threw the lighter as far as she could towards a large thicket bush. It disappeared into its prickly heart. She turned back looking triumphant until Mary held out her other hand and in the centre of her palm rested another lighter. Her face dropped and so did she to her knees.

'Now that's sorted let's see what we have in the pouch.' Mary's hand delved in and she retrieved the watch. 'What a lovely piece of craftsmanship in gold and such sweet diamonds.' Turning with finger and thumb the small knob on its side she then held it to her ear. 'It works!'

She passed it to Gwendolyn, who instinctively held it up to the light as she enjoyed the jewel-encrusted treat, before clasping it to her wrist. Mary's hand once again disappeared into the pouch, then out again, this time holding a key. 'This isn't much use now.'

'What is it?' asked a bemused Wolf, but Mary didn't go into further detail. She just tossed the car key onto the floor before pulling out the final item from inside. It was a picture. She turned it over. She said nothing, just starred at the photo.

'What is it, Mary? Are you all right?' She didn't reply to Gwendolyn's question. 'What is it, Mary? Say something.' Gwendolyn nudged her arm.

'Mummy. Daddy.' Mary brushed the picture gently with her finger. Tears started to well up in her eyes and she sounded like a six-year-old child. 'Mummy, Daddy, I have missed you so much.' Mary's hand suddenly shot to her mouth as she yelled out before slowly turning to look at Daniel, 'How come you have a picture of my mum and dad?'

Daniel felt stunned at Mary's sentence. 'What are you talking about, Mary? They aren't your parents. They're my grandparents.'

'No, you're wrong. This is where I used to live before the Over-seers turned up, and this is Mummy and Daddy standing outside my old home. I was rescued from here by the resistance. They found my here at the bottom of our driveway.'

Mary's hand was shaking and a couple of times she had to wipe her cheeks with her sleeve. Suddenly Daniel was startled into the realisation of how significant her words were. At first he chuckled, not knowing if he should laugh or cry, but in the end it turned to laughter.

'So after all this you're not Mystic Mary. You're my Aunt Mary.'

Mary was too shocked to say anything. She just leaned into Daniel, wrapping her arms around him, and started to sob with joy. Jack jumped up, clapping enthusiastically, while Wolf said nothing. All this family talk wasn't his scene, so he walked over to the horses leaving the rest to it. Gwendolyn was silent, also shocked at the news, but there was something else. It was eating at her. It was something she didn't normally feel, and that was envy. She had always been Mary's only family, and now she had a whole new family with a real-life blood relative. For the first time since she had met Daniel she now wished she had left him at the mercy of the Over-seer. She wished she had never saved his life and that she had let him be executed.

'Right, you lot. Let's get going.' Gwendolyn hoped her words would bring an end to this family reunion. Anger was swelling within her heart after it had consumed the envy, and she was ready for a fight. Mary was still hugging Daniel as he struggled to his feet, when everyone was stopped dead in their tracks by the blast of a mighty horn.

'We need to go.'

Mary pulled out a hanky, blowing her noise noisily as everyone hurried over to the horses and prepared for the Achievement Centre as Daniel fired out instructions.

'You two need to carry on in a straight line through the trees until you reach the dirt track, and then follow it up the hill. You will know when you are at the Three-ways because at its centre is a Tribute hut and there will be crowds of people. You need to get there by the third call of the horn and then just follow all the others as they walk pass the large boulder. You will need to hurry.'

Mary looked at her wrist. 'Gwendolyn, let's synchronise our watches. Give us an hour to get into the Centre, then another hour to come looking for us. We will try to find the others and get them prepared to leave.' She turned and gave Jack a kiss on the cheek. 'I have faith in you and your contraption to open the doors, so do your best, and stay brave.'

Wolf nudged Mary's arm. 'Let's go before I change my mind about this whole crazy adventure.' And with that final word he headed into the trees. Mary had time just to give Gwendolyn a goodbye hug before following Wolf, as she called out.

'Remember everyone, positive thinking. Whatever the problem you come across just keep cool, think positive, and find a way through it.'

With that they disappeared. Within the minute the other three had also darted into the trees, loaded down with any weapons they could carry, so in the end only the horses were left tethered to trees while they munched peacefully in the shade.

24

TIME IS RUNNING OUT

The panting increased and without a helping hand no further steps could have been taken, for the body was exhausted although the spirit was willing. A shock wave of sound unsettled nature, but for the hopeful few it brought joy. A round of clapping singled the end of one journey and the beginning of a new one for the expectant crowd. *En masse* the mob moved forward up the winding path that disappeared into the distance, shrouded by the surrounding trees.

'Come on Mary, time is running out. Just a few more steps and we will be there.'

She was struggling to keep up with Wolf, but his arm was interlocked with hers tightly, so giving enough support to make the last final dash to join the other Achievers. Wolf pulled up his hood over his head, and although they were the last people they had just managed in time to join the group as it meandered its way towards the Achievement Centre.

By the time the path came to a sudden stop in front of the cliff face Mary had regained her breath, and she could hear Wolf mumbling to himself under his hoody, 'I must be utterly crazy to be here. Whatever came over me back at camp I just don't know.'

She held his hand and gave it a tight squeeze for assurance just as rumbling began to emanate from behind the cliff, which made loose gravel underfoot dance as if enchanted by an unknown force. Slowly a gap appeared and increased in size until it moved no more, and two silver-suited Over-seers stood motionless, pointing into the darkness of the inner chamber.

Slowly the crowd moved forward. Mary and Wolf had managed, by means of gently nudging their way past people, a position in the middle of the crowd. As everyone shuffled in no-one took any notice of them as they blended into the mass of human excitement that tentatively waited for the doors to close and darkness to descend. When light appeared by magic from the roof people began to clap and cheer, until a Dominator came striding out of a door at the far end, barking out orders to the new arrivals.

'Silence!' The noise settled down. 'I am the Dominator. You will follow my commands at all times.' Without saying another word it pointed through the open door and people began to file in one at a time to the various rooms that lay off either side of the long tunnel stretching into the distance. There didn't seem to be any particular order in which people were placed and concern began to grow in Mary that she would be separated from Wolf. He was behind her at one stage, but then there was an eager scramble by everyone to get to their just rewards, and it ended up being a bit of a scrummage. She reached the next open door, and in a fleeting glance her heart missed a beat when she realised that they had somehow became separated.

Suddenly she felt her arm being grabbed, and before she could protest she was un-ceremonially shoved through the nearest entrance into a side room by an unforgiving Over-seer. Someone else was forced in then another and the wall began to slide shut.

'Wolf!' cried out Mary in desperation, then with just inches to spare Wolf elbowed his way through the remaining gap to join Mary just as the door slid shut. 'That was a close call. I don't know what we would have done if we had become separated.'

Wolf agreed, but their thoughts were soon onto the next task. The room was packed with people. Some were sitting on benches that ran the length of the room while others just stood, or wandered around.

'I hope John is in this room,' whispered Mary, 'and not in one of the others.' She paused. 'Or worst still, already been taken to the feeding chamber. For all we know he may already be in the belly of the beasts that were standing in the corridor. I will approach all the men sitting down and discreetly ask is they are called John Jones, and you do the same with all the others standing up.'

Wolf agreed and they went to work. One by one they made their greetings with their fellow strangers, and one by one they failed to find their man. Wolf approached Mary.

'I've asked everyone standing up, but no one is the person we are looking for.'

Mary had found the same with all the men sitting down.

'What about asking the women?' Mary discreetly suggested. 'Maybe we can find Daniel's mother. Maybe they got separated like we nearly did.'

'What's her name?' Wolf asked and Mary was left stumped.

'I don't know. I never got around to asking Daniel. All the same we will have to check everyone out.' As Mary turned to make her first enquiry she noticed someone sitting on the floor in the corner all on their own, their head buried between their legs. She prodded Wolf. 'Have you asked that chap his name?'

'No,' he replied. 'I was just concentrating on the men standing up.'

Mary walked over and stood over the forlorn soul. 'Daniel's a lovely name for a son.'

The man wearily looked up. 'I have a son called Daniel.'

Using the wall for support Mary plonked her backside onto the floor. 'I take it you must be John Jones.'

'Yes,' the reply came. 'Do I know you?'

'No, you don't, but I know a lot about you because I have had the pleasure of recently meeting your son Daniel.' John's face lit up. Mary held out her hand and he shook it. 'My name is Mary, and I have a story to tell you, but you must promise to keep an open mind and not to do anything rash that will draw attention to ourselves, but before I go on I want to introduce you to Wolf.'

Mary looked up and winked. Wolf instinctively knew she had found John so joined them both by sitting on the floor.'

'Please tell me Daniel is safe,' said John.

'Yes, and he is closer than you think. With luck you should see Daniel in the next hour because he's coming here to get us all out.'

The colour seemed to come back into John's face. He had looked so sullen before, almost deflated, but suddenly he looked alive again. 'Tell me more. I want to hear everything. I have so many questions. Why did he run away? Where did he go? Did it have anything to do with the Over-seers?' His voice became more excited and louder with each question. Mary held a finger to his lips to stop him drawing attention to them.

'Yes, it has got something to do with the Over-seers, and I will tell you as much as I can, so be quiet and let me explain.' Mary leaned over and spent the next fifteen minutes whispering in John's ear, explaining all about Daniel's journey into her life, and the following sequence of events that led to finding the Golden Shield. The truth about the Over-seers and what happened in the Achievement Centre, and finally the plan for their rescue. Mary fumbled in her pocket and then, using her hand to hide the lighter, she lit it to show John the flame, before hiding it back in her pocket. She had to keep the information as basic as possible, but by the end there was still one question she needed to ask John.

Wolf had sat quietly looking at the expressions on John's face that changed with every new discovery he was told. They went through the whole range, one minute showing delight, then the next shock. He couldn't hear what she was saying, so every now and then would glance around the room checking out that no one was suspicious of their behaviour. He needn't have worried as everyone else in the room was engrossed in their own little world, eagerly waiting for the pleasures they had been promised all their life. His attention was drawn back to Mary when he heard her speak.

'We understand that your wife is with you in the centre. Is she here in this room?'

John's reply was short. 'No.'

Mary feared the worst, but this one word just led to another question from her. She didn't like asking it, but she didn't have much time left and needed to find out. 'So do you know where she is?'

'Yes. She was taken to the Orb for special pleasures whatever that means. Not everyone is taken, only certain women, but she's definitely not been taken to the feeding chamber.'

Mary glanced at her watch. 'You three. Where are you? Time is running out.'

There was one final thing she wanted to tell John and that was the discovery of the picture, and the fact that they must be brother and sister. She wished she could have done it in a more relaxed atmosphere. Somewhere like John's home while they all sat in front of a roaring fire with a belly full of succulent food, but this wasn't going to happen. She would have to tell him now. She wasn't sure of his reaction. John had had a lot of new information to absorb in such a short period of time and she wasn't sure if this final piece of the jigsaw would be too much for him to take.

It was now or never. Mary had made up her mind. The other three could turn up any moment and then all hell will be let loose. She took a deep breath and just as she was going to tell John her attention was taken by the sound of the wall sliding sideways as the doorway appeared.

* * *

The clank of metal on metal got louder as the Dominator marched down the hallway until it reached its destination. Two silver-suited Over-seers on guard duty clenched their fists to their chests in salute. Clicking sounds emanated, and in response one touched the wall, making it slide to the side as a doorway appeared. The Dominator walked in the room. Everyone was standing in line, and naked, expect for a woman at the back who was still undressing while throwing all her possessions down a chute. The guard pointed up the hallway and meekly the bodies walked out until the room was empty and the door slid shut once more.

'We need one more for the feast,' the Dominator instructed. 'Open the next chamber.'

As instructed the Over-seers walked over and touched the wall making it slide sideways, then it and its colleague followed the Dominator into the room. People inside made way and stood expectantly. The room had fallen silent as the Dominator raised its arm, pointing to three people sitting on the floor against the corner.

'You, single male, are due your rewards.' There was no reaction so the Dominator stepped forward and pointed to the door. 'You are to go as instructed.'

Again it was ignored, forcing the Dominator to take action. It raised the arm that clasped its rod of punishment and thrust it hard into John's chest. He convulsed in agony on the floor. Mary tried unsuccessfully at her first attempt to get to her feet, but Wolf was quicker off the mark. He jumped up and swung his fist into the side of the helmeted beast. He recoiled in pain holding his hand, and before he had a chance to use his thick leather boots as a weapon in his next attack, the grey rod was thrust into his chest, which paralysed his muscles. The force sent him crashing to the floor and his head hit the side of the bench on the way down, knocking him unconscious.

Mary was now on her feet and had grabbed the Dominator's arm.

'You beast, you're nothing but a nasty bully.' She wished she had her umbrella so she could stab the metal tip of it into the monster's eye as it glowed behind it protective glass slit in the middle of its helmet. Instead she tried to distract the Over-seer by pulling at its armour while calling out for help from the other humans within the room.

'Help me get this monster. There are no rewards. They are going to eat you all alive.'

No one moved. Some people sat down, refusing to listen to what seemed the mad ranting of an old woman. Others turned their backs, while the rest just stood motionless on the spot.

'Help me, you lot. Can't you see what monsters these are? Help me.'

Her scream for help was ended when the rod of pain was pushed into her throat. Quivering uncontrollable on the spot she momentarily fainted, before collapsing to the floor next to Wolf. John was just recovering when he was once again sent into excruciating pain by the Over-seer.

'You have been instructed to move.'

Slowly John raised his body, but didn't have the strength as yet to get to his feet. Once again the Over-seer's rod electrocuted his body, sending out a screech of pain. He crawled forward on all fours until he was at the door.

No one came to his aid. No one said a word. No one offered help.

Mary gained consciousness just in time to cry out, 'No John! Don't go, don't go.'

John stopped crawling at the door, but one final prod was enough to force him into the hallway. Wolf started to stir, woken by Mary's pleas. 'Help him someone, anyone.'

Wolf got to his feet still dazed, but able to focus enough to make once last charge at the Over-seer as it walked out the door, following John as he crawled along the floor. The wall began to slide shut. Wolf let out a wild scream, and with shoulder lowered he went crashing into the door as it shut. He fell to the floor in pain.

The room fell silent, then someone whispered, and then another, until the room was full of chatter as people went back to their previous discussions as if nothing had happened.

* * *

'It's here somewhere?'

Daniel was scanning the sandy cliff face.

'Hurry up Daniel, the third blast of the horn went off ages ago,' Gwendolyn called out in frustration, 'At this rate we are going to run out of time.'

'Stop nagging me. It's here somewhere. The last time I came in a totally different direction, and the others knew where it was as well so we guided each other.' Daniel was getting just as irritated with Gwendolyn as he was with himself for being unable to locate the tunnel entrance.

'Is this it?' called out Jack, while he peered through a very large prickly bush. The other two rushed over and Daniel shot around the edge of it.

'I think it could be. Well done, young Jack. Follow me you two, and keep your backs pressed against the wall.'

Daniel started to edge his way sideways, desperately trying not to get any of his clothing caught in the sharp thorns that protruded from every branch. Finally he reached the overhang, and slumped onto the soil kept cool by the constant shade. He waited for the others to reach him. His heart was pounding, and it wasn't all caused by the frantic search for the tunnel. The images of his last visit were still vivid in his memory, and his palms became clammy. He wiped them down his trousers just as Jack, followed by Gwendolyn, flopped down next to him.

'Right. I will warn you that the tunnel will get smaller and smaller, but eventually it will turn into a metal duct. It will be dark and these lighters aren't going to give us much light. Now let's have one final check.' They all flicked their lighters. Three small flames appeared. 'OK. We have weapons too and Jack has his iPad, so I think we are all set to go.'

Daniel didn't say another word as he turned and then crawled forward on all fours, holding out his lighter, followed by Jack, as Gwendolyn guarded the rear. The tunnel got smaller and smaller and the memories became more and more garish. Once or twice

Daniel had to stop to catch his breath and calm his nerves on the pretence of checking the others were still all right.

'Is everything all right behind me?'

'Yes,' was the unified reply, forcing Daniel to plod on. Loose bits of dirt kept being dislodged, falling into hair and eyes, and then all came to a stop. The way ahead was blocked. Then it came back to Daniel.

'How could I have forgotten?' he cursed under his breath. The tunnel had partly collapsed when he had made his escape the last time he had crawled through it, and this very same blockage now stopped all further progress.

'What's up?' Gwendolyn called. 'Come on. Get moving.'

Daniel could feel his anger swell up within at Gwendolyn's constant pushiness, and he had to fight the urge to explode at her. 'Some soil has come loose and is blocking the way. We should be able to clear it by shoving it backwards.'

Daniel had no choice now but to let his lighter go out as he started to shovel earth back to Jack with both hands, while Jack could only use one of his. The darkness closed in on them and all three became panicky in the tomb that now enclosed them. Just one small flame was all they had to beat away the fear and the creepy crawlies that scuttled about. Even though the soil was cold to the touch, and the air chilled, they sweated profusely as they burrowed away like moles. Daniel stopped and retrieved his lighter. With a quick flick a flame appeared and he held it out in front.

'I think we have cleared enough just to squeeze through, but it's going to be tight and be careful not to dislodge any more dirt.'

Suddenly Gwendolyn shouted out, 'Do you know what time it is?'

Daniel's annoyance finally erupted. 'Of course I don't. I don't have a watch. What a stupid question to ask me.'

Gwendolyn was holding a lighter to her watch. 'It's time we were in the Achievement Centre, that's what it is.'

Jack could sense the stress was getting to everyone and hoped his encouragement would help. He pulled out his iPad and turned it on. Using the light of its screen it lit up the surrounding tunnel.

'It can't be too far. Here. Use this to see further ahead,' and he passed it through Daniel legs. Up ahead the light flickered off the walls, indicating the start of the metal duct, and Daniel yelped out a joyful call to arms.

'We've done! Let's get going.'

They all pushed forward on their bellies, over the raised earth, until they slivered onto the smooth metallic surface of the air duct. Up ahead a faint light could be seen and as they carried on it became brighter. Then there was a sudden rush of air pushing against them as it hissed around their ears and the light started to fade.

'Quick,' Daniel called out. 'I think the doors are starting to shut!'

He lowered his head and charged forward as the light became smaller and smaller, while the hiss of air being expelled became louder and louder. They clanked their way in a frenzied panic to get to the doors to the feeding chamber before they were shut for good. Daniel reached forward, but it was too late. They clicked shut barring any access into the Achievement Centre.

* * *

John crawled along the floor towards a procession of naked people waiting patiently for their next instructions. When he reached the back of the queue he used the wall to get to his feet and stood, a defeated man, with the others. Suddenly the door opened. Overseers at the head of the column marched in. Their boots made a fearful clank as they moved, and everyone moved forward into a large chamber full of metal tables, and more followed from behind. The Dominator now gave instructions.

'I am the Dominator. Do as instructed. Lie on the tables. Silence at all times.'

Some people looked bemused but no one protested except for

John. He turned and tried to push his way back through the Over-seers, but an explosion of pain once again sent him to his knees. Two Over-seers grabbed an arm each and dragged him across the floor to an awaiting table. Another two beasts joined in the preparation of their meal by grabbing his legs, and the four of them picked him up, hauled him onto the top of a table, and then held him down by force.

'Stop!' John cried out. 'Don't let them do this to us.' The Dominator stormed over with a dreadful shout.

'Silence at all times.' And it once again inflicted punishment to poor John's body until the seizures stopped and John was semi-unconscious. Silently and without protest people began to lift their naked bodies onto the tables. Some giggled as their flesh touched the cold surface, but no one dare question their masters as they readied themselves like sheep for the slaughter.

The sound of whirling brought John back to the land of the living just in time to see two throngs come rising from the side of the table, and clasp around his upper and lower body. His captives no longer needed to hold him down and they started to communicate to each other with excited clicking.

Dribble was running down John's cheek as he turned his head to the side to make one last plea for mercy, but no sound came from his paralysed mouth. The air began to weaken and it became harder to breath. The sound of hissing filled the room and as the air became stale the immobilised bodies on each table began to contort as desperate lungs fought for oxygen. People pleaded for air but their masters took no action. The light suddenly went out, to be replaced by a florescent glow that made the veins under the flesh pulsate a vibrant blue.

A siren engulfed the room, blanking out the sound of the obnoxious gas that was being pumped into the area. When it stopped it indicated it was time for the Over-seers to feed. Each one removed their helmets allowing them to stretch out their jaws, revealing deadly fangs that dripped with poisonous saliva. Their eyes shone an evil red and each and every one now looked down on the human flesh that wiggled in panicked fright as they gasped their last gulps of air.

John turned and faced his demons. Four stood around each table and they now raised their hands in the air removing their protective gloves. Spindly fingers increased in size as the nails of each hand, as sharp as razors, extended like the claws of a cat. The last image in John's mind as he closed his eyes to the impending doom were the swish of the Over-seers arms as they ripped at his clothes.

* * *

'Damn.'

Daniel cursed again. His mind was whirling away and Mary's last words kept repeating in his head. 'Positive thinking, whatever the problem you come across, just keep cool, think positive, and find a way through it.' By now Jack had squeezed next to him and Gwendolyn had got as close as she could.

'What do we do now?' she enquired, not wanting to make it sound like it was Daniel's fault that they had failed to make it in time. Daniel held up the iPad and its light reflected off the metal shutters. He ran his finger down the central groove. He dug his nails in and tried to prise open the door, but it was useless. Then he started to grapple with his belt. It was a struggle in the confined space, but eventually he released his sword.

With a shuffling of bodies Daniel manoeuvred the tip and pressed it as hard as he could in the groove to use as a leaver. He couldn't get enough leverage when he tried to heave the sword. Trying a second time only confirmed it. He looked at Jack.

'Here, Jack. You will have to hold the sword for me while I use the blunt end of my axe to knock it as far into the groove as possible. Leave your iPad on so we have some light.' He handed over his lighter to Gwendolyn. 'I need extra light so use both lighters and keep them as close to the sword as possible so I can see what I'm doing. If we get…' Daniel paused, remembering Mary's words, and rephrased the sentence. 'When we get these doors open take a deep breath, and hold it as long as you can because whatever is on the other side won't be breathable until it has been vented.'

All three were on their sides. It was very uncomfortable and hot. Jack was next to Daniel holding the sword while Gwendolyn was at their feet with arms stretched holding the lit lighters as close as possible. Daniel picked up his axe and hit the end of the sword, and then again, and again and for a fourth time, then dropped it and heaved on the sword.

There was a high pitched hiss and a foul smell filled the duct. He heaved again and the groove opened enough for him to thrust his hand in the open gap that had been created, and to start pulling the doors apart. The hissing turned into a rush. The doors tried to close in, but Daniel shoved his axe head between them in the open space, and sparks started to fly from their hinges.

The rush of deadly unpleasant air seemed to take for ever to empty. The sound of hissing was overwhelmed by fearful screeches. Red light now lit up the duct and a warning siren blasted from the walls, making the eardrums ache.

The three rescuers covered their heads as the sparks increased with density the more the automatic doors tried to crush the steel of the axe head. In one final blast of light they gave up the fight, and both doors fell dead.

Loud distressful clicking could be heard in the chamber below. Daniel, still holding his breath, edged forward. Wanting to take a peek into the room below his curiosity was startled when a leathery hand shot into the duct. Its skin was bubbling with boils that leeched yellow puss as it frantically felt around the area trying to close the opened doors.

Daniel froze, and it that split second the hand had grabbed his hair and yanked it hard so forcing Daniel's head out of the duct. He tried to pull the hand away, but its grip was too tight and he yelled out, 'Dagger. I need a dagger.'

He could hear Gwendolyn calling out, and then an object was thrust into his hand. He couldn't see what it was, but instinctively he brought it forward, and dug it deep into the beast's hand. A loud squeal echoed around the chamber and the hand retracted, releasing its hold on Daniel.

Looking over the edge the first sight to greet Daniel was a naked man strapped to a table by two metal prongs. The flesh of his belly had been torn away, hanging in large shreds. Underneath his body fat glistened in the violet light as his body contorted in agony. Still alive, froth was bubbling from his mouth with every breath it took as his eyes flicked wildly in distress.

Surrounding it were three Over-seers. Two were collapsed on the floor as green liquid putrefied from every orifice. Their skin bubbled as if boiling in a pot; pools of puss increased with every desperate attempt they made to breath. The third had hold of a helmet and was in the final throes of putting it back onto its head.

The next table had a woman lying on it. One of her eye-balls hung from its socket, dangling on its nerve ends. Her flesh too had been ripped away with large chunks of blooded body fat strewn across the table and floor, as once again Over-seers struggled in various frightful states of difficulty.

Daniel had now run out of breath, and gulped desperately for air. A coarse mixture of atmosphere filled his lungs, making his head fell woozy, but he could breathe. Oxygen was now rushing into the chamber, filling the lungs of all the humans while at the same time attacking the flesh of the Over-seers.

Looking at the third table made Daniel gasp. On it was his father, tethered down. His clothes had been stripped off and blood covered his naked chest. He didn't move. His head was turned to the other side and Daniel couldn't tell if he was alive.

With one almighty push with his knees he went head first out of the duct, crashing to the floor, half landing on the still alive Over-seer as it grappled with the knife in its hand. There was no hesitation. Daniel got to his knees, pulled the knife free, and as the monster wriggled in pain while its skin blistered with poisonous fluid, he stabbed it right through its throat. Its body went inert.

Daniel jumped to his feet and called out, 'Jack! Come on down.' Jack's head appeared and then instantly shot back in fright at the bloody scene that lay before him. 'Jack, I need you and your machine to set my father free. It will be all right.' The siren kept on sounding so Daniel shouted out. 'Gwendolyn, give Jack a hand.' And with one hard push he shot out of the duct like a child on a slide. Daniel just caught him in time in his open arms.

'Throw me my axe.'

It shot out, clanking to the floor at Daniel's feet, followed by a bow and a quiver full of arrows, and then swords. By the time he had bent down and picked it up there was a charge of clanging and roaring coming towards him, and Daniel turned in time to see the Over-seer who had put its helmet back on coming after him with outstretched arms. It had no gloves on and it claws were out for the kill.

Daniel tried to raise his axe, but there wasn't time. With a swish they came clawing towards his face and sliced through the skin of one cheek. Blood spurted out and the instant pain made Daniel drop his axe. A second claw now made for Daniel's scalp and as he flinched in terror he heard a whoosh and his eyes closed in expectation of the worst.

The siren kept on making a dreadful din. Then there was a thud followed by a loud squeal. Daniel opened his eyes to see Gwendolyn on top of the Over-seers. She had come thundering out of the duct and the Over-seer had cushioned her fall.

Once again there was no hesitation from Daniel. He picked up his axe. Gwendolyn just had time to roll off as Daniel kicked the Over-seer onto its front, raised his axe high into the air, and just like he did the first time he had killed one of these beasts he went for the weak spot at the back of its neck where the helmet met its suit of armour. He brought down the axe and buried it deep into the fold. The monster slumped forward, motionless. Green liquid spurted into the air and when it hit the floor it bubbled away, hissing like cold water thrown onto hot rocks.

Daniel rushed over to his father's table, dragging a petrified Jack with him. As he approached an Over-seer was on one knee with the helmet it had retrieved, and was just going to place it back onto its suffocating head when Daniel took a swing with his foot, and kicked it away like a football.

'Father, are you alive?'

Daniel turned his father's face towards him.

25

NO OTHER WAY

Mary sat down on the bench and moved over to make room for Wolf. He was still feeling groggy and lowered his backside with a huff.

'What do we do now, Mary?' he asked, still shocked at what the Over-seers had just done. Up to that point he still had doubts whether what he had been told was the truth. He still wasn't even sure why he was following this quartet on their mad quest to the Achievement Centre.

'I think we need to warn this lot in here. I just get the feeling they won't easily follow us once the others arrive. But they will have to because there is no other way.'

Idle chit chat reverberated around the room as Mary got to her feet and cleared her throat. No one took any notice so she coughed a bit louder. Still people kept talking to each other.

'Quite please.' It quietened down a bit, but not enough for Mary's liking. 'Will you lot just shut up for one minute?'

The room fell silent and all eyes were locked on Mary. 'Now what I'm going to tell you might sound out of this world, but it's the truth. Hopefully any minute now we are going to be rescued.'

Someone laughed, which made a couple of others follow suit, then a voice asked mockingly, 'Rescued from what? The Over-seers are rescuing us from a life of toil.'

Mary was annoyed and you could tell by her voice.

'Don't be so silly. There are no rewards. The Over-seers have conned you into believing that they will look after you, but they won't. They are aliens who want to feed on your live flesh.'

The whole room burst into laughter as someone called out. 'What's an alien?'

Mary took a deep breath, trying to stop her annoyance turning into open anger. 'They're monsters who have exploited humanity for decades and we are here to save you.'

The laughter now became gut wrenching in its ignorance until a loud siren sounded, startling the crowd. Mary looked at Wolf. 'I think they are on their way.'

Wolf jumped to his feet and stood by the door in anticipation.

* * *

'Father – are you alive?'

Daniel held John's head and turned it carefully towards him. His eyes opened, and when Daniel's face came into focus he smiled faintly.

'Quick, Jack. Can you get these prongs off father? Now.'

Jack's hand was shaking uncontrollable. The mixture of human screams, Over-seers distressful squeals, the continuous blast of the warning alarm, mixed with the stench of human blood intermingled with the quickly rotting flesh of the Over-seers, was too much for Jack's senses to handle. He was desperately trying to connect the interface when something took hold of his leg.

Jack looked down and screamed out. An Over-seer lying prostrate on the floor and in the final throws of death had grabbed his ankle and was making one final attempted to stop the intruders. The sight of its flesh, liquidizing like a stranded jellyfish on the seashore, was just too much to take, and he froze in fear. He couldn't move.

'I'm here father – just hold on and we will have you out any second.'

Some words seeped out of John's mouth, too quiet to be heard over all the din and commotion. Daniel pressed his ear against John's mouth.

'Daniel, I knew you would come back. I love you, my son.'

Daniel hugged him, then pulled back to find out why the prongs were still binding his father to the table. It was then that he saw Jack stuck in a moment of time. Not moving, just looking down at the beast that had hold of him while another one was crawling ever so closer to help its colleague.

'Get off him, you monsters.'

Daniel swung his axe and it sliced through the Over-seers arm. Green liquid splattered all over Jack's trousers and started to sizzle on the cloth. Daniel took another swipe and this time its arm was severed, leaving behind its hand which was still gripped around Jack's ankle.

Jack's nerves couldn't take it any more, and he started to cry.

Gwendolyn came rushing over with an arrow in her bow and dispatched it into the skull of the Over-seer, finally ending its life. With a flick of her wrist she had another arrow in the taut bowstring, and sent it flying straight into the throat of the second crawling Over-seer. It gurgled while grappling at the arrow, but before it had time another was sent hurtling towards it, and this time death was instant.

Daniel took hold of Jack, bringing him out of his trance. He kicked at Jack's ankle and after the second attempt the claw dropped to the floor.

'Listen to me, Jack. I promise you no other Over-seer will get near to you. We are both by your side and will protect you, so please focus on the table and get these prongs off.'

Jack started to look around the table for somewhere to connect his interface.

'There's a problem, Daniel. I can't find any sockets.' Daniel started to yank at the two prongs hoping to force them free, but his sheer brute force was making no inroads.

Then Jack called out, 'I have a theory,' and with that he picked up an Over-seer's glove from the floor. Looking inside he fumbled about with his fingers, then inserted the lead into it before pressing the glove against what looked like a control panel. It started to flash and the prongs started to retract into the sides.

'Well done, Jack,' cried out Daniel as he hugged his father once again, but his moment of joy was short lived. A Dominator at the far reaches of the room had managed to replace all its uniform and now came clanking towards them with an arm extended, and in its clasp it held its rod of pain. Gwendolyn sent an arrow flying towards the slit in its helmet that glowed red, but it splintered off its armour. She just had time to send a second one that hit the bulls-eye, but only cracked the protective visor.

In the next instant Gwendolyn felt an over-powering shock that took hold of her body, sending it into uncontrollable spasms of muscle-aching pain. When it stopped she slumped to the floor and even then struggled to stop her body convulsing. A Dominator stood over her ready for the kill.

Daniel picked up his axe and sent it crashing into the beasts back, but it didn't penetrate the armour. It made a loud clonking sound as it made contact, and sent a painful shock wave up the handle, which made Daniel drop it to the floor. In a flash Daniel charged at the Dominator and went crashing into. They both fell to the floor. Daniel banged his head and for a few semi-conscious seconds he didn't know where he was. By the time his memory came flooding back the Dominator was prostrate over his body with its large metal-clad gloves firmly gripped around his throat.

Daniel couldn't breathe. The grip became tighter and tighter. Loud, almost excited, clicking emanated from the Dominator as Daniel's vision, and sense of sound, began to fade. He knew his spine was just millimetres from being crushed, and only seconds away before his life was snuffed out.

Suddenly the grip loosened and the Dominator slumped onto Daniel, crushing his body under its great weight. He took in a deep desperate gulp of air and his mouth could taste the stench of human blood. The acrid smell of burning Over-seer's flesh filled his lungs, and as he heaved the monster off he gagged for breath.

The beast was dead and protruding from the back of its neck was his axe. Looking up he could feel the presence of his father standing over him, and when his vision quickly came back into focus there he was standing motionless as blood dripped from the many deep wounds across his chest.

Daniel got up and they both hugged once again.

Gwendolyn had regained her composure and was in the throes of taking joyful revenge as she dispatched another two Over-seers before retrieving her arrows from their rotting flesh. They made a squelching noise as she pulled them out, and cleaned each one in her ritual manner with a rag.

The remaining Over-seers had suffocated to death.

Jack was going from table to table using the glove he had picked to up to release each prong, but it was too late for the humans who lay on top. They were either dead, or barely alive, their skin torn away with large chunks of bodily flesh missing, devoured by the Over-seers, or hanging off their bones as blood continued to gush all over the tables.

'Leave them, Jack. Open the door,' Daniel called out, his shirt now covered in his father's blood. John was as shocked and sickened as Jack, and stood in silent disbelief in not only the human carnage that now lay about moaning their last breaths, but also in the fact he had just killed an Over-seer. The Over-seers were more than just a way of life. They were treated as god's, and now he had slain forty years of religious belief in the Seven Procedures in just a couple of seconds with a swish of an axe.

Daniel put John's arm around his back and helped him hobble to the door. Every step taken was accompanied by a groan of pain. Jack was now in his element. With iPad and glove in hand he pressed it against the wall and another control panel magically lit up. Strange symbols appeared which Jack eagerly studied.

'I know what some of these mean. I have studied them before.' He touched the panel. 'See this? It's the symbol for 'close', and this one is for 'open'.' He touched it but nothing happened. He touched it again with the same result. Looking perplexed his expression suddenly changed, and as the others impatiently waited he hesitantly put his hand within the Over-seers glove.

It was cold to touch and too big for his small hands, but when the glove touched the symbol the wall in front of them began to slide sideways, and the hallway behind appeared.

'We need to rescue the others. Where do we go now, father?'

John croaked and bloodied words spluttered forth. 'Go straight ahead to the door at the very bottom that leads to the way out. The others are kept in rooms on either side of the hallway.'

Jack was last out while he continued to play with the control panel. Suddenly the alarm went off and all went dark. The violet light had gone. The control panel light was all there was until Jack tapped another symbol and normal light was restored. He let out a yelp of victory and darted out of the door to join the others. As he did so the door closed behind and there was silence. No more groaning of human misery, no more Over-seers flesh, blistering and bursting with puss, only silence until suddenly the sound of hissing came from the ceiling.

Looking up it was obvious to all that oxygen was now being vented from the Achievement Centre. The air was being made ready for Over-seers to breath. More were on their way, but more frightful than that, soon they would all be disabled by suffocation.

* * *

Thud.

It caught every ones attention. The incessant alarm had stopped as quickly as it had started and now the sound of a woman's body collapsing to the floor had people looking down in disbelief. Above her head a vent had opened and from it came a slow but persistent hiss. Others next to her started to gasp for air while looking unsteady on their feet.

Mary's throat felt sore after her unsuccessful exchange of words with the unbelieving audience who stoutly refused to take her seriously. Now this new event had spooked the crowd and Mary sensed it. Not only that: she knew it also spelt danger so reacted without hesitation.

'Wolf. Take off your coat and use it to plug the hole.'

Mary was pointing to the ceiling, but now Wolf was rammed against the wall as people pushed ever closer to get away from the mystery stench that was slowly filling the room. By the time he had pushed his way through another person was on their knees gagging for breath, and when he finally got his coat off they had fallen forward semi-unconscious.

Wolf stuffed it into the duct. It helped to stem the flow, but not to stop it.

'I need another coat and a big one too.'

Wolf grabbed the nearest man he could find.

'Give me your coat.'

He didn't get a reply.

'I said give me your coat and I mean now.'

This time there was a reply and Wolf didn't like it one bit.

'I'm not giving you my coat.'

Wolf was in no mood for arguing. He retracted his fist and sent in flying into the stranger's jaw.

'Now give me your coat.'

He started to retract his arm once again, but the man had got the message and was swiftly taking it off.

'Here it is. Take it. I don't need it anyway. The Over-seers will give me all that I need in the future.'

Mary wanted to laugh, but her head was feeling woozy. She had to take a seat as Wolf tried to finally stop the inrush. Then suddenly a scream from the far end sent fear throughout the whole room as others joined in the horror.

Mary got to her feet trying to see through the masses at what was causing all the commotion, but all she could see was that the door had once again opened, and there, standing in the entrance, was something. What it was she couldn't see, but by the horrified screams and shouts it was something frightening.

* * *

'Where do we go now Daniel?' Gwendolyn asked, at last able to catch her breath.

'We must find the others,' he replied, but Jack was already onto it. He was now in his element and once again used his new found toy to open the first door to his right. The room was empty. Turning to his left he pressed the appropriate symbol on the control panel and another door opened. This time it was packed with people gasping for air. Bodies started to fall through the open door.

Gwendolyn helped a lady to her feet, then another.

'Can you see Mary and Wolf?' Daniel asked, as more mystified helpless souls came stumbling through the doorway. Jumping up and down on the spot she tried to see over everyone while calling out their names.

'Mary. Wolf. Are you in there?'

John held up his arm and tried to talk, but coughed instead. A trickle of blood seeped from the side of his mouth.

'Jack, I think it's the next door, open it up.' But he wasn't taking any notice while scrambling through the throng of people calling out.

'Daddy. Mummy. It's Jack. Where are you?'

John was shaking his bloody face from side to side. The wounds across his chest wept, matching his shredded trousers as his legs too dripped with blood.

'Orb. The Orb.'

John's strength gave way, and Daniel just managed to stop his weakening body from falling to the floor.

'What are you trying to say, father?'

John steadied himself. 'The Orb – the women have been taken to the Orb. Mother – she has been taken to the Orb.'

Daniel looked shocked and hoped he had misheard his father, but there wasn't time to react. They had become caught in a human stampede and were pushed further down the hallway. Gwendolyn grabbed Jack's arm and dragged him after them.

'I don't think your dad is in there, and it sounds like your mum may have been taken to the Orb. You need to open the other door that John was pointing to. We need to find Mary and Wolf.'

Gwendolyn pushed her way through. She could see Daniel desperately trying to stop John from getting crushed under foot as they leaned against the wall. Jack reached up with his gloved hand and touched the wall and it slid sideways. Daniel and John both fell backwards onto the floor into another room soon followed by a howl of screams.

Gwendolyn called out in despair, 'Daniel. Daniel. I'm coming Daniel.'

It became harder to approach as the screams set off a full blown panic sending people fleeing out of the door, and the hallway became a log-jam of human anguish. Gwendolyn lost Jack's grip. His body was taken in the swell of individuals that flowed in an ever-increasing terror. She now forcibly pushed all and sundry aside without a care until she had reached Daniel who was kicking out like a ranting mad-man.

'Get back. Get back. I need to help, father. Get back. Get back.'

John lay helpless on the floor, too weak to lift himself. Daniel was getting more frantic as it became a mass brawl for survival. The air became foul. People began to hyperventilate. Trampled bodies lay on the floor. A green mist hovered over their heads.

Jack, in his desperation to find his parents, opened another door, releasing a third tide of choking human wretchedness into the already cramped passage. The heat was stifling and the metallic floor became slippery with human fear.

Then a pair of helping arms appeared.

'I've got him, Daniel. Let's lift him together.' Daniel had distrusted Wolf when they first met and had disliked him even more when he unexpectedly joined their little group, but at this very moment he couldn't had been happier to hear his voice.

By the time they got him to his feet the room had emptied enough for Mary to be able to reach them, and took command of the situation.

'We need to get the door open at the bottom because it leads to the large outer cavern and from there to the outside world. Where's Jack?'

Gwendolyn darted back out into the mayhem just in time to see another door open. Its entrance was blocked by bodies piled on top of bodies as if they were a human step ladder, then suddenly the mass of dead or dying tumbled onto the hall floor, adding another layer of crushed flesh. She could hear Jack calling out, 'Mummy, Daddy, where are you?'

But she couldn't see him at first, only hearing his repeated requests for them: 'Have you seen my mummy and daddy?' His head appeared, choking in the mist, and there he was standing as if he was seven feet tall on a mass melee of writhing, panicking, pitiful humanoids that resembled squirming eels caught in a river trap. Gwendolyn called out to him, catching his attention. She waved him on, and he had started to climb towards her when he was knocked sideways by a stranger more intent on his own personal wellbeing than that of a child. He hit the wall painfully, rubbing his shoulder, and then innocently opened another door when he used the wall for support to get back onto his feet.

A pungent cloud bellowed forth followed by an Over-seer. It was not in uniform and the form of its ghastly naked frame sent nightmarish shrieks echoing off the walls from the horrified humans still battling for a way out.

The Over-seer grabbed the first person it saw by the throat, then extending its neck it widened its jaw so wide it was able to consume a third of the poor man's face as he stood there paralyzed with terror. As the beast pulled away so did half the man's skull, revealing the soft-tinged yellow of his brain, which fell away in pieces.

As the Over-seer spat back the facial remains the man dropped like a quivering wreck. It now clawed its way into the hallway, followed by another, and then another, as the vapour became all consuming.

Jack had started to scramble his way back to Gwendolyn as she let fly with an arrow. She missed her target as it clanked off the wall. With so many petrified people all pushing and shoving it was hard to get a clear line of shot. When Jack reached her he wrapped his arms around her lower waist and held on tight which impeded her even more.

She let loose a whole salvo, but only one hit its intended target and only then through the monster's shoulder. She could hear Mary barking out orders.

'Wolf and Daniel – drag John to the closed door at the very far end. Jack, you come with me. We need you to open that door. Gwendolyn, can you hold them off as long as possible?'

With that she could feel Jack being tugged free by Mary. Now there were too many Over-seers to count as they came storming into a frenzy of mass slaughter. No one was being spared. Any flesh that came into reach was torn asunder until its owner was dead and no longer a threat to the Achievement Centre. They were getting closer and closer to Gwendolyn.

Her normal steady hand had deserted her in all the carnage. Her head was also feeling faint. The acrid smell of the Over-seers and of human death made her stomach churn, and she wanted to be sick. She gagged for breath and felt the acid of her gut burn the back of throat. It tasted sickly and she spat out a mouthful of phlegm mixed with some half-chewed remains of her last meal. Hands now clawed at her body pleading for help as the Over-seers came ever closer.

Gwendolyn took another arrow from her quiver and steadied her thoughts. She aimed for the skull. She was all that stood in the way of the Over-seers catching the others. Pulling back the string until it was taut she aimed, then let it loose while screaming out sarcastically, 'Nice to see you again.'

It went straight through the Over-seer's eye. It didn't have time to cry out in pain. It just slumped forward, lying on top of the other dead. There was no respite though because another Over-seer came towards her holding in its hand a long grey rod. Quickly she got another arrow and aimed, and with this shot it sliced into the monster's chest. For a second it stopped and looked at the protruding arrow. Then it took hold of it and yanked it out. Green fluid spurted out, dripping onto the flesh of the dead that lay under foot, and when it made contact with flesh it started to boil and hiss, sending small plumes of smoke rising that smelt like over-burnt meat on a barbecue.

The Over-seer steeped forward, then stopped, then took another step as if unsure if it should live or die, before finally taking one final step, leaning forward just in reach of Gwendolyn. She desperately reached for another arrow, but her hand could only feel emptiness. She glanced back hoping to see the shaft of an arrow, and in that fraction of a second her worst nightmare had happened again. Turning back while grappling for her dagger the Over-seer thrust his rod of pain deep into her belly. She started to convulse wildly. The pain seemed to go on for ever until finally the Over-seer crashed dead to the floor, Gwendolyn collapsed beside it.

The others had momentarily lost eye contact with her as Jack opened the remaining door. Fresh air came surging in from the pitch darkness. A lone light of a control panel on the other side was all there was to see with. Then Mary screamed out, 'Gwendolyn!' Wolf and Daniel looked behind. 'I must get Gwendolyn.'

Wolf grabbed her arm. 'No. You stay here with Jack and make sure he opens the chamber door to the outside world.'

There was no choice other than to put John on the floor, resting his back against the cold stone walls of the outer chamber, while Jack studied all the symbols, looking for a way out of the darkness.

Wolf darted back into the hallway followed by Daniel with his axe. They had to fight their way through the onrush of people who now sensed the darkness ahead was the best place to be, and the mad dash for freedom sent both Mary and Jack flying to the floor. They were lucky not to be crushed alive in all the confusion.

Finally Wolf reached Gwendolyn and scooped up her slender body with his muscular arms, then headed back towards the darkness. Daniel was now the rearguard, and was soon in combat with an Over-seer who came lurching towards him. Its fangs were exposed and its nails were as sharp as a butcher's knife. Saliva dripped from its open mouth while wild clicking sounds emanated from its foul breath.

Daniel swung his axe to his left and to the right as he slowly took steps back while trying not to fall over all the dead and dying bodies that littered the floor. The atmosphere was almost impossible to breath. It was thick with poisonous smog and Daniel longed to get back into the darkness so he could taste the cold sweet air that filled the outer chamber. In front of him was a never-ending line of Over-seers, two abreast, slowly edging ever closer to him forcing Daniel to retreat. He courageously continued to hold off the attack with nothing more than his axe.

He knew he had reached the outer chamber when at last he could let go of the breath he had been holding and could replace it with fresh air. The lead Over-seer made a lunge for him, but then pulled back screaming as it held its arm in pain. It too could feel the air and knew it was too dangerous to go any further. It turned and started to fiddle with the symbols on a control panel. Hissing could be heard in the darkness and choking sounds soon followed.

'Get the chamber door open now,' Daniel cried out, just as a rumble shot through the floor.

A sliver of light appeared at the far end and Jack could be heard celebrating. The light became ever brighter with the increasing noise of the rumbling, alongside the screams of panicking people who now rushed towards the entrance and to the outside world.

Wolf was heading there too with Gwendolyn still in his arms. Mary bent down and tried to lift John's semi-conscious body, but had only lifted him a few inches off the ground when her back gave way, and pain shot through her spinal muscles. She tried to straighten herself, but doubled over in even greater pain. Slowly she managed to take a step with the help of Jack's arm.

John held out his hand as words gurgled from his blood-filled lungs, seeping out in ever greater frothy amounts from his mouth.

'Give me the lighter.'

Mary froze. She hadn't even had the chance to tell John she was his older sister and now he was asking her for the means to end his own life. John spoke again, but with all the commotion going on Mary had to be painfully helped to one knee so she could hear.

'No other choice.' John repeated himself. 'No other choice'

A tear rolled down Mary's face and she gentle stroked away hair from his bloodied head.

'No other choice.' John voice was getting weaker. Mary held his hand clasping in tightly. She kissed it and said.

'I will never forget you, John, I promise.' When she let go of his hand it now contained a lighter. 'Help me, Jack.' He did as instructed.

'Come on Daniel, let's get out of here.' Mary hobbled her way with the aid of Jack towards the light.

Daniel turned and could see his father smiling at him. His arm was raised, and between his forefinger and thumb was a lighter.

'You have to the count of ten to get out of here, my son.'

'No father!' Daniel cried out.

'Ten.'

'No, father! There must be another way.'

'Nine. Tell your mother and sister that I've always loved them and always will. Eight.'

Daniel was perplexed. The hiss of the Over-seers gas was mingling in a deadly fight with the on-rush of air for supremacy of the chamber. He couldn't hold off the Over-seers anymore and wouldn't be able to drag his father away in time.

'Seven.'

There was another problem. The entrance had stopped opening and was now retracting shut. Daniel wasn't even sure if he could make it before the door to the outside world closed on him for the final time.

He ran for it while his father's voice repeated in his head.

'Six.'

He thought about dropping his axe just to give him another split second of advantage, but it was the only thing left he had from his previous life, the only memento with which to remember his father.

'Five.'

The light was starting to fade and the hiss became ever louder.

'Four.'

Daniel's lungs cried out for oxygen.

'Three.'

He was now the only one who had failed to make it through.

'Two.'

Now only a step from the outside world the final number was said.

'One.'

There was a violent shockwave. It felt as if a giant hand had grabbed Daniel by the scruff of the neck and thrown him through the air. Then searing heat struck his back. He didn't even see the light. It was blinding, and his hearing stopped for a second to be followed by an incessant ringing tone. Soil splattered his face at first, but then larger debris began to hit his body, which was now curled up into a tight ball while his arms covered his head. The dusty air became unbreathable. The ground shook so violently his body felt it was being bounced about like a ball on a trampoline, and Daniel feared that any second now he was going to be swallowed up by Mother Earth.

* * *

Mary held tightly onto Jack, who was hiding under the long hem of her dress like a baby kangaroo in its mother's pouch. They had just made it to the first line of trees when an almighty explosion had kicked them to the ground, where they now hid behind the trunk for shelter as giant boulders came raining down. The last thing she did see was Gwendolyn resting against a tree further into the woods recovering from her shock treatment. She was conscious and seemed to be responded to Wolf's questions.

Mary didn't know why she felt so surprised when the Achievement Centre went up in flames, though deep down she was hoping that maybe Daniel could have made it through with his father. As she took shelter from the storm of dust that engulfed everything within the immediate area she pondered if she would have had the guts ultimately to have lit the fuse. Could she have done it? One second her hatred of the Over-seers was all-consuming, but the next her zest for life made her wonder if she could have really ended it with such self-sacrifice.

For the moment she wouldn't find out. As the dust began to settle new concerns filled her. Dare she take a look? Had her plan been a success? And more importantly had Daniel made it out in time?

Once the final boulder came crashing to earth the sound of mother nature's wrath was taken over by the cries of frightened and confused souls, who crawled about the debris, calling out the names of loved ones as if it could comfort their distress. The thick cloud that had blotted out all daylight began to clear, and once Mary could breathe without choking she raised her head. Wolf was staggering to his feet, his face ash white, his body covered in dust. Gwendolyn too was shocked, but as least alive. Jack's head appeared from under her skirt.

Slowly Mary looked back to where they had just run from. The ground was a whirl of soil still concealing everything in its grasp, but behind it was nothing. Where once stood a cliff face, the entrance to the Achievement Centre, there was nothing. It looked as if the very earth itself had been consumed. The ground that once soared so high had collapsed on itself, and now there was just a crater that stretched out into the distance. Anything left inside had now been consigned to history, buried for eternity.

Mary's heart sunk. It should have been full of joy, but it wasn't. Slowly the final swirling mass of fragments settled and there under a mound of rubble laid a single body curled up into a silent ball.

* * *

Slowly the vibrations began to seep away while the patter, patter, of small loose stones rained down. The incessant ringing in his ears was annoying, but at least it indicated one thing. He was still alive!

Daniel couldn't hold his breath anymore and took in a gasp of dust-filled air which made him choke. He wanted to pull his shirt up to his face to use as a filter mask, but his movement was being restricted. Squirming like a worm he moved his body to the left and to the right until he manoeuvred his head free and it popped up. Eventually he managed to get to his knees. His vision was still blurred and he was deaf with the continuous ringing of his eardrums. Grit filled his eyes which made them water profusely, helping to clear away the itching grime.

He had just managed to stand when he was nearly knocked over. Something had grabbed him tightly. He could just about hear, but couldn't distinguish the words. For a second he thought he had been grabbed by an Over-seer, but then there were more arms around him and as the ringing abated he could hear cheering. With his vision improving with every second it wasn't long before he could tell that all the others had made it safely and were now congratulating him.

Finally the ringing stopped and the tweeting of birds in the distance was a welcome sign. The air had cleared, and Daniel delighted in taking big gulps. Finally he was let go and able to brush off the dirt that caked him from head to toe. When he turned to face the Achievement Centre a string of different emotions swept over him. Pride at what had been achieved; sadness at the price that had been paid.

'Well done, Daniel. We've done it. It's all over.'

And then a third emotion seeped from his lips in answer to Mary.

Looking defiantly into her brown eyes he replied, 'It's not over, Mary. It's not over until I have my revenge.'

THE AUTHOR

Mark King is a free spirit, lover of life, family, friendships, good food, and travel. He lives in Norwich in the county of Norfolk in the UK. Norwich is one of Britain's most historic cities and a hub for present day literature.

Mark is the author of the internationally acclaimed book *Frenzy, a Daniel Jones story* and writer of the world-wide blog at www.always-hanging-around.blogspot.com.

You can also follow him on Twitter @author_king and contact him at markkingtheauthor@gmail.com